INTIMATIONS
OF EVE

Intimations

of Eve

BY VARDIS FISHER

The Vanguard Press

NEW YORK

Manufactured in the U. S. A. by H. Wolff, New York, N. Y.

INTIMATIONS
OF EVE

I

He was lost. This he realized with fear that burned in his skin like the heat of his home fire; that twitched in his muscles, grasping with little spasms at his cheeks and eyelids and lips, or running in shudders down his frame as if hordes of insects were feeding on his nerves. When, like one dazed or blinded, he put a hand to his brow, his palm felt the cold sweat; and sweat in big drops fell from his nose to his naked chest and ran like tiny feet across his skin. Tense and expectant he listened—and heard only the labor of his low deep breathing.

While hunting, he had wandered farther from his home than was his custom and had entered a strange wilderness, thinking that he could quickly push through it; but almost at once he had found himself in dank gloom, with the sun shut out by a vast and luxuriant ceiling. In turning like a trapped beast to seek a way out, he had lost all sense of direction; and when realization of his plight burst from him in a strangled sob of terror he began to fight desperately with the impenetrable walls of ferns and vines, of

3

brambles, of dense perfumed clusters and thorny nightshade, of reed and moss and lichen, trying in the darkness to open a path where no path had ever been. It seemed to his frenzied mind that everything in the jungle was striving to entangle and bear him down. Cool, moist, and invisible vines coiled like serpents round his body and neck, and when he strove to tear them away or to drag them down under his feet, his hands closed on brambles or the deadly teeth of razor grass.

After an hour of frantic and futile struggle he stood still, damp with sweat and quivering from head to feet. He could hear a sound. At first it was a very low and gentle humming, as if the forest were drawing a deep, full breath. Then it grew in volume, still muffled but with menacing overtones, as though ghosts of the jungle had been aroused from sleep and were breathing fiercely in the sweltering undergrowth. For him it was not the sound of beetle wings echoing in their own hard shields. For him all sounds made by invisible things were the sounds of spirits; for he lived, and all his people lived, in a ghost world, and all things that they did not understand were the doings of ghosts. The world was haunted by day and by night, and sleep was troubled, as now, when a man tossed in his dreams while his soul wandered abroad and got itself lost in a jungle built less by the man's own experiences than by the dim memories of a time long ago.

The muffled and insistent and menacing sounds which he heard were the breathings of many ghosts that had gathered here in the gloom. He was so terrified that, while he stood and listened, his head shook on his neck as if twitched by the pounding of his heart. He moved backward, his naked feet sinking soundlessly in the mold and

4

decay—backward very slowly, step by step, in the rotting leaf depth; but he was now shaking so uncontrollably that he almost screamed when, in one moment, the thrust of a bramble was like the sting of an insect, or, in the next, the sudden cool and sensuous brushing of a vine was like the touch of a snake. He felt an urge to kneel and supplicate with moist hands all the invisible and unfriendly forces around him.

After he had withdrawn a few steps, using his rump as a prow to thrust his way through the tangle and holding hands before his face to ward off sudden attack, he paused again to listen. He heard a low moaning and, very faintly under it, the breathing of ghosts. He felt a little more secure, and for a few moments he stood as still as the windless growth around him, trying to quiet the tremors in his frame. Realizing that no member of his family would ever find him here and that his escape depended on him alone, he became cunning and deliberate. He took his hands away from his face and tried to see, but the roof above him was so dense that he stood in midnight. He knew there was blood on his hands, and on his arms and body; he could still feel the bite of thorns.

Looking up, he could see only darkness, but his mind was sly now and wide awake—and one watching the sleeping man would have seen him smile. He thought he might climb a tall tree and look across the ceiling and so learn which direction would lead him home. Turning, he groped forward, his hands warily seeking a bole, and when he found a tree large enough to support him, he felt over its cool wet bark. Not knowing how tall this tree might be, he put arms around it and tried to shake it. Failing in this, he tugged at a network of vines. At once

5

a multitude of insects lost their footing and swarmed in dense clouds, swirling downward at first like a shower of leaves and then rising in a bewildered and murmuring fog. Clasping the tree, he strove to climb, his arms hugging the trunk, his right foot pressing an instep against it, his left leg reaching round to cling. There were no branches on the tree, nor even old scars or moss pads to make his grasp more secure, but by hugging it tightly and using both arms and legs he climbed thirty feet or more; whereupon, breathing heavily, he paused to rest. Straining his head backward he looked up, but there was only the midnight of millions of dark leaves. Despairing, he loosened his clutch and gently slid down, the bole moving like a huge moist serpent between his arms and legs. He stood again on the deep mold and listened.

He could hear no sound except the low moaning. Knowing that if he moved noiselessly he would not disturb the ghosts, he left this tree, his outstretched hands exploring like antennae, his feet testing each spot before accepting his weight. Very softly, as if all the nerves in his body were quivering in his skin, he parted a wall of vines and advanced step by step, with the leaf mold of the jungle floor like wolf fur under his feet. Not even with his breathing did he make any sound at all. The climbing vines, hanging like rope draperies, hardly rustled when he moved them, and across his shoulders and back, when he passed under them, they were like the caress of silent hands.

If he heard a sound, he would stop short and stand very still and listen. He knew that spirits liked to sleep during the daytime—or at least those did of which he was most afraid—and that they resented anything which disturbed their rest. When angered they could be very malicious, and in ways sly, and often unpredictable, they could torture a man. These ghosts around him were of dead birds and small forest creatures, and though one of them alone was not dangerous, a multitude of them could attack like a swarm of destroying hornets.

Sick with despair, he moved again in the darkness, parting the walls of growth which centuries had built. The sun had set long ago, and the day had deepened into night, but this wanderer, lost in a jungle, did not think of that. No light ever reached the floor on which he stood; noonday and midnight were always the same, and now, as in a long-ago time when his ancestors in terror conceived of ghosts, no darkening of the gloom warned him that the sun had left the world.

There were sounds around him now. Somewhere, not far away, in the deep and sunless interiors, perhaps the nightjars were rising from their day beds to soar into the higher corridors and catch the moths, or perhaps it was an old woman whispering in her sleep. But neither for the man, restless in slumber, nor for his soul lost abroad, were the sounds those of nighthawks and owls and bats. They were the sounds of ghosts, and while he listened he could hear their anguished breathing, and then their moaning full of menace and pain.

For him and for his people all the ills of life, all its sorrows and sickness and famine and blight, and all the terrifying manifestations of lightning and flood and storm, was the vengeful work of ghosts or the anger of the Moon Woman. Their own dead, unhappy and restless and spiteful, came back from their graves to trick and deceive the living, to torture them, to contrive pitfalls and snares, or to creep into their bodies, there to build sickness and

7

pain until sometimes in utter hopelessness a possessed person would yield as the prey of his malign persecutors. There was such a person in his family at home. A spirit had entered her and now used her as its house, and the wise one of the family, an old woman, had not been able with all her magic to drive it away. It would live in this woman until she died, and then it would crawl out of her, like a rodent driven by flood from its burrow, and enter another.

This woman moaned all night in her sleep.

And he knew also, and all the living knew, that the spirits of the dead were not only malicious; they also skulked invisibly. Stealthy and lurking, they hid in crevices and holes, under rocks, in hollow trees, in fluttering reeds and agitated seed pods; or they entered thickets, there to hide and sleep in daytime and come abroad at night like any other prowling and predatory thing. You could never see them, but often when they were careless you could hear them.

While listening to the ghosts around him, this man put an open hand over his mouth. Ever since entering this forest he had kept his lips tightly closed, knowing well that a ghost preferred to enter a living thing by way of its mouth. After a few moments he placed hands over his ears, and while trembling with apprehension he listened to the dangers around him and wondered what he could do. He was confused and sickened. He could keep his mouth closed and cover his ears and nostrils, and all these he now did. His left arm he placed up and across his left ear, with the forearm lying across his skull and the hand reaching down to cover the right ear. His right palm he placed over his nose.

Thus protected, he felt a little more secure. Ghosts

never attacked in the manner of visible enemies; the sly and treacherous things always sneaked into a person, usually through his open mouth, though sometimes they entered a nostril. When one entered a person's nostril, he would sneeze violently, trying to blow the invader out.

Having protected himself as well as he could, he began to move, his body bent forward, with head and shoulders parting the vines. His naked feet reached out to test the soft cool floor. He went very slowly because he was now moving through a dense tangle of nettles and brambles, or among trees festooned with mosses and lichen and hugged by enormous draperies of blossoming vines. He was still sweating, and because he was faint with thirst he removed the hand from his nose and explored for succulent reeds. Some of them were so filled with juice that a man could bite into them and feel the liquid gush in his mouth, and one, a leafless and black and snakelike vine, contained pure water. In searching for such vines he clutched the jeweled hardness of spined grass and felt a wetness in his palm which he knew was his own blood. He paused to lick the blood off and again cover his nose. . . .

The man at home turned in his sleep, and there was a lacuna in the slow journey through the wilderness; but after a little, the wanderer there moved forward again, and on looking up saw a tiny skylight in the ceiling far above him. Moonlight was falling through the window and bathing the uppermost leaves with the radiance of stone mirrors. He stood very still in the darkness; the window above was such a friendly thing that he did not want to leave this spot. The trembling in his body was not constant now but came and went in spasmodic seizures. Lis-

9

tening, he heard the ghosts in muted journeyings around him, searching tirelessly in the gloom. Because so much water had poured from him, and because terror even more than exertion devours a person's strength, he felt weak and sick and, dropping softly to his heels, he rested and looked up at the patch of light. He thought again that he might find a tree and climb and look over the forest, and presently he arose and explored, keeping all the while the window of light within view. He found a big tree, clothed with colonies of orchids and hugged by large moss pads that were as soft and friendly as cattail down. Leaning against the tree, he put his face to a cushion of moss.

It was a large tree, so large that he was unable to reach round it and touch his fingers; but because from its lower branches arching vine galleries hung like dead snakes he thought he would be able to climb it. In the first part of the ascent he clutched the vines, using them as rope ladders, and when he was thirty or more feet above ground, he came to branches that would support his weight. He now strove to climb while keeping his ears and nose covered. Finding this impossible, he would ascend a few feet as swiftly as he was able and then stand on a limb and protect himself. During these periods of rest he would lean his chest against the trunk; and the beating of his heart was so strong that each throb moved him back a little from the tree and kept him moving in and out to the rhythm of his pulse. He could feel the sound of his heart in his whole body and hear its muffled echo in his covered ears, above this sound he could hear the low and constant moaning of a ghost.

The wilderness seemed to be alive with ghosts now. Most of them were above him in the leaf valleys, under the arched canopies, or upon the prairies of the topmost levels. Now and then a wail would rise and tremble and break, as of a dying ember in a fire, and then fall in a tortured sigh, swallowed by the growth and the gloom; or up out of the depths would come a shriek like a sudden arrow of sound. Every menacing cry made him stiffen and clasp his ears and nose tightly and try to draw his whole body into a small hard knot that nothing could enter.

After he had climbed to the topmost branches of the tree he felt dismayed, even though the view before him was one of incomparable splendor. Overhead in the sky was the Moon Woman, full and white, warm and softly glowing, and her brilliant light flooded a deep depression in the jungle roof. This depression was a green valley, bordered by taller trees, each cloaked with the prodigal wealth of all the things that clung to it, reaching upward to light and air; and the innumerable leaves, of all sizes and of all shades of green and russet and gold, were like millions of mirrors, flashing in a breeze that spilled over the enclosing walls and down into the basin. A hundred feet or so from him, and standing high above the valley floor, was a lone tree, embraced by vines that had climbed to the very pinnacle and now seemed to fall downward in enveloping blankets of foliage and flowers. On the foliage were countless fireflies like faintly burning jewels. It was a tree aglow with the living light of the Moon Woman and the flies, a solitary sentinel of dazzling radiance—but not for this one who gazed at it for a moment and turned away.

For children and for primitive people there is no beauty in nature: There was none for this soul of a man that stared across the night. He did not see a great basin filled with moonlight. He saw only a friendless waste that was homeless and strange, and alive with the portents of invisible and malicious things. For him the solitary sentinel was not a gemmed tree, not a marvelous thing of light and loveliness, standing in a fairyland high above the jungle.

When he looked up he saw not the moon but a woman, an old woman, because she was round and full tonight. For all his people this moon was a woman. Sometimes they thought of her as three women, one young, one middle-aged, and one old; but usually they thought of her as one woman who eternally renewed herself. When she was young she was not frightening; but when she was old—and she was very old tonight—her countenance seemed to foretell disasters. Old women were tyrants like the one in his home. They were morose and vengeful; they were barren; they were sick and impatient; and they terrified men with their whims and tantrums and their vast and mysterious knowledge of magic.

He now looked at the old woman in the sky, not boldly, not with any wish to defy her—no, but humbly, fearfully, as if to read her mind and will. She could, if she wished, hurl him from the tree; or with her effulgence she could wither him like a beetle in his home fire. She could roar at him with the most awful wrath anywhere in the world or she could menace him with a flickering white tongue. She was fate and destiny because she had found the secret of perpetual renewal; she was the caretaker of the eternal because she was the woman who never died.

The women among his people were much like her, save only that they were not eternal. Nevertheless, they did change, as the Moon Woman changed, with the change in their bodies governed by her. They shed blood, sometimes when this woman was young; and that was a good sign. Or they shed it when this woman was old, and that was not good. They completed their cycle every time the Moon Woman completed her cycle from youth to age; and so they knew that the moon was a woman and was like all women except in her discovery of the secret of youth. Because she had discovered this secret and now lived above the earth, eternally in her own special home, it was in her power to fertilize the earth's women or to make them barren, to give babies or deny them, and to control, in ways wholly mysterious and unpredictable, the whole pattern of human life. . . .

For a long moment he looked at the serene face, bathed in its own smile; and when convinced that, though old and weary tonight, she had no unfriendly will toward him, he turned his gaze to the roof of the jungle, trying to see beyond the tall trees. In the direction facing him there was only the shining wall and its gleaming mirrors, but when he turned and parted the foliage to look the other way, he thought he could see the smoke of his home fire. He thought he could see familiar landmarks in the hills beyond.

But he did not descend at once. Again like a suppliant, with his will softened by dread and his body limply submissive, he looked up at the Moon Woman. Before leaving the tree and seeking his way out of this leafy haunt of ghosts, he wanted to be sure of her friendliness; and so he gazed at her, his eyes half-veiled, his ears and nose covered by his arms and hands. She seemed to wear a benign countenance tonight. Perhaps she had eaten well of choice foods; or perhaps, with the magic known only to her, she had relieved her aches and pains. Sometimes, for reasons never clear to her people, she gave way to violent tantrums and skulked about in sky darkness, now vanishing completely or now appearing suddenly to look down, angry and scowling, with darkness streaming across her face. Sometimes her voice thundered through the world. Then her anger made him and his people tremble and crawl into their huts and shake with terror through the wild night.

But she was calm now. To be sure that she had no mischievous designs, he slyly tricked her, looking away for a little while and then turning swiftly to see if he could surprise anger in her face. But there was no anger. There was only age and weariness and quiet. Aloof, calm, and alone in her untroubled home, she looked down at him, her gaze tired but without any hint of gathering tantrums. Reassured, he glanced the other way to mark the direction of his home. Then he slid down, but in the long descent to the jungle floor he faced always toward his home fire, knowing that if he confused his directions he would again be lost.

On the soft carpet he stood for several moments. He knew which direction to take, though again he was sunk in midnight, with the ceiling black above him save for the small window. When at last he moved, he went with extreme caution because all around him were long recurved thorns and sharp brambles. After a little while he dropped to hands and knees and crawled like a beast, moving noiselessly, with his shoulders hunched up to protect his ears. Upon seeing a hint of light he arose to his feet and emerged from the jungle.

14

The first thing he did was to glance anxiously at the Moon Woman to learn if she had changed her mood, but she was still serene and plump and old. She had traveled up the sky and now stood in her tallest position, so that she could look everywhere and spy out the happenings below. When she was highest in her home, her people knew she was most suspicious, and then they were doubly careful not to offend her. This nocturnal wanderer, sensing in her tall position the sharper intent of her mind, now turned away like one too humble to breathe. He wanted to run but he knew that if he ran she would think he was plotting mischief, and so, much against his will, he went slowly and softly, as befitted his helpless station of life.

He and his people never blamed themselves for any illness or unhappiness or misfortune; all unpleasant things that happened to them were the sinister doings of ghosts or punishment of the Moon Woman. If their house fell down on them, if they were sickened by overeating, if they were poisoned by certain plants, or even if they were wounded when moving carelessly, they never thought their craftsmanship was poor, their appetite unreasonable, their choice of food ill-advised, or their movements clumsy. If they were tortured by rheumatic pains or leached by fevers, it was because malicious spirits plotted against them. They looked beyond their own lives, beyond what they did or had power to do, for the cause of all things. For them, no object, not even a stone, a tree, or a river, was inanimate; everything had its own indwelling spirit, or was possessed by a ghost seeking a home.

While standing like a naked and defenseless and fearful thing, this wanderer remembered a grave. Only two days had passed since his family had buried one of its members, a very old man who in his younger years had distinguished himself as a hunter. The more important a person was, the more his ghost was feared by the living after his death. To this old man they had given a painstaking burial, laying away with him all his weapons, his trinkets, and his cutting tools. They had also buried with him some choice food, striving in every way they could think of to propitiate his spirit and invite its good will.

This wanderer was troubled by memory of the old man. As persons today are said to seek again the scene of their crime, or of any spot where they once endured emotional crisis, so this being, a man or a man's soul, was drawn on the homeward journey to seek the fresh grave. He wanted to be sure that the old man was resting well. If the old man were unhappy in the spot chosen for his grave, or if any of his belongings were missing, or if his food had been stolen, then his ghost would be vengeful and would return to haunt and derange the living. Ghosts were unpredictable in their whims and fancies and often seemed to be spiteful for no reason at all. The living never could be sure what the spirits wanted, or what unhappiness or loss impelled them to malicious acts. It was far better not to offend them; it was better to yield than to strive against them.

And so, worried by the old man's spirit, he left the most direct pathway home and turned aside to look at the grave. Now and then he glanced anxiously at the Moon Woman and sighed with relief when he found her countenance unchanged; or from time to time, while going softly like one who expected rebuke, he paused to listen to the night sounds and to interpret them. Most of them he heard as the cries of unhappy spirits, wandering discon-

16

solately in the brilliant night. Those that were the ghosts of animals cried constantly as if tortured by unrelenting pain. The ghosts of human beings, sly and treacherous and everlastingly up to mischief, moved as soundlessly as a snake. Invisible, nevertheless they were always present if a man only had power to see them. Ceaselessly, with never a moment's rest at all, the unhappy ones devised cunning ways to torment and sicken the living. Often, in the dead of night, they would enter your home, and then you would hear a sleeping person cry out in pain or you would see him sit up and strike out angrily as if to drive an invader away. If a ghost had succeeded in entering a person, then the possessed and tortured one moaned all night in his sleep.

On coming within sight of the grave he paused and gazed at the dim mound. He was now trembling as if chilled. The very sight of a human grave was enough to make a person shake with dread; the thought that an un-friendly ghost might be lurking there was almost more than a man could endure. Covering his ears and nostrils and keeping his lips tightly shut, like one expecting a bad odor or a blow on the head, he softly advanced, his fasci-nated gaze on the mound. When close enough to see that the grave had not been disturbed, he felt overwhelming relief that surged through him in warm nausea. He freed his ears and nostrils and let his arms fall; and then for a long moment he stood erect and bold, as if he had scattered the nameless terrors and looked far into the future, far beyond this, our present-day world, to the time when men would not be the slaves of their fears. . . .

His home was a small dirty hut close by a stream and a thicket. From a hole in the roof smoke issued like pale cloud shadows of the Moon Woman's wrath. Some families had wolf-dogs, but there was none sleeping by the man who turned restlessly on his bed and none to meet the wandering souls when they came home. This man had been awakened, and at once he knew that his soul had left his body and had got lost in a jungle and had paused on the way home to look at the uncle's grave; and he arose and went outside as if to meet this recklessly adventurous part of him. Realizing that his soul had not deserted him, that he was still alive, he felt a great gladness; and then, remembering how the other part of him had stood tiptoe by the grave and looked beyond the sky and the Moon Woman, he stretched his arms to the night and felt a sensuous hunger in his groin.

Turning, he paused by the doorway and looked inside. In the gloom he could see his family asleep and he could hear one of them moaning, and the sound took him back to the dank jungle and the wet tree and the basin of moonlight. Remembering that a ghost was housed in this woman who moaned, he slipped in silently and dropped to hands and knees and crawled to his mattress of skins, not knowing for a certainty whether he was awake or asleep. Lying on the bed, with knees drawn up to his belly, he protected one ear by laying it against a pelt and the other by placing a palm over it. With the other hand he cupped his nose. Then he listened for unfriendly sounds, but he could hear only the embers bursting on the hearth fire or the moans of the woman who lay by the opposite wall. It was the way of people then, as now, to feel childlike joy in life when freed from care; and this man, looking back on the terrible midnight adventure of his soul, strove to shut out the terrors and remember only the friendly things.

18

He wished he had a dog to reach out and caress. Having none, he moved a hand over the friendliness of his bed, softly stroking the fur. Another ember burst in its dying flame, and the suffering woman, with an alien ghost lurking in her abdomen, moaned in her sleep. When the man himself was half sunk in slumber, he seemed to be living two lives, one as an anxious creature drowsed in dreams and waiting for the morning and one as a naked and lonely soul standing in a treetop and looking at the age and weariness in the face of the Moon Woman. The flesh, tormented by fear, tossed on its bed; and the spirit, housed in racial memories and oppressed by the intolerable brevity and casualness of its body, fed on the storehouse of the unconscious mind and wandered in that allegory of darkness which still has no meaning beyond pleasure and pain.

2

At the first faint signs of daylight, the grandmother of this family, the guardian of the fire and keeper of the hut and the food, left her bed and went to the hearth. People long ago had learned to bank their fires with ashes for the night, and so her task now was to sweep the ashes aside with a green stick, stir the smoldering embers, and lay on grass and twigs and wood.

Completely naked, and squatting on her heels, with her withered breasts hanging to her knees and her unclean hair falling like a short gray cloak from her skull, she peered at the embers while stirring them; and when she saw that they were alive and glowing she made a clucking sound of pleasure and reached for a handful of grass. On the grass she saw a crawling beetle, and this she picked off and thrust into her mouth. When the grass curled in flame she laid on some twigs, and then across these she placed some small pieces of wood. The chimney was only a hole in the roof, but this morning the smoke hastened upward as if eager to escape. Sometimes it was lazy and spread out and downward as if seeking a bed, and then they had to leave the hut to get away from it.

When the fire was blazing, the old woman stood up on lean brown legs and turned to the sleepers. There were so many separate beds that they almost covered the floor.

"Get up," she said.

Those lying on the beds had known that this command would be given, but they had hoped that the old woman would need a long time to build the fire and so leave them a little while to drowse. On hearing the sharp words they stirred and rubbed at the sleep in their eyes. The first to sit up were a daughter and a granddaughter. The latter was a pubescent girl. These two were healthy and firm of flesh, but some of those lying on beds were sick. One of these seemed to be the special favorite of malicious and mischievous ghosts; it was this woman who had moaned in her sleep.

There were two old men, one of whom, petulant and self-pitying and given to tantrums, the others thought of contemptuously as a spider. The other aged one, having never had a name, or whose name had been forgotten, will be known here as Old Man. An elder brother of the grandmother, he was very old, so old, indeed, that his teeth were gone and his hair almost white, and his body was gaunt and stooped. Racked by degenerative diseases, he was slowly wasting away.

There were five women in the family, including the girl. The fifth, another daughter of the grandmother, was a pathetic creature who had always been sterile; and she, too, was held in contempt, because a barren woman for the people of this time was a monstrous thing. For reasons dark and mysterious, and related somehow to all the other forces in the world that were unfriendly to human life, she squandered her precious blood and had done so since puberty. The others, and especially the women, felt that she was stupid and unclean, that she had offended the spirits of the dead and was being punished for her clumsiness.

These people all lived, day and night, while awake and asleep, in almost constant fear. In their world there was nothing very friendly, and such friendliness as they found now and then was capricious and might, without a moment's warning, turn on them in vengeful anger. They were the prey of many living things, including flesh-eating beasts and birds, and hordes of insects that bit and stung or sucked their blood; and even more helplessly they were preyed on by the ghosts of the dead.

Long ago, before deciding that living things had a soul and that the soul survived physical death, human beings had lived in a happier and more carefree time. The only world they knew then was the visible world. Then they had been afraid only of things they could see. In that far-away time they had used their minds as well as they were able, and sought the truth, and striven to determine the logical relationships of cause and effect. The explanation of all baffling things they had looked for in natural phenomena. There was no superstition in them, no dependence on magic, no notions of good and evil as absolute values, and no fixed and harrowing anxiety in regard to the present or the future. In their own simple way they had all been scientists in a world where all things could be explained by one with enough knowledge. In that time, and only in that time, have human beings been free.

After they came by the notion of the soul and of the

ghost that survived the dead body, they entered the long terrifying night of spiritual bondage, the end of which is not yet. They then sought explanation of baffling events not in natural but in supernatural things. Indeed, they forthwith abandoned reality and enveloped themselves with an invisible world. The invisible became by far the most important meaning in their lives; in it they looked for the cause of sickness, of pain, and of misfortunes, even in very simple matters where their own laziness or fumbling was the sole cause. If the grandmother's fire had died, she would never for a moment have thought the wood was too green or too wet; she would have believed at once that a spiteful ghost was vexing her.

If a man, out hunting, was stabbed by a thorn, or if he stepped on a sharp splinter of stone, it never occurred to him that he was unwary or awkward. He thought that a ghost had thrust at him or had maliciously placed the stone in his path. If food made them sick, it was because a spirit had poisoned it. If they were taken by a fit of sneezing or coughing or hiccoughing, it was because a ghost was trying to enter their bodies and dwell there and torment and convulse them. And when in sleep they were tortured by unhappy dreams, it was because the spirits of the invisible world were plotting against them.

It would hardly be too extreme to say that they were only dimly aware of the visible world. To be sure, they perceived the visible things around them; but all these, including trees and stones and running water, were the dwelling places of spirits. The visible world was little more than the tools and materials and strange changing patterns of the beings who were invisible.

And so they lived, day after day and year after year,

23

haunted and anxious, in a baffling and unpredictable borderland, with the real dissolving into the unreal like smoke into a sky, and with the restless and unhappy energy of the invisible permeating everything they could see and hear. The phenomenon of physical death had forced their ancestors to think; but after a few generations the mind became the abject and impotent vassal of the emotions. The only function of the mind now was to formulate in concepts, as if it were a mere robot, the conclusions which fear drove the emotions to accept.

These people had many such concepts. In fact, there was almost nothing in the world that they had not explained. Innocent of both doubt and criticism, and with childlike acceptance of their few ideas, they had deduced logical conclusions. This was especially so of the women, and particularly the grandmothers. Women have always been more cautious than men, more confined by habit and routine, and more unwilling to alter their fixed ways. Men have been more reckless and adventurous and therefore more receptive to new ideas.

Among the people of this time, the grandmother was the boss of the family group, the guardian of the essentials, the firm core and anchor of all the habits and customs. She tended the fire and stored the food and made or supervised the making of such tools as were used in the home. She used resinous woods or twisted fibers as torches; the sap of olive or beech or the wax of bees for candlelight; and she found natural stone urns or baked crude clay pots or made skin pouches in which to carry water, mix her simples, or ferment juices. Her position was unquestioned, and her demands were law.

24

"Get up!" said the old woman, and they all knew that they would have to leave their beds.

The man by nature was a hunter and a wanderer, but he was chained to the hearth by the stored food and the friendliness of fire. Like his dog, if he had one, he preferred the anchor of a home to a life of vagrancy, because a home made him feel more secure. There had come to be a division of labor between the sexes, with the men hunting and the women tending the children and the home. The division had been made, not because the woman was less able as a hunter but because she was more confined by pregnancy and the care of offspring. Once the two spheres of action became distinct, each sex tried to make a monopoly of its sphere, the women suffering no male interference in the management of the fire and home and children, and the men striving to enrich the leaner destiny of hunting by turning to simple forms of art.

In the fulfillment of egoistic hungers, the women for a long time had had enviable advantages. In the miracle of birth, the male did not, so far as these people knew, participate at all; the child came from the blood in the mother's body. It belonged to her. It had uncles and aunts because its mother had brothers and sisters; but it had no father because these people had no concept of fatherhood. The mother gave birth, aided only by the fertilizing rains, by the magical fragrance of flowers and fruits, and by the Moon Woman; and the mother's will became law in the home because the home was for children and the care of young life was the mother's task.

For many generations the man had felt cheated and left out. So far as anybody could see, he was useless save as a provider of food. Sensing that he was of small importance in comparison with mothers, he had turned to art, striving to find in it an extension of his meaning; or, when he had one, he turned to his dog. In comparison with the maternal feeling, the paternal urge was weak, as it still is; but it was there, in this long-ago time, and it drove the man to be more than a hunter, more than a mere provider of food who lived like a handy servant on the margin of family life.

When the young man arose from his bed this morning, the first thing he did was to go outside and look round him for a dog. During the early part of the night he had dreamed again and again that he was lost in a deep jungle, that he had climbed a tall tree and looked at the Moon Woman, that he had descended and found his way out of the wilderness and fled home. Over and over he dreamed this until it became a kind of allegory of all the fears and strivings of his people during the long past. He knew, to be sure, that his soul had left his body and had been lost in a wilderness. Then he had dreamed that he owned a dog, and so now he looked round him expectantly, hoping that his soul had fetched one home. After searching in vain he looked up at the sky. Usually the Moon Woman hid when morning came, though sometimes she was visible, even in broad daylight. There was no sign of her now. The man sniffed the air for scent of wild beasts and explored the yard for their footprints. Then, because by nature he was lazy, but also because he had nothing to do, he went over to sit by a tree and wait for breakfast.

Inside, the other members were rising. The sick woman who had moaned in her sleep stood up in her bed and clutched her groin. When she gave a low cry of pain, the grandmother turned to look at her. Sick people were the objects of suspicion and fear; with the cruel consistency of logic it was believed that they were tormented by malicious spirits. The barren one also arose, and then the grandmother looked at her with scowling resentment. For many years she had squandered her precious menstrual blood and had never given birth to a child. She still squandered it.

Even though she was looking at one of her own daughters, the grandmother eyed her with loathing and sharply she said, "Go outside!"

"No," said the woman. But when her mother grasped a stick and menaced her, she quickly left the hut. She went over and sat by a bush, looking more hopeful than unhappy. Sniffing the air, she searched the sky for signs of rain—because when rain fell she would dash around in it, sometimes like a woman out of her mind, trying to absorb its fertilizing magic into her own barren body.

Of the others rising from beds, two were old men. One, contemptuously called Spider, was emaciated, with sunken cheeks and cavernous eyes. The only teeth he had left were rotted snags, and he suffered constantly with toothache. He was also a victim of rheumatic pains, inflamed joints, and nervous tics and twitchings. They all believed that this man in a strange way was in league with spiteful ghosts; and this he proved, time and again, by flying into wild tantrums and racing about as if demented, leaping up and down and smiting himself, or rolling and tumbling until exhausted.

Some families, less indulgent or more fearful, killed their sick and barren members; but this grandmother tolerated Spider and the sick woman and the barren woman.

She hated all of them. If there had been children in her family, then for their own well-being she might have tried to drive these three persons away. But there were no children; and the old woman, deeply unhappy because there were no young ones to care for, became more tyrannical with the passing of time and felt more empty and desolate. To be sure, the fire belonged to her, the food, the hut, the tools; she had more vital meanings than the others had. But the most precious meaning for a woman was a young child.

All of her fertile daughter's children except the oldest, the girl, had been born dead or had died soon after birth, having been killed by ghosts; and the fact that this family seemed to be a special victim of malicious forces was an oppressive blight on all of them. It made the barren woman more frantic in her repeated efforts to fertilize herself. It aroused Spider to such dreadful tantrums that he seemed obsessed by a wish to knock out his brains. And even the girl, a handsome and healthy lass, rarely smiled or yielded to that spontaneous joy which in moments of security it was natural for all of them to feel.

After they left their beds each morning, nobody save the grandmother had anything to do. There were no morning chores. Personal cleanliness has developed out of religious practices and not out of a natural wish in human beings to be clean. They never bathed or washed their faces and hands or made any effort to unsnarl their hair. The dirt of years clung to them, was in the pores of their skin, on the hair of their bodies, under their nails and in their ears. It was a thick brown covering on their scalps. They had no beds to make because their beds were only animal skins, turned fur side up. The wolf was the only beast these people had domesticated, and this family had no dog.

So there was nothing to do but to sit and wait while the grandmother prepared breakfast. In this task she would accept no help because women of her time found their richest meaning in waiting on others. Tending the fire and preparing the meals was a privilege that belonged to the oldest woman in a family group, and if one of the daughters had been indiscreet enough to offer to assist, the grandmother would have turned on her in fury.

And so they all waited while she prepared a gruel of ground barley and water or reached under a pile of skins in a corner for pieces of dried meat. Sometimes they had an abundance of food, but this was the spring season and their store of provisions was lean. The old woman took her time. Getting breakfast was a pleasure, not a chore to rush through; she spent almost an hour heating water, and she spent several minutes dropping the meal into the water, letting it sift slowly between her fingers. When the breakfast was over with, she would have nothing to do all day long until the evening meal, and so she dallied in the preparation of the food, making a kind of ritual of it, as if each small task were to be savored in all its precious details.

After leaving his bed, Old Man did not sit by the hut or by a bush or tree, as most of the others did, but walked around as if to straighten muscles that had been cramped by sleep. He was a half-brother of the grandmother and, like her, he was crippled by degenerative diseases. His kidneys, his intestinal tract, his heart, and all his other vital organs functioned very feebly. His shrunken face wore a sickly pallor; his ears looked like two brown leaves curled by frost; and his eyes watered when he left the hut and entered the bright morning. He looked like one who, pushed over, would die quietly where he fell.

As a young man he had been tall and strong; but now, slowly walking back and forth, he was bent over, with long fleshless arms hanging uselessly, with the bony nebs of his shoulders thrust forward beyond his sunken chest. Seeing the younger man sitting by a tree, he shuffled over to him and leaned forward, with hands on his knees, to sniff and peer.

"You eat?" he asked.

"No."

The old man sniffed. In his younger years his sense of smell had been almost as trustworthy a guide as his sense of sight. He seemed to think that the young man had eaten breakfast and, like a timid but persistent pest, he continued to sniff and peer.

"You eat?" he asked again.

The young man raised a menacing hand. "No!" he shouted.

There was no sympathy in the young for the old. Save in mothers for their children, there was no compassion in any of them for one another. Sympathy is an imaginative process, depending largely on foresight and the power of projection. Of foresight these people had little, and what they had was confined, like their emotions, by inflexible habit. The young man wanted the old man to go away, and when he again moved to strike, the old fellow went over to Spider, who was sitting by the hut.

Bending down and sniffing, the old man asked, "You eat?"

That inoffensive question aroused Spider to a tantrum. He struggled to his feet, his old bones shaking with rage, his lips drawn back in a snarl across the snags of his teeth. With venomous ill will he spit at the old man and then jumped up and down on his calloused feet and howled with abuse. His jawbones were aching this morning, his whole body was racked with pain; he felt misunderstood and tormented; he hated everyone. His cries were so shrill and goaded that the grandmother heard them and came out of the hut like a huge angry bee.

She advanced on Spider as if to strike him down, but the moment he saw her coming his manner changed completely. He lived in deadly fear of her. A grandmother's abuse was the worst of all punishments because she could summon malicious spirits to torment you. She was a woman, like the moon, and all women, but especially old ones, were in possession of mysterious and dreadful magic.

Spider ceased jumping up and down and yelling. Cringing, he retreated, his loose wet lips twitching with fear, his insane eyes supplicating the old woman. His shrunken hands covered his nose and ears, lest she summon a ghost to enter him. If he had been more intelligent, or if he had not been such a helpless victim of the simple logic of his time, he might have realized that he was already possessed by an alien ghost and could hardly be more defenseless and unhappy than he already was. But no such thought entered his mind. All men cowered in terror when the grandmothers began their furious clucking as if they were talking to the Moon Woman.

The moment she came out of the hut, Old Man discovered in himself an amazing nimbleness and ran away to hide. Even the young man by the tree stood up and began to tremble; he looked anxiously at the sky to see if the Moon Woman was there and then hid behind the tree and peered round it.

But the old woman's anger quickly cooled when Spider supplicated and whined and behaved like an abject creature. Eyeing him with distaste, the grandmother said contemptuously, "Spider!"

"Yes!" he quavered, gladly admitting that he was a spider.

"Be still!" she said.

"Yes," he said, nodding eagerly.

"You want food?"

He continued to shake his head up and down.

"Be still," she said, dismissing him, and returned to the hut.

The girl had stood back and watched the scene. When the grandmother vanished, she came forward, slowly, tentatively, her handsome face very grave, but without any hint of compassion or friendliness. She was thinking that this man had a malicious ghost in him; and when she advanced now to stare at the cringing fellow, she was wondering why the Moon Woman was punishing him with such torments. Unclothed and unashamed, she looked at the man, her brown eyes winking thoughtfully, her parted lips revealing strong teeth. She stared at him as she might have looked at any strange and baffling thing. During the more recent years of her girlhood she had watched his insane antics and heard his wild and terrified babbling. She had known that a ghost was dwelling in him because she had heard the grandmother say so, but she had been too young and was still too young to understand the matter very well. She was only eleven. But she did understand now that a spiteful spirit was in him and that he had jumped up and down and yelled because he was tormented; and by gazing at him, solemnly, steadily, she hoped to realize more fully why he behaved as he did.

Spider did not like her searching and unwavering stare. Nobody liked to be stared at. This was especially so of the men; they resented women who looked at them, because women had strange knowledge of magic. Spider wanted to leap at this girl and strike her down but, instead, he slowly retreated, still covering his nose and ears, his suspicious and despairing eyes slyly watching her. The girl's mother was also firm and healthy and rather well poised, considering the kind of haunted world she lived in. She came up and stood by her daughter, and the two of them looked at the man.

After a few moments, the girl turned to her mother.

"Ghost there?" she asked, and pointed at him.

"Yes."

"Spiteful ghost?"

"Yes."

"Tiger ghost? . . . Human ghost?"

The mother did not know, and nobody knew whether the ghost in Spider was beast or human, but she said, "Rabbit ghost." She chose the rabbit because this creature screamed when captured.

"Ahhh!" said the girl. "Rabbit ghost spiteful?"

"Yes, spiteful. It cries. It screams."

"Ahh, yes!"

Spider could not hear what the women were saying but he had no need to hear to be convinced that they were plotting mischief against him. He retreated again, his eyes hating them.

The grandmother now came out, bearing a crude stone dish filled with barley gruel, and a piece of meat. These she gave to the girl's mother. The next serving she gave to the girl. The third she gave to the young man of the family because he was the hunter who provided most of the food. The others she served as she came to them, singling none out for special attention; in her opinion they were all ghost-riven or sick and useless. Unlike some grandmothers, she was too indulgent to starve them, though little she would have cared if the useless members of her family had wandered away to be slain by beasts or had crawled into thickets to die. She felt compassion only for small children; among adults she felt friendliness only for those who served a useful purpose in her home.

Life for these people was so bitterly cruel, and the struggle to live was so hazardous, even for those in good health and sound mind, that the well ones could afford no time or patience for the sick. To be sure, now and then they did so, when more vital matters did not press on their energies. The old woman concocted various brews of herbs and juices, and these the sick ones drank; or sometimes, but only in extreme cases, a sick one was operated on with crude instruments in an effort to drive a ghost out. The grandmother wondered now and then if she ought to open Spider's skull to see if there was an alien spirit in it or make an incision in the sick woman's abdomen. Perhaps some day she would. Meanwhile she kept a suspicious eye on them and waited for them to die.

Nobody had yet devised an unfailing protection against malicious spirits. Because a woman in her menses was very vulnerable to invasion, she had to withdraw from

34

the family group and hide in dense growth or fence herself around with sticks and grass. She wore a menstrual apron as a sign of her wanton squandering of precious blood, but the apron was not yet regarded as a barrier against ghosts. In regard to protective devices these people were still in an experimental stage, obeying chiefly momentary impulses, such as clapping a palm to their nose when they sneezed or covering their ears and nose and mouth during thunderstorms.

Thunder and lightning were very dreadful things for them. Gentle rain they loved when it came from a friendly sky, because rain fertilized all things it touched; but thunder was the voice and lightning was the angry gestures of the Moon Woman. When she roared overhead and struck out with blinding fingers, they knew she was outraged by something her people had done; and then they cowered in helpless terror, not knowing in what way they had offended her or with what self-abasement they could recover her good will.

Having a curious and alert mind, the young man of this family thought about matters that the others took for granted, and there was developing in him a new and revolutionary notion. It seemed to him that perhaps it was not all the people who offended, but only a certain one; and if this were so, and they could tell who the offender was, then they could drive him away or kill him and so quiet the Moon Woman's anger. But this was still only a dim notion in him, slowly feeling its way toward certainty. He would continue to think about it, feel out its logic, silhouette its truth, and come at last to a conclusion that would make a great change in their way of life.

This morning he was not thinking of the Moon Woman;

she was nowhere visible, and there was no sign that she was angry with the people. Not with *her* people: he did not think of it that way. Nobody had yet come by the idea that the Moon Woman was the First Mother. For them she was only a woman who constantly renewed herself; who had knowledge of all magic; who spent most of her time watching them to see what they were doing; and who, when they displeased her, convulsed the whole world with her wrath.

No, he was remembering a dream. A large part of the moral and spiritual values of human beings today have come from the dreams of their ancestors. During their sleep, these people dreamed constantly, as people do still, and their dreams were always rich with meaning for them. They always knew what their dreams meant. Sometimes the soul went abroad while the body slept, a solitary wanderer, hunting or being hunted, pursuing or fleeing, seldom triumphant and often defeated. Now and then, but only rarely, the soul did not return to its body, and the sleeper was found dead when morning came. The men especially were haunted by the fear that their soul would not return, that it would find and enter a more acceptable home, or that, with deliberate malice, it would leave its body to die. This fear troubled their dreams and made them moan in their sleep or sometimes sit up suddenly and cry out to the soul to return.

This young man, who was a hunter, had dreamed a dream that he had dreamed many times. His soul was wayfaring when it came to a jungle by a deep and gloomy river. There it heard a continuous and dreadful uproar. In the jungle were the sounds of the hunted and the hunters—the rending and tearing of flesh, the crunching of bones, the screams of living things that were being eaten alive, and the snarls of the eaters. Then came the hush before dawn, the brief peace and quiet that always intervened between the killers of the night and the killers of the day. The whole world, so far as this man knew, was filled with ceaseless struggle and terror and death. Some creatures spent all their time fleeing and hiding; others hunted down the defenseless, the sick, the old, to kill and devour them. That was life; and everywhere above the terrifying carnage hovered the ghosts of man and beast, restless and vengeful, striving eternally to enter and possess the bodies of the living.

His dreams were nightmares because, like the dreams of all other men, they used the experiences, the sights and sounds and smells, the frustrations and loneliness, the anxieties and terrors that filled his life when he was wide awake. His body slept but his soul never slept. His body could be destroyed, but not his soul; it never died but like the Moon Woman was deathless. His soul could leave its body and wander at will, and every night it did so, prowling in the most dangerous places and troubling his sleep with its foolhardy and unpredictable adventuring. The souls of all people did so, though those of women did not race over the hills or enter jungles but stayed close by their homes, busy with their gardens and children and fires.

When the old woman came over to this young man and offered him food, he glanced at her fearfully, knowing that a little later she would command him to go hunting. If she did not abuse him or threaten him with her dire magic, he was resolved to do no hunting today. He felt too apprehensive to wander far from his home. He was wor-

37

ried by the grave of the old man, because it seemed to him now that the dead man's ghost had been present during the night and had been very unhappy. After eating his breakfast, he would steal over and look at the grave and see if all was well.

3

At a little distance from the grave he stopped, aghast, and looked at a dreadful sight. On the mound stood a raven. It was eating something, and the man knew with a shudder of horror that it was eating the dead body. Before coming to the grave he had gone to the jungle to recover his weapons, and he now fixed an arrow to his bowstring. But a moment later the bird ascended on great black wings and perched in a tree top. The man hastened forward to the grave and was appalled by what he saw.

Wolves or some other digging beasts had come during the night and uncovered the body. They had eaten a part of it and had torn open the chest cavity; and what was left of the heart lay red and naked in the morning sunlight. The raven had been eating the heart. Realizing this, the man laid his weapons aside and looked up at the bird, and the bird looked at him. This raven, the man told himself, had been eating the old man's heart, and that alone proved that it was a wise creature. He himself always ate the heart of beasts he admired. If you ate the heart you absorbed the animal's virtues, because the heart was the seat of the soul. This man had eaten the heart of wolf and hawk to absorb their courage, and of the deer for its speed, and of the snake for its cunning. Here was a raven that had been eating the heart of a man.

Overwhelmed by wonder and amazement, he resolved to be sure that the bird was as wise as it seemed to be. First, he knelt and stared at the piece of heart to engrave on memory an image of it, and then, picking up his weapons, he entered a thicket of trees to hide and watch. The raven left its perch and descended. For several minutes the man waited, thinking meanwhile of a bird that was wise enough to choose as its food the home of the human soul. It did so, of course, because it wished to be more like a man. And it would be. It would be an extraordinary bird—more wary and resourceful—and less vulnerable to its foes. It would be more human because of what it was now eating, and it would have a kind of kinship with human beings.

Excited by these thoughts, the man left his hiding place and hastened forward; and again the raven ascended on broad wings and perched in a tree. At the corpse the man fell to his knees, but there was no need to examine closely; the remainder of the heart had been eaten. He looked up at the bird as he might have looked at anything he admired. He felt for it a kind of kinship. With simple logic he identified himself with it and thought of the raven as a member of his family and people. Because in times past he had eaten the hearts of ravens, he was part raven, and this raven was now part man. Not for anything in the world would he have thought of killing it; on the contrary, he would have been overjoyed if he could have taken the bird home with him.

40

While staring at the handsome black creature he was taken by a thought: he would call himself by this bird's name. Among his people he would be known as the raven. Neither he nor any of his people had totems, but this man was feeling that kinship out of which, in a later time, the totem would come. So far as he was aware, all kinship was based on assimilation. A child was made of its mother's blood. If a man drank the blood of a wolf, he established kinship with the wolf; or if a raven ate a man's heart, it became related to all men. If Raven had been asked if all things that were eaten became the relatives of the things that ate them, he would have said yes, especially if the parts eaten were the blood and heart.

He himself was related to many things. Some creatures in the world he wanted no kinship with, and these he would not eat. Though women ate the timid and slinking rabbit, he would not. Women would eat any bird he brought home, but he ate only those he admired. After killing a hawk, he would first drink its blood, and then he would tear out the heart and eat that. The remainder of it he would take to the women.

While he was busy thinking of himself and his new name, the bird rose from its perch and flew away; and after it had disappeared, Raven was possessed by two impulses. He wanted to bury what was left of the old man, lest its ghost should become angry and punish him, but he also wanted to rush home and tell the family of his new kinship. The first impulse grew out of fear; the second out of joy in his greater meaning. In looking at the body he observed again that beasts had eaten a part of it, and he knew that its spirit would be angry if he left its home exposed. No ghost, of man or beast or bird, liked to see its body

destroyed. Quite as people today make war on one another, yet implore their gods to believe that their motives
are worthy, so Raven, before setting forth to hunt, always
supplicated the ghosts of his prey, asking them to understand that he and his family needed food and that he had
no ill will against them, and after he had killed a beast he
again talked to its spirit, trying to convince it that he was
its friend.

Now he was so filled with delight that not even fear
could restrain him; and so he picked up his weapons and
ran homeward, with a sense of new strength warming his
body and mind. On coming within sight of his family he
began to yell because he was bursting with joy; he danced
toward them, waving his weapons, shouting his new name
and believing all the while that he was afraid of nothing in
the world. The old woman came out of the hut and stared
at him. She had thought at first that he was bringing food,
but when she saw that he had none she began to cluck
angrily, as if tormented by insects. Then she thought he
was preparing for a hunt and was yelling to frighten his
enemies.

"What is wrong?" she asked, sternly eyeing his wild
capers.

He continued to dance, his head bobbing, his arms waving up and down as if he were trying to fly. Indeed, he was
simulating the flight of a raven. He felt lighter on his feet,
swifter, more eager, more venturesome, because the raven
was his relative now and its power was a part of him. The
members of his family stood in a group and stared. They
knew he was not troubled by a ghost because his face was
too radiantly happy for that; his whole body danced and
sang, and his mouth was singing a song of triumph. He

was telling them he was a raven, and there was no reason for any of them to doubt it.

Human beings could be many things. They thought of themselves less as human beings, sharply set apart from all other living creatures, than as the sum of all the things they had eaten. All of them were wolf and deer, bird and fruit, and the fertilizing rains. Sometimes they were more of one thing than another, as this man was now.

"Raven?" asked the old woman, wondering what he had been doing.

"I am Raven!" he cried, and waved his arms.

The old woman grunted. She supposed that he had been eating a raven and she wondered why he had brought none of it home. When, a little later, he told them that a raven had eaten the dead man's heart, the women were horrified. The change in the grandmother was sudden and violent. The dead man was her brother and the uncle of the children, and when she understood that he had been dug up by beasts and that his heart had been eaten, she was overwhelmed by dread. She began to run back and forth, uttering anguished cries and supplicating with her hands. The dead man's ghost would be outraged by such neglect of its body; it would haunt them all to the day of their deaths.

Turning on Raven, she cried, "Fool!" and ran over and slapped his ecstatic face. "Uncle unburied out there?" She pointed to the hills.

The question sobered Raven. His delight in closer kinship with the raven had made him forget the unburied corpse. Now, remembering it, and seeing the horror in the old woman's face, he was frightened. His joy was snuffed out like a burning ember thrust into water. His notion of kinship left him completely; in his mind was only one

43

image: that of an old man, half-eaten and lying unburied on top of his grave.

All the women were lamenting. The awful sound of their fear and grief threw Spider into a tantrum, and he began to dash back and forth like a demented creature, his eyes rolling in terror, his hands striking at the air as if he could feel a ghost clutching at his throat. Now and then he would pause and turn rigid and utter a wild scream. Old Man was so overcome that he slowly sank to the earth, as if his legs had melted. The lamenting women paid no attention to the men but looked up at the sky and wailed in the manner of dogs.

The grandmother was the first to come to her senses. She rushed into the hut and came out, carrying some digging tools.

"Come!" she cried to the others, but nobody seemed to hear. She hastened away in the direction of the grave. Observing that no one followed her, she swung furiously and came back and, dashing up to one of her daughters, she struck her across the skull with a stone spade. The blow interrupted a long mournful wail that broke off and died in a strangled sob.

"Come!" the grandmother cried. "We will bury him!"

Like one in a trance, the daughter looked at her and, though her lips moved, she made no sound. Thrusting a stone spade at her, the old woman ran over to Raven and gave him another digging tool; and again, calling to them to follow her, she started off. The daughter followed, moving like one drugged with grief. The girl went next, Raven fell in behind her, and the others, sensing that they would be left, moved off in single file, one by one.

With the grandmother leading, bent by age but driven

44

by an indomitable will, the family went out to the grave. When she saw that Raven had told the truth, that indeed the body had been dug up and the chest cavity torn open and the heart devoured, the old woman shuddered with pain and closed her eyes; but after a few moments the dizziness left her and she knelt and began to dig. The tool she used was a natural stone spade to which had been attached a wooden haft. It was not a sharp tool, but the earth here was soft and friable.

They had piled small stones on the grave, and these the grandmother now brushed aside. Her well daughter and Raven came up and knelt, and the three of them dug with their crude tools while the others stood back and watched.

For the people of this time, burial of their dead was a difficult task. They knew that a body had to be placed beyond the reach of enemies or its ghost would not rest in peace. They knew also that the ghost would be unhappy, and very probably spiteful, if they did not bury with the body all its weapons and trinkets, as well as choice food for its spirit to eat. To please the ghost they did everything they could think of; if they could have thought of more to do, they would have done it eagerly.

The case before them was especially dreadful because the body had been dug up, mutilated, and degraded. To placate its ghost now, it would be necessary to bury more than tools and food, and while the old woman thought of the matter, there came to her a flash of insight. Perhaps the ghost would be content if they were to bury with the body another heart—because a heart was the spirit's home to which, when weary of wandering, it returned to rest.

To Raven she said, "Look here. No heart."

"No heart," said the daughter.

"Raven ate it," the man said.

The grandmother was impatient. The important thing was not what had eaten the heart but that the heart was gone.

"Ghost needs home," she said.

Nobody questioned her statement; its truth was obvious to all of them.

The daughter said calmly, "Ghost needs heart."

Those who had been standing back fearfully now advanced and looked at the body; one by one they said that the ghost needed a heart, as if by repeating the statement they could fix the truth in their minds.

"Man heart?" asked Raven at last.

The grandmother had not pursued the idea to such a logical conclusion, but now that the question had been asked, she realized that the ghost would prefer to have a man's heart as its home.

"Yes," she said.

Raven looked away at the sky. He had asked a rash question and now he was troubled.

"What man heart?" he asked.

The grandmother was troubled too. It had been easy to realize that the ghost needed a home, but where to find a home was another matter. If a heart were taken from a living man, then its spirit would be restless and vengeful. Among the human enemies of these people, living beyond the farthest hills, there were men, but she did not ask herself whether, if a heart were taken from one of them, its ghost would come to haunt her. Her mind was weary and confused; it understood only that the uncle's spirit needed a home.

Raven had been thinking of another matter. Blood was also the home of a ghost.

He said, "Ghost needs blood."

The grandmother looked at the bloodless corpse. "Yes," she said impatiently. Of course it needed blood; anybody could see that. It needed a home. If they did not provide a home, then it would skulk around day and night and at last enter a living body. There was her sick daughter, for instance; a homeless spirit had entered her.

Indiscreet and eager to please, Raven asked, "Man blood?"

"Yes!" said the old woman sharply.

Raven pondered the matter. There were people, living far away and unknown to him, who drank human blood; but Raven and his people were not cannibals. The notion had never occurred to them that by drinking the blood and eating the flesh of their own kind they could strengthen and prolong their lives. If they had been told that this was so, they might have believed it, and the men might have begun to track down strange men.

But Raven was thinking now that the blood of wolf or hawk would satisfy this ghost. He thought it would be content with the heart of anything it had admired. Nevertheless he did not look cheerfully at the task of getting these things. He did not like to hunt alone. Until recently other men in his family had gone hunting with him, but one of them was now dead, and the other two were old and feeble.

Meanwhile he and the women had dug a fresh grave, though it was only about three feet deep and barely wide enough to receive the corpse. After the body was laid in it, they dug in the other grave to recover the weapons, and

47

these they placed by the body within easy reach of its hands.

"Food," the grandmother said.

She rose to her feet. She was racked by rheumatism, and when she straightened, her face was distorted with pain. It was the pain that made her sharp and querulous.

"Food!" she cried, turning to Raven with a menacing gesture. "Ghost needs food!"

"Yes," he said, rising hastily and going over to his weapons.

"Go find food!"

"Yes," he said.

He picked up bow and arrows and a stone knife. The arrows stood in a skin quiver which he suspended from a rawhide string around his waist. He drew a troubled sigh and looked away at the unfriendly world.

"What kind?" he asked.

"Choice food."

"Fish?" he asked slyly.

"No."

"Bugs?"

"Fruit," she said. "Eggs."

It was an unreasonable demand. Eggs he might find, but there was no fruit at this time of year. As for bringing a heart, the old woman knew very well that he could not hunt animals without making preparations, and these would take at least a day and a night. Did she not realize all this, he wondered, staring at the wrinkled old tyrant and hating the sight of her.

"No heart," he said, hoping she would change her mind.

"Heart, yes!"

"Where?"

48

Pointing to the world, she cried, "Go!"

He turned away like a man going to his doom. He hated this old woman because he was afraid of her, of her mysterious knowledge of magic, of her kinship with the Moon Woman, of her tyrannical furies. The grandmother of any family lorded it over the men, driving them away to find food, giving the choicest portions to the children when there were children and scraps to the men, and sometimes cursing the men. Having no gods, they did not really curse them, but their wild abuse was as terrible as a curse. It so frightened a man that it paralyzed his will and made him the easy prey of sickness and enemies.

Raven went out of sight but he had no thought at all of hunting larger game. Before hunting any beast or bird whose ghost might be vengeful, he had to prepare himself with a long and careful ritual, strengthening his body and will, filling his heart with boldness, and pleading with the ghost to be friendly after it was driven from its home. He now searched bushes for fruit, though he knew there was none, and he climbed trees to look for eggs in old nests.

After an hour or more of aimless and unhappy wandering, he remembered that the old man's body needed blood, and so he went home to get a skin pouch. Then, like one oppressed by a great weariness, he went over the hills, his naked feet leaving clear prints in a dusty path. He looked for squirrels and mice and rabbits, or for any other creatures of whose spirits he was not afraid.

After a while he surprised and shot a rabbit and, running forward, he seized the beast and tore its throat open with the stone knife and let the blood run into the pouch. When the blood eased to a drip, he set the stiff skin vessel between his legs; whereupon, holding the rabbit above it,

49

he squeezed downward along the carcass to force out all the blood. Then, hoping to get a little more, he laid the creature on the earth and massaged it, rolling and kneading it with strong hands, pressing on the bones and flesh, and at last grasping it by the hind legs, he held the open throat above the pouch. When convinced that he had emptied the creature of all its blood, he rose, taking his bow and the rabbit in one hand, the pouch in the other, and set out for the grave.

He found the family there. They had buried the corpse but had kept one corner of the grave open.

Seeing that he had fetched only a rabbit, the grandmother snorted with disgust and marched over to look into the pouch.

"Blood?" she asked.

"Yes!" said Raven, eager to please.

"Rabbit blood?"

He was tempted to lie but he knew she would not believe him.

"Rabbit blood?" she repeated angrily.

"Yes."

"No deer blood?"

"No." He stood like one who expected to have to run for his life.

"No wolf blood?"

"No."

Clucking with disgust, she took the skin vessel and went to the grave and knelt. With a long sharp stick she thrust downward through the soft earth and turned it round and round to make the ground firm where it banked the hole, and then very carefully she drew the stick out. Next, she tipped the pouch and spilled the thickened blood into the

hole. Bending low, she peered for a long moment; and Raven, anxiously watching her face, felt relieved when she seemed to be satisfied.

"No food?" she asked, looking at him.

"Rabbit!" he said eagerly, as if rabbit were the best food in the world.

She took the rabbit and thrust it down in the open corner of the grave, but she was troubled and made low angry sounds. She did not believe that the uncle's ghost, having no heart to rest in and no more than rabbit to eat, would be satisfied. Rising to her thin brown shanks, she looked at Raven.

"No heart?" she asked unreasonably.

As if she could be sure only if she called off the items one by one, she asked, "No eggs?"

"No," he said.

"No fruit?"

"No."

"Ghost will be unhappy," she said.

During all this time, none of the others had spoken or moved. Spider, standing back from the group, but anxiously listening, heard her say the ghost would be unhappy. He made a queer sound, as if choked by a sob. The fertile daughter looked up at the sky to see if the Moon Woman was there.

"Bury now?" she asked her mother.

The old woman said yes, and the two of them pushed earth into the grave, covering the rabbit and filling the hole. They spread stones over the mound. The grandmother gazed round her for a moment, wondering what else could be done, but, unable to think of anything more,

51

she gave a sign that the task was finished and started for home.

She knew the ghost would not be pleased with what they had done for it. Her brother had been an important man among men—or as important as any man could be who lived in a society dominated by women. At least he had been an able hunter who had set cunning snares and had trapped and killed beasts as large as the wolf and the deer. He had gone to the river and floated on a log in deep water to spear fish. He had climbed the tallest trees to look for eggs, and he had explored the gloomiest jungles, searching for strange nuts and fruits. He had been bold and resourceful in providing food for his family, and his spirit would be outraged now by the stingy way in which it was cared for. But in the way of all people the grandmother moved against logic and reason and hoped for the best.

That trait in human beings known as conscience has developed largely out of fear. When a primary instinct is exhausted when it has been satisfied, the organism feels weakened in its defense against its enemies, and fear ensues. Fear becomes a warning against excesses, and the conscience is the repository of that fear.

It would be extreme to say that the old woman was conscience-stricken. Such sense of right and wrong as she had was very vague; but nevertheless she did feel that they were neglecting the uncle's ghost. In that feeling were the faint beginnings of conscience. She was afraid; and because she was weary and old and very tired tonight, she felt deeply anxious. As the wise seeress of the family she knew that trouble lay ahead, and when at last she stretched out on a skin mattress to sleep, she moaned softly. She was lonely; she was sick with age and weariness; and against all the troubles that daily beset her, her remedies and defenses were often unavailing, no matter how shrewdly she devised them, no matter how hard she tried.

4

As DUSK approached, the others anxiously watched the grandmother because she was the wise one of the family and had more knowledge of unfriendly things. She could anticipate dire happenings. When her old witchlike face was serene, when she sat and let her chin sink to her breast, closing her eyes and dozing gently, they knew there was nothing to fear. But after she came in from the grave, her face was terribly awake and full of trouble. Her gestures were nervous and impatient. Now and then she glanced up at the sky to see if the Moon Woman was there, or she sniffed the wind, as if it were a messenger bringing tidings. All her movements had told them that this would be an unhappy night.

In the dusk Raven went over to sit by his tree, resting his back against it and drawing his knees up to his belly. He had watched the grandmother as anxiously as any other until he became engaged in a little ritual with mosquitoes. They were a humming swarm around him, flying lazily, with their legs dangling. When one stood on his

trayed any awareness of the frantic questions. Nothing in this moment could have invaded that strange and secret world in which she was queen.

Receiving no answer, the others again stared at the Moon Woman; for all of them she seemed to be calm and untroubled tonight. She was plump and old, but soon she would renew herself and appear as a young girl. Now she sat there in the sky, with no sign around her of anger or unrest—a gentle woman looking down at the earth and its people.

The grandmother nevertheless felt in her bones that there would be trouble tonight; and so, with the eyes of a seeress, she saw in the Moon Woman what the others missed. She saw hints of gathering wrath. She stared long and hard until she saw what unconsciously she had wished to see; whereupon, turning slowly, as if coming out of a trance, she said:

"She will be angry tonight."

The answering cries were full of alarm. They looked at the Woman again and saw what they had not seen before. There were signs of anger, all right; they were sure of that; and while Spider stared and trembled he became convinced that she was looking at him. He saw her move, as if shifting her position for a better view of him, and with a strangled cry he turned and dashed into the hut. The sick woman followed him, no less terrified; then one by one all save the grandmother slipped softly out of sight.

She stood for several minutes, looking at the Woman and feeling out the possibilities of her mood. This she did by becoming very sensitive to the emotions in her own body, with their burden of ache and pain, the twitchings in her skin, the pangs in her joints, the choked and suffocating deadness in her throat—as if her body were a barometer of all the woes of the earth. She stared until convinced that her first surmise had been right.

An hour later they were all lying on their beds, but none of them was asleep. The fire had been banked, and there was no sound, though each of them could hear his own breathing. Each of them was lonely and afraid. Outside, a wind had entered the night, and they could hear it whispering across the dry roof of their home. But for them it was not a wind. It was the mournful breath and the cries of innumerable ghosts, unhappy and homeless and eternally searching for homes. Some of the ghosts were timid, like those of rabbits and certain birds, and these only whispered in a plaintive and despairing way. During the time of light these hid in dark burrows or in the jungles or under stones. But the spirits of human beings, and of all flesh-eating beasts and birds, were bold and wild and often cried out with angry voices. These prowled through the darkness, plotting mischief against those who had eaten their bodies or had carelessly buried them.

This family, lying on beds and listening, knew that the wails and shrieks and moanings were the cries of ghosts both beast and human. It was a dreadful world, especially in the nighttime when darkness enveloped the earth and the disembodied creatures wandered at will. These people, and all the people of their clan, now lying in beds beyond the hills, were afraid of the dark. Daylight held its terrors, too, but then a person could see, and he could use his weapons or run without dashing into bramble thickets or falling into pits and snares. In a pitch-black night he was helpless and unprotected, save for the thin walls of his home and a buried fire.

58

Raven was convinced that among the ghosts crying in the night was that of the old man. Hearing a sudden and fearful sound, he sat up, but beyond the entrance he could see only the light of the Moon Woman. Glancing round him, he saw that the grandmother had risen and was looking out. Something in her face chilled him with dread. If terror could have been poured over him like an icy substance, he would not have been more rigid. He tried to speak, but his throat was paralyzed. One of her daughters asked the old woman:

"What is it?"

At the moment of speaking, the grandmother had not decided what it was, but as the matriarch of the family, in whom all knowledge rested, she always gave answers to riddles, choosing from her intuitive feelings the one that was most urgent.

"Uncle ghost," she said.

For all of them this answer had the weight of logic because they had expected the old man's ghost to be unhappy tonight.

Remembering that the sound had been a kind of terrified howl, the daughter asked, "Uncle ghost enter wolf?"

This question alarmed the grandmother. Years ago her family had owned a wolf-dog that a ghost had entered; the beast had become violently wild, frothing at the mouth and attacking everything in sight. She arose and went to the doorway to look out.

"Enter wolf?" the daughter asked again in a loud whisper.

"No," said the old woman, looking out and sniffing. There was no sign of a wolf anywhere.

Next she glanced up at the Moon Woman and saw that

59

she was preparing to leave the sky. She was barely above the treetops now and in a little while would withdraw to her mysterious hiding place. Her early departure was ominous and sinister; it meant that she was disgusted with the people and weary of watching them.

Returning to her fur mattress, the grandmother said, "Moon Woman disgusted."

"Why?" asked the daughter, still whispering.

The old woman did not know why, but again she chose the first of her intuitive responses.

"Uncle ghost has no home."

"No home!" whispered the daughter.

"No home!" said her sister.

For women nothing could be sadder than anything without a home. They took up the cry as a kind of lament; and because they had so few words with which to express anxiety and sorrow, they added low and melancholy syllables.

"No home—ahhohhh—no home!"

"Ahhohhh—no home—ahhohhh!"

In these sorrowful cries, Raven sensed a rebuke to himself. He was the one who had been told to find a home for the ghost and he had provided only a timid rabbit. Now the old man was out in the night, wailing like a lost and abandoned thing; if he did not find a home, he would come into the hut and try to enter one of the persons there. His ghost might come in the form of a snake, or it might hide in the wind and so be drawn in on a breath. While listening to the women and feeling that they were rebuking him, he covered his nose and ears.

In voices vibrant with a mother's sadness and pity:

"Ohhahhh—no home—unhappy—ohhahhh!"

"Ohhahhh!"

"No home—ohhhh!—no home—no home!"

Turning in her bed and looking over at Raven, the old woman said sharply, "Uncle has no home!"

"Rabbit," he said timidly.

"No!"

He shivered. She might order him out into the night to find a home for the uncle. He hated her because he was afraid of her. But she did not order him out. Perhaps she knew that he would be only a sly and cunning fellow, slinking close by the hut for a little while and coming in at last, out of breath as if he had traveled a great distance.

In the darkest corner of the hut was a lone bed, and above it now something moved like a spectral substance in the gloom. It moved very slowly, back and forth, back and forth, and Raven, watching it with fascinated and terrified eyes, felt his flesh creep and his throat tighten. He did not know that it was one of the sick woman's hands.

When ghosts were near her she could feel their presence. She lay now with eyes closed, with a piece of fur over her ears and nose, and explored with a hand, softly back and forth, to learn if spirits were hovering above her. Like one searching the atmosphere for areas of greater density, or for a palpable floating substance, or for variations in warmth and coolness, she quietly moved her hand back and forth in the darkness; all the while she pressed the other hand to the pain in her groin. Now and then she would press hard and then open her mouth wide under the fur to let the ghost come out; but all the while she passed the other hand slowly from side to side.

Many times, while lying alone in darkness, she had been

able to feel a ghost's presence—its breath on her hand or a faint movement in the air when it stirred or a pricking pain in her skin when it touched her. She could feel such a presence now. It was hovering above her, seeking a way to enter her body; but by moving her hand back and forth she kept it confused and baffled and she hoped that after a while it would go away.

Across the room, Raven still stared at her hand and waited.

For an hour or more this woman, lying apart from the others because she was sick and detested, and striving with all the courage she had to solve her problem without aid, had been moving one brown and wasted hand back and forth in the darkness and from time to time pressing the other against her belly to force the ghost out. The pressure caused severe pain, but she only gasped faintly and opened her mouth wide. On many a night, alone in the loneliness of one whom healthy persons abhorred, she had done this, trying to cure herself, never asking for pity or help, knowing well that none would be given, and seldom crying aloud with pain, save in her sleep. Night after night. . . .

And now, pressing against the ghost and opening her mouth wide like one yielding to surgery, while the other hand searched patiently for sign of relief, she did not know that anybody was looking her way. For all that her family meant to her in kindness, she might as well have been alone. Whether the alien spirit in her was that of human or beast, she did not know; but she knew it was there, nesting in her like a devouring parasite.

After a few minutes she summoned enough courage to press with all her strength; then the pain was so sharp and terrible that she screamed. In the same instant, her moving hand vanished, and Raven, who had been watching it, knew he had been looking at a ghost. He gave a yell of terror that brought the others upright in their beds.

"What is wrong?" demanded the grandmother, staring at him.

"There!" he cried, and a trembling hand pointed to the far corner.

"What is there?"

"Ghost!"

The old woman went to the doorway to look out. The Moon Woman had gone. The world had darkened. The trees swayed and tossed in the night as if cloaked with terror. Far away across the hills she could hear the baying of wolves.

Returning, she knelt by the hearth, uncovered the embers, and laid grass and twigs on them. While the fire was awaking, she went to the far corner and looked at the sick woman who was now sitting up, with both hands clasped across her belly. She was rocking gently and moaning.

"Ghost entered her," Raven whispered. He stood up and shook like one who had risen from a warm bed to stand naked in icy air.

"Uncle ghost?" asked one of his sisters.

He did not know, but he told them it had been in the form of a snake. He had watched it for a long while. He had seen it writhe across the floor and climb the wall by the sick woman's bed; then it had floated in the air above her, moving back and forth and waiting for a chance to enter.

"How big?" asked the grandmother.

"This big," he said, indicating that the snake was as long as the span of his two arms.

In the waking firelight the people looked at one another. If the snake was that long, then indeed it was a big ghost, the ghost of a man or a wolf or a tiger. They all knew that he had seen it and that it had entered the sick woman because they had heard her scream. They could tell now that she was in pain by the way she rocked her body and moaned.

Kneeling by her, the grandmother asked, "Ghost enter you?"

The sick woman bowed her head.

"Uncle ghost?"

"Yes."

"Ghost snake shape?"

"Yes."

One of the women laid wood on the fire, and soon there was light dancing on the walls. They could see one another clearly, and they looked at one another, their eyes anxious and questioning. Still, there was nothing much to ask, nothing to tell. The uncle's ghost was angry because its body had been buried carelessly and its home had been eaten; it had returned to the family to find another home. The grandmother had told them that it would. They remembered now that she had asked Raven to find a new home and that he had returned with a rabbit.

Raven had three sisters here. One was sick, one was barren, and the third was the mother of the girl. Women felt less need than men to have personal names, but now and then, especially when pregnant or when striving to be fertilized, they identified themselves with something they admired. Men identified with animals, but women chose fertilizing agencies such as rain or growing things whose color or fragrance pleased them. The favorite flower of the third sister was the rose, and she had sometimes thought of herself as a rose. The barren one had been forced to think of herself as one whose kinship was with still water, stones, and certain plants that bore neither blossoms nor fruit.

Rose had been scowling at her brother. "You lazy fool!" she said.

"Coward!" cried the grandmother, and the word came off her tongue like mucus.

Raven slunk back, hating both of them. He went to the darkest corner and sat by the wall. The grandmother called the sick daughter over to the fire, and with words and gestures told her to kneel, facing the light, and open her mouth. Then she peered into the mouth or spread the gristle of an ear to look in or tilted her head back and squinted at the nostrils. If this woman now housed two alien ghosts, that could mean, for the grandmother at least, only that the Moon Woman was angry. She was disgusted with the whole family.

For Raven, whose curious mind had often thought of these things, she was angry only with the sick woman. He came forth boldly, though he did not feel bold at all, and he tried to explain to them that when the Moon Woman became angry it was not because of the doings of all people but only of one of them. This notion was so revolutionary that the women were unable to grasp it. Indeed, they suspected him of plotting mischief, of having in mind some sly scheme, and they drove him back to the corner, rebuked and crestfallen.

Nevertheless, for Raven the truth of his idea became all

65

the more certain after he had tried to formulate it in words. In his confused but persistent thinking, he had come close to the notion of individual sin; whereas for the women, all members of the family had been offensive to the Moon Woman. They did not know how they had offended, save in the matter of careless burial. As for the sick one, she could hardly be guilty at all, inasmuch as she had not participated in the burial and as an ailing one had no important duties of any kind.

Raven's mind was trying to probe beyond family responsibility. He had put two facts together and drawn a conclusion from them. The sick one had already housed a strange and unfriendly spirit, and now the uncle's ghost had entered her; and so, for some mysterious reason she seemed to be the choice of ghosts seeking a home. If she had not offended the Moon Woman, why, then, was she singled out for torture?

While thinking of her as the offending one, he looked round the hut and his gaze fell on the barren sister; and at once his mind, like a battalion of attacking suspicions and conjectures, turned to her. She had never had a child. During all the years of her womanhood she had wasted the precious substance of birth, even though from time to time she dashed around like a frenzied creature in the fertilizing rains or sat in running water or bathed herself with the blood of such fertile things as rabbits and mice. Was not the Moon Woman angry with her? It seemed so to Raven, now that, with extraordinary insight, he had woven all his suspicions into the texture of lucid thought.

Rising eagerly, he went over to her bed and sat on his heels and looked at her. If a person stared at an object,

66

thinking about it was less difficult. Rose and the grandmother, busy with the sick one and exclaiming over her,
paid no attention to him; and so Raven gazed hard at his
barren sister, trying to discover by staring at her in what
grave way she had offended. For a few moments she suffered his earnest gaze, but her unhappy face darkened, and
all through her body she hated him. Squatting on his heels,
with arms clasped round his knees, Raven looked at her as
he might have stared at a strange insect, and he was taken
by surprise when she suddenly stood up and pushed him
off balance and yelled:

"Go away!" Her dark brown eyes were like melting
fire.

"No," he said, speaking like a patient and kindly inquisi-
tor. "Let me look."

"Look what?"

"You," he said.

Their eyes met; a man and a woman stared intently at
one another. Barren did not know that sexual embrace was
necessary to birth; she did know, and now remembered,
that Raven had not embraced her in a long time. When,
now and then, she had made it plain that she was receptive,
he had spurned her. He was afraid of her—as all men were
afraid of women who followed faithfully in the Moon
Woman's cycle, yet never gave birth but merely grew old,
without the Moon Woman's power of renewal. There was
a feeling in him, as in all men, that such a woman was
unclean. He had never thought of her as guilty and sinful;
but now, in a very obscure and baffled way, that is how he
was thinking of her.

In his eyes she read the suspicions of his mind. With a
burst of fury she leapt up and smote him and then stamped

67

her feet and screamed. The other women turned to look at them.

"What is trouble?" the grandmother asked.

Raven was standing now. He had backed away, conscious that every member of the family was looking at him, including Spider and Old Man.

"No baby," he said, and pointed an accusing finger at Barren.

That she took as a taunt. Maddened with grief and fury, she uttered a strangled cry and rushed at him, striking with both hands. She attacked with such frenzy that under her blows Raven stumbled and fell, sprawling on his back, with his arms and legs threshing; in the next moment Barren looked down and saw his genitals. Something in her unconscious mind awoke as a wild impulse and she threw herself on him. She hugged him with insane ardor and strove to pull him to her in embrace, but Raven howled like a small lad being mauled and tried to fight her off.

Then the grandmother intervened. She seized Raven by his long tangled hair and yanked his head back. She told her daughter to go to her bed, and Barren did so, shaking all over with grief, with the desperate hunger of a woman who had never been a mother. Lying on her bed, she pulled a skin over her and began to moan.

Raven crawled over to his bed and sat there like one who had been whipped. Gone completely from his mind was the brilliant notion he had been considering. From somewhere across the hills he could hear a wolf-dog baying. By a blazing fire, the old woman and her daughter, with the girl looking on, were ministering to a sick woman tortured by two ghosts. They were pouring down her throat a bitter medicine that the grandmother had concocted, the secret of which was known only to her. It was a mixture of herbs, dried blood, tree sap, fermented plant juices, and the broth of a piece of animal placenta that she had boiled. It was her cure-all for everything.

The sick woman yielded without protest and gulped one mouthful after another; but when, long past midnight, she returned to her bed, she was racked by severe pains. She stretched out on her bed and moaned, with one hand pressed to her groin and the other moving above her in the gloom, softly, tirelessly, its fingers slowly closing now and then as if to feel a presence. Instead of lying on his fur, Raven crawled under it and drew it snugly around his head. He lay face downward, with his nostrils pressed to an arm and his hands cupping his ears.

5

SOMETIMES a family burned its house and moved away if it became too infested with tiny blood-sucking creatures or too filthy with their offal or too haunted. The next morning the grandmother arose from troubled sleep and looked round her with distaste. She decided to burn her home and move to a clean spot and build another. She announced her intention not with words but by moving the furnishings outside. Perceiving what she had in mind, Rose and Barren and the girl assisted, carrying out the skins which were used for bedding, the few crude utensils, and the small hoard of food. All these they heaped in piles at a safe distance.

Before allowing any of the women to touch the food the grandmother examined them to learn if they were menstruating. A woman in her menses was never permitted to handle food or the household dishes. Such a woman was unclean and poisoned everything she touched; even her presence could so contaminate food that it would cause bellyaches and vomiting.

In turn the old woman faced her two daughters and her granddaughter and looked at them and asked, "Blood?" They all answered no, not resentfully, but as a simple statement of fact. They all knew that Rose was pregnant; but Barren still had regular menstrual periods, and the grandmother looked at her more sharply. She bent over to peer and sniff and when she straightened she looked at the woman's eyes.

"No," Barren said calmly.

Raven had gone over the hills to look at the uncle's grave. It was his task to keep it covered with stones, to pour blood into it from time to time, and to bring to it, if he could, a heart that a proud ghost might accept as a home. But Raven was a lazy fellow; he did no more than to look at the grave to see if it had been disturbed. Besides, the uncle's ghost was now in the sick woman, and until it was driven out of her he saw no reason why he should worry about it. A ghost was much like a mosquito; if you let it have what it wanted it ceased to be troublesome.

Raven was a kind of specialist in the ways of ghosts. He had a curious and scientific turn of mind; and after he returned from the grave, he gathered his weapons and dyes and trinkets in a pile and lay on his back in full sunlight. He closed his eyes against the sun and watched the ghosts that then became visible. The world he looked at with his eyes closed was full of them. Some were only black spots that darted nervously back and forth and up and down, acting like insects at twilight; all these, he supposed, were the spirits of insects and other very small things. Others were wraithlike and reminded him of smoke. These also moved constantly, and when he tried to follow them they often vanished completely; but they waited, he had learned long ago, just beyond his vision, and darted back into sight the moment he gave up trying to see them. He did not know that he moved his eyes under their closed lids. He did not know that it was bright sunlight on his eyelids that gave warm golden colors to some of the spirits. Nor had he ever decided what kind of spirits these wriggling smokelike creatures were. Perhaps they were the ghosts of flowers and other plants.

While he was studying his tiny world of darting things and speculating on their nature, the grandmother came up and kicked him. She struck him with a tough heel against his ribs, and he felt a twinge of pain.

"Get up!" she cried.

Raven opened his eyes and looked at her. Then, beyond her, against the sky, he saw some of the dancing phantoms and, pointing to the sky, he said, "Look! See ghosts there."

The old woman turned to look but she saw only the pale blue emptiness of space. Suspecting that he was trying to put her off with some of his unpredictable fancies, she said more sternly, "Get up!"

Raven stood up and felt the warm dust close round his calloused feet.

"What?" he asked, resenting her intrusion.

"Go hunt food."

When freed from care, these people strove to enjoy life, sometimes quietly, as Raven had been doing, and sometimes with impulsive and boisterous fullness. In spite of the anxiety of the women he felt unmolested today and wished to lie in the sun, warming himself like a lizard and thinking of the strange world in which he lived. But there was work to be done. Instead of driving him away to hunt, the grandmother assigned him the task of carrying the old stiff bedding-skins to the new home site. The spot chosen by her was only a few hundred yards away, but after taking only a couple of skins instead of an armful, Raven trudged along like an old and overburdened man. After covering a part of the distance he lay down on the skins, as if intolerably weary, and closed his eyes again to watch the ghosts dance.

The grandmother came up, stooped under a burden many times as great, and smote him on the side of his skull. The blow of her heel made his senses swim. For a moment he was aware of an extraordinary number of spirits swarming in his vision, as if, like wasps, they had poured out of a nest when the blow fell, but in the next instant he saw a wrinkled face full of disgust and anger.

"You lazy man!" she cried.

"What?" Raven asked innocently.

"Get up!"

He struggled to his feet and picked up the two skins. She thrust her armful against him and almost pressed him down; and again he trudged with his burden, feeling cruelly done by and going like one who had known only hard labor all his life. In his body was wild rebelliousness against all women and their ways. It was a man's desire to be a wanderer, but he was anchored to a home and a hearth, not because of love for women and children, not because a family relationship had any deep meaning for him—no, but only because of the security of fire, the constancy of warmth and food. The ways of a woman were unfriendly to his strongest impulses and his most sleepless instincts.

Raven was not, of course, thinking of the matter so clearly; he was feeling it. He knew intuitively that the women had contempt for him. They had their busy little world of duties, customs, labor, and fireside; and outside all these was the man, looking in—a lackey who brought food, a cunning pest who hungered for sexual embrace, and in nearly all hours a superfluous intruder. Raven felt so debased by the blow on his skull that he groaned and dropped his burden of skins and pots on the new home place and then looked round at the world, his lips parted, his nostrils aquiver, and his eyes strangely intent, as if he had caught a vision of the man he might be. After staring beyond horizons, his obscure dream of himself became mixed with the smell of smoke and flame.

The hut was made of interlaced vines and branches, long since dead and dry, and so it burned swiftly in sudden violent passion that shot up in yellow tongues and engulfing fury, with its hot breath pouring over the earth and its cries ringing to the distant hills. How many things died when a home was burned, these people never knew; but they could hear both human and animal cries in the devouring hunger. There were happy spirits in water, because it sometimes whispered and laughed and sang; there were unhappy spirits in trees, for they often moaned and sobbed all night. An old hut was full of ghosts hiding in the cracks, under the bedding, in the hearth ashes, and even in the earth of the floor. Nobody thought that these were burned and destroyed; they wailed so with anguish only because the fire drove them from their hiding places.

After choosing a spot close by a jungle of vines and not too far from running water, it was the women who built the new home. Even if they had wished to help, and had been allowed to, the men would not have known what to do, never having built a house and knowing nothing of the art of weaving vines in a firm network for the roof and walls. For a woman, a house was the core of her world. For a man, it was merely a shelter against the sun, a barrier against wind and enemies, a storehouse of food.

When Raven saw all the women but the sick one go into the thicket to gather vines and supple green branches, green ropes and poles and leaves, his gaze followed them lazily and without interest. He had made a luxurious bed in the shade of a tree and stretched out on this like a lord at his ease, untroubled and indolent. No fears sucked his strength like leeches, no riddles pestered his mind. It was a glorious and gentle day in the spring season; the earth was roofed by a sky as soft and friendly as the moss pads on an old tree, and after he looked at the sun steadily for several moments, it became a round warmth in this roof.

When he first glanced at it, this fire above him seemed to be only a dazzling brilliance; but now he observed, as he had observed many times before, that if he gazed at it fixedly he could drive away most of the glare and the leaping and splashing of light. Then he saw something about the size of the Moon Woman, with a golden circumference and a glowing face. He had also learned that after looking for a little while at the sky-fire he could close his eyes and study the insect ghosts against a background that was luminous and warm. Then the smokelike spirits seemed to be clothed with an extraordinary radiance.

He was lazily experimenting and enjoying himself with childlike delight when the women returned, each carrying a load of vines. They dropped their burdens not far from where Raven lay, and for a few moments they murmured happily like bees getting ready to build a hive. Then the

75

grandmother saw him lying on a pile of fur bedding and with a grunt of disgust she marched over.

He rolled off the bed like one who expected indulgence if he eschewed all luxury and sought the hard ground; and when she came up and stood with hands on her scrawny hips and stared at him, Raven tried to look as if he were unhappy and sick. It was not his help in building a house that she wanted; such labor was the privilege and joy of women. Providing food was a man's work; and while she looked at him the old woman was thinking of her small hoard of provisions. She had not tasted fresh meat for many days.

"Lazy fool!" she said with contempt.

"What is wrong?" he asked.

"No food!"

"Food is there," he said.

"No meat!"

"Seeds," he said, as if by naming the foods which she had he could take her mind off meat. "Carrots. Barley. Fruit—" He was naming not only the foods she had but all those he could think of. "Fish—"

"Ahhh!" she cried, suddenly aware of what a cunning impostor he was. She had almost believed his catalog of foods; at least she had been wondering, until he mentioned fish, if all these good things were over there in her pile. But they had not had fish for two or three seasons, and when he named it she realized that he was trying to trick her.

Gasping with amazement at his audacity, she advanced to smite him, but at once he fell over like a man stricken with death and stretched out on his back and began to moan. He said he was sick. Bending over, with bony hands

76

clenched and her taut muscles ready to strike, she stared at him, unwilling to punish a sick man yet afraid he was tricking her again.

"Sick where?" she asked.

Obeying a luckless impulse, the cunning fellow clasped his belly; at once the old woman hastened over for her medicine. When he suspected what she was going to fetch he sat up in alarm, not because he doubted the efficacy of her simple but because it tasted so vile, and he was not sick at all. She came back, bringing a filthy skin-pouch half filled with her bitter concoction.

"Open mouth," she said.

He knew it would be folly to argue with her. She loved to doctor the ailing, because this was also one of her special and enviable rights. Making a face of disgust, less for her than for himself who had blundered, he opened his mouth, and she poured into it about an ounce of the medicine. Lest he might spill and waste it, as sick persons sometimes did, she quickly set the pouch aside and grasped his chin, as if it were a hanging and helpless half of a hinge, and snapped his mouth shut. Then a strong calloused thumb and forefinger squeezed down along his gullet, massaging his throat and forcing him to swallow. A moment after swallowing, his eyes opened and winked swiftly a few times and then looked stricken.

"You feel better?" she asked hopefully, and seized the pouch.

He nodded vigorous assent and arose to his feet, resolved to go hunting rather than to swallow any more of the bitter stuff. He knew, and they all knew, that her medicines were marvelous; they could cure any ache or disease, if malicious ghosts would allow them to. Only the grandmother knew how many ingredients her simple contained, though they were never twice alike, inasmuch as she was guided not by prescription but by intuitive impulses. Her remedies depended largely on the mood she was in when she wandered across the hills to gather the materials.

"Go find food," she said, studying his face to see if he intended to puke. She regarded it as a special merit of her simples if they made the sick one vomit—because severe vomiting could sometimes eject a ghost.

Raven said he would go hunting, but he intended to do nothing of the kind. He really felt sick now. For into her last concoction the grandmother had put not only the juices of several aromatic plants and the sap of different trees but also lime and a kind of pepper. The mouthful Raven swallowed had burned down his throat and scalded his stomach; and instead of going hunting he intended to drink cool water to ease his pain. But to deceive her he took his weapons with him and sped over a hill and out of sight.

Without pausing to eat, the women labored all day, the grandmother and Rose building the hut and the others bringing vines. The old woman had built many huts and took pride in her workmanship, though her methods were very crude and often improvised. She used a large limb of a tree, thrust out parallel with the earth, as a roof anchor, draping the vines across it and then over a slender framework of poles. The supporting structure of the walls was a kind of trellis work of wooden battens; upon this they wove the long vines, as if they were making a huge basket. They set two poles upright to mark the doorway and tied vines around them.

The hut had no windows save the hole left in the roof for the smoke to escape; and it had no door, though some of their distant neighbors used doors that were bundles of interwoven branches. Its floor was the earth, upon which the women would put old leaves and dry moss after a while; its fireplace, set against one wall and under the hole in the roof, was completely fenced with large stones. Fire was always a hazard, especially after the walls and roof became dry, and because of the dry covering on the floor. They never dared to leave the fire unbanked or to let it blaze up joyfully even when closely watched.

The women did not expect to build a new home in one day but only to shape it and put on a part of its covering. For many days they would add to it, particularly to the roof, because if they were skillful and used plenty of materials, they could make the top almost rainproof, as well as insulate the interior against the hot sun.

When she saw that dusk was approaching, the grandmother made it known to the others that they would now carry in the bedding; at once the women sorted the skins, each taking the ones she had formerly used. Inside the hut, the old woman took her choice of the bed places, Rose took second choice, and the girl took third. The fourth and fifth positions fell to the other women. After these five beds were laid, the men would have to sleep where they could find room.

Spider and Old Man, sitting back under the branches of a tree, scratching their dirty skins and fighting off pests, had watched the women all day long. Not once had they moved off their haunches. There had been nothing to move for. They had no right to touch the hoard of food,

79

and though they had felt thirsty they had been too indolent to go for a drink. When they saw the women take
their beds inside, they realized that the time had come for
them to move and, looking at one another with comical
gravity, as if to say, "It's now or never," they crawled
out like enormous brown bugs and rose to their legs. After
approaching the skins, they saw that the women had taken
all the best ones, as was their custom—and, indeed, their
right—and so it was with no resentment at all that the
men looked at the scabbed and worm-eaten hides that
were left. They were stiff, and in patches they were hairless.

"Not good bed," said Spider, holding up a skin and
staring at it.

"Not good," said Old Man. He also picked up a skin.
Each gazed with distaste at the hide he held up, and then,
with inquiring eyes, they turned to look at each other.

It was at this moment that Raven returned and, sensing
at once what was happening, he rushed up to the men,
yelling at them and menacing them with his lance. They
dropped the skins and retreated. Thereupon Raven
pounced on the pile and turned the hides over and over,
seeking for his own use those with most hair or fur. Having made his choice, he left three almost hairless skins for
the two men and, with the others clasped to his breast,
he entered the hut.

Still clutching his bedding, he stood for a long moment
looking round him, observing where the women had laid
their beds and the spaces available to him. The grandmother had made a fire, and the smoke from it, instead
of ascending through the roof hole, spread out in a lazy
fog that filled the room. In an effort to dodge it, Raven

went to the hearth; and now, having chosen, at least tentatively, a place for his bed, he held the skins in the firelight to choose the least desirable one to lay next to the earth. Soon he was holding them up like enormous stiff leaves and while thus engaged he almost encircled the fire, with the skins standing like a fire screen around the hearth. He was about to turn away and make his bed when he noticed that the smoke was not spreading out but was rising to the roof hole. Looking over a skin and down at the fire, he observed next that the pale smoke seemed to be crawling up the hair. Curious, he moved the hide away, and at once the smoke spread out and enveloped him. He returned the hide to its upright position and now, in an effort to enclose the fire completely, he placed skins upright on the hearthstones from wall to wall.

He did not realize that he was making the first chimney.

Looking across the top of the hides and down, he saw the smoke rising in a column; then, looking up, he perceived that most of it was rising to the roof. Eagerly now he experimented. He tried to hold up the skins and make a chimney clear to the ceiling, and when he was unable to do so he called for help.

The grandmother had been watching him. At first she had thought he was warming his bedding, a foolish thing to do on a hot night, but after a few minutes she realized that he was trying to do something with the smoke. When she came over, Raven thrust a skin at her and said:

"Hold it there."

Rose and her daughter came, and Raven gave them skins to hold; but he soon learned that if the skins rested on the hearthstones, the fire acted sick and helpless. So he indicated that they were to hold the skins a few inches above the stones, and he knelt and peered under at the fire and observed the behavior of the smoke. The women were now excited too. Observing that the smoke climbed when it was imprisoned, they gave cries of delight or shifted the position of the skins, trying to improve their crude chimney. It occurred to the grandmother to suspend the skins from the ceiling, but while she was searching for her wooden needles and rawhide thongs, Raven became bored and turned away. Shouting at the two women as if they were trying to steal his bedding, he tore the skins from their grasp and went back to make his bed.

The sick woman had gone to bed and was moaning like one in constant pain. The sound she made was almost continuous, because each indrawn breath was a strangled gasping and each exhalation was a sobbing release, with the tone rising to a shrill pitch and falling down and away in a low murmur of despair. Nobody paid any heed; they had heard her moan night after night for a long while. But when making his bed Raven became aware of a new and strange quality in her breathing; and after listening intently for a few moments, he crawled over to the sick woman's bed to look at her.

Her eyes were closed, but he could see twitchings in the lids. Her mouth was closed, too, except when she exhaled; then the slow rush of breath puffed her cheeks a little and made tiny spasms in her lips. Her hands were clasped over her ears. If Raven had not been so ignorant of such matters he would have known by the ghastly pallor of her face and by her bloodless mouth that the woman was very sick. To be sure, he realized that she

82

was ill, but only because a malicious ghost was tormenting her. The strange and different quality of her moan held his interest because there was in it such chilling loneliness. He believed that this loneliness came from the uncle's ghost.

Sitting back on his heels, with his forearms resting limply across his knees, he studied the woman's face; and while he was wondering what could be done to expel the spirits, the grandmother looked over at him.

"What is wrong there?" she asked.

"Ghosts in her," said Raven.

"Uncle ghost."

"Yes."

"Uncle ghost unhappy."

"Unhappy," said Raven.

"No home."

"Uncle ghost talking," said Raven.

This statement brought the grandmother to his side. She knelt and looked at the woman.

"Listen!" Raven whispered.

For a long moment they listened. The old woman's ears were not so sensitive; she did not hear in the moaning a ghost's voice that was lonely and pleading.

"What is uncle saying?"

"He is unhappy. He wants home."

"Ahhh! No home!"

"Listen! Uncle is hungry. Uncle wants food."

He was guessing now, but it did not seem so to him. To put an impulsive notion in words was to give it the certainty of truth. From the point of view of his own self-interest it was foolish of Raven to say that the uncle wanted food, because food for the ghost, as well as a home,

83

was what the grandmother had asked him to get. He was calling attention to his own lazy neglect of his chores.

"Food!" the old woman snorted. "Lazy man! Uncle wants food!"

"No," said Raven.

"Listen! Uncle wants food."

Realizing that he had blundered again, Raven began to crawl backward, retreating like a ground creature to its hole. He was afraid the old woman would order him out into the darkness to find food for the uncle, and so he wished to slink away and crawl under his bedding and hide. He was willing to go without his supper, to hunger and thirst until morning, if only the angry tyrant would not drive him out into the night's terrors. Noiselessly, like a crab backing off, he crossed the earth floor and reached his bed and strove to hide under the skins. He could hear the old woman crying out of shrill, blind anger.

She was telling him that he was foolish and lazy and worthless, and she was looking round her meanwhile with rheumy and half-blind eyes, wondering where the sly rascal had gone to.

"Uncle ghost hungry!" she cried, and her voice made the green leaves whisper in the ceiling. "No food, no home! Ahhh, no home!" She broke off and squinted in the gloom for a sign of her worthless son.

Under his bedding, Raven was peering out and watching her. Rose and Barren had taken up the cry and were lamenting for the dead one.

"Ahhh, no home!"

"Ohhh-ahhh!"

"Listen!" the old woman said.

They all listened. Some heard the lamenting cries of ghosts as they wandered, homeless and lost, through the wild night, but Raven heard the awful loneliness in the sick woman's crying.

6

THE next morning the sick woman was no more ailing than she had been for days, but after stirring the fire the grandmother went over to look at her. It was not the woman she was thinking of. It was the uncle's ghost, unhappy and homeless, that worried her—the spirit of her brother who, among all the men she had known, had been the most faithful provider. For his ghost especially she felt that something must be done; but first it would have to be driven out of the sick woman or it would nest in her as long as she lived. When she died it would be homeless again, and more restless than ever.

The grandmother told the woman to come with her outside. Frightened and obedient, she rose to her feet and then bent over and clutched her groin and stifled a cry of pain at her lips. The grandmother wanted her patient to go out into the bright sunlight where she could look at her and speculate on what to do, and so she led her from the hut and spread a skin and told her to lie on it.

"Put arms out," she said.

86

The sick one thrust her arms out at right angles to her body.

"Put legs out."

She then spread her legs. In this moment there was an intuitive recognition like a flash of lightning in the old woman's mind. But she did not speak of it. She was a cunning physician who kept her secrets, or did so at least until she had good reason to share them. Besides, though the recognition had been like a flash of light, it was gone in a moment, leaving the old woman more startled than enlightened.

It was an intuitive perception's way then, as it still is, to come as a sudden and brilliant illumination and then vanish, leaving a kind of afterimage that faded and escaped, or slowly grew into an idea, depending on how receptive and tenacious the beholder was. The grandmother was by no means so receptive as her son Raven, but she was as tenacious as a leech, and what was revealed to her she struggled to keep. She turned a hard stare on the sick woman's pelvic area and then knelt by her and laid a hand on her groin.

"Ghost here?" she asked, pressing a little.

"Yes."

"You feel ghost?"

"Yes."

The grandmother stared at the brown hairy belly and remembered that there were two ghosts in this woman. Moving a hand up and across the abdomen, she pressed again and asked:

"Ghost here?"

"Yes."

The grandmother made a clucking and satisfied sound.

87

She had suspected there were two spirits, a fact now confirmed, and such a shrewd surmise, it seemed to her, proved that she was a remarkable seeress.

The other members of the family were watching her. None of them had any notion of what she intended to do; but they had great faith in her ability to drive a ghost out, once she put her mind to it and used all her wisdom, and they would not have been surprised if a spirit had leapt from the sick woman and run away with hisses of amazement and alarm. There was a look in the old woman's face that refreshed their confidence. Her wrinkled lips were set in a firm line; her eyes were half-lidded, as if a little burdened with so much knowledge; her hands, moving over the body, were bold and unerring. She was at her best this morning, and they all believed that they would see remarkable things before she had finished with her magic.

The grandmother was enjoying her role to the fullest. A man's meaning was in ideas and symbols, but a woman's was in the work she did—in caring for children, the fire, the home, and in manifesting her mysterious and boundless knowledge. Unlike some of the matriarchs among her distant neighbors, she had never used surgery, though she had some crude tools with which she could have opened a skull or a belly; nor had she ever experimented with certain powerful herbs that put people to sleep. She sometimes privately suspected she had her peers as a wise woman; but for her family, or at least for the other women, she seemed to be omniscient.

Raven was a little dubious, but that was only because he had a curious and skeptical turn of mind.

"Two ghosts?" he asked.

88

"Two," said the grandmother, again clucking with pride in her knowledge.

"Three ghosts?" asked Raven, speaking with perverse impudence.

"No!" she cried sharply. "Two."

"Three," he persisted.

The grandmother turned to look at him, wondering if he had observed something she had missed; but when she saw how inoffensive and humble his face was, she decided he was only a foolish man with nothing to do but to ask stupid questions.

But Raven was not stupid and he was not being malicious. While staring at the prostrate woman it had occurred to him that she might have a ghost in her skull. Sometimes, as the grandmother knew as well as any other, a ghost housed itself in the head and could be driven out only if a piece of skullbone was removed. Kneeling, Raven gently touched the woman's head.

"Ghost there?" he asked, looking at his mother.

At once the old woman began to press the skull, and when the woman winced under a prodding finger, the grandmother examined the spot and asked:

"Ghost there?"

"Yes," said the poor woman, who was too sick and tortured to care what questions were asked or what answers were given.

"Ghost here," the grandmother said, looking solemnly at Raven; and meeting her gaze with eyes equally humorless, he said:

"Three ghosts."

"Yes, three."

The others had been anxiously waiting. Now Rose

89

turned to the woman behind her and in an awed voice said:

"Three ghosts."

Barren turned to Spider and said:

"Three ghosts."

As if the fact could be fully realized only if it were repeated again and again, Spider announced to Old Man that there were three ghosts.

The grandmother meanwhile had not taken her finger from the spot under which the third spirit was hiding. It was an inch above and a little behind the right ear. With a hard finger she probed around the spot. Then she bent forward and stared into the ear but, seeing nothing suspicious, she next seized the gristle of the ear and spread it back while she tried to look deeper inside.

"Ghost entered here," she said.

The statement was so logical that nobody questioned it. Bending forward and looking in turn at the spot under which the spirit was hiding and at the ear just below it, they all understood how the ghost had entered; and after staring for a long moment, they looked round them and up at the sky. Raven clapped his hands over his ears.

What to do now, the grandmother hardly knew. She lived in a time when there was more logic than ritual in curative practices. Nobody had ever thought of stroking a sick person with a leaf, of putting the leaf in water, of pouring the water into a hole—or of doing many other things which in a later time people would do. The grandmother had not learned to gather her herbs by the light of the moon in a certain phase; or to talk in the gift of tongues, the exact sense of which would be unknown to her but understood by the evils to be exorcised; or to weave sorcerous spells or wear protective or good-luck amulets. Such methods as she employed she had inherited from generations of wise old women like herself, but she had never been a person of lively fancy, and so to the knowledge she had been given she had added almost nothing.

She knew there were various ways to drive malicious spirits out of persons. Sometimes it could be done with purges and emetics; sometimes by starvation—because no ghost would live in a home without food; and sometimes it was necessary to cut open the unfortunate one and expel the ghost by exposing it. But in this woman there were three, and she was at a loss to know what to do.

While prodding and inspecting the hapless woman as if she were a carcass about to be skinned and quartered, the grandmother observed again that the genital looked strange. Urging the woman to take a position that would allow a fuller inspection, the old woman rested on knees and elbows, peered and squinted, and made a low clucking sound as if she were savoring some remarkable data. Then she moved aside and asked the other women to look, and in turn they knelt and did so; and when Rose saw the turgescence, she turned to her mother and asked:

"Baby soon?"

"No."

"Baby there," said Rose, and pointed.

"No!" cried her mother impatiently.

Rose stooped again to peer; she looked at the woman's swollen belly and, convinced by the evidence, she said firmly:

"Baby is coming."

"No baby," said the old woman, and her statement was so final that nobody dared to dispute her. She now folded her arms under her chin and rested her face on her arms and began to pace back and forth; the others watched her and waited. The grandmother never entered trances the better to read the secrets of the invisible world; nor did she, like some of her distant neighbors, drink fermented juices to sharpen her powers as a seeress. But she did have a manner of pacing back and forth, with head bowed on her arms and with her stomach muscles moving in and out like a slow bellows. In such a mood she pushed away everything that was trivial or malicious and focused all her powers on the question that troubled her. Whether she was engrossed for a few moments or for a long while depended on the importance of the question.

The matter she pondered now was as serious as any she had ever faced, and so she walked back and forth and back and forth until the others became fearful and anxious; until the sick woman, overcome by dread, sat up and stared at the faces around her; until Raven pulled his arms tight against his stomach in an effort to keep from vomiting; and until Spider, unable to endure the suspense, suddenly screamed and began to leap up and down and smite himself.

As if she had waited on his outcry to bring her out of a hypnotic communion, the grandmother turned calmly to her family and pointed to the sick woman's genital and said:

"Ghost entered there."

Nothing that she might possibly have said could have amazed them more. They were speechless. They all stared at the sick one, and like a person sentenced to death by their stares the woman looked in turn from one to another, her eyes filling with terror. Nobody moved. Nobody dared to move. The old woman again bowed her head to her arms, and they knew that she was reviewing the evidence to be sure her conclusion was right. When at last she raised her head and looked away at the sky with eyes clouded by more than human knowledge, her daughter Rose softly asked:

"Ghost entered there?"

"Yes."

Rose turned to the others as if she were an interpreter; she pointed to the sick one and said:

"Ghost entered there."

"Ahhh!" cried Barren.

"Three ghosts?" asked Rose in an awed whisper.

"Yes, three."

Rose knelt by the sick woman. "Not enter here?" she asked, indicating the nostrils.

"No."

"Not here?" she asked, and touched an ear.

"No."

The grandmother had the proud bearing of an oracle. She was an oracle. She was so sensitively in tune with the invisible world that in this moment she could have answered any question without hesitating, without feeling any doubt at all.

It did not seem strange to these people that they had never perceived all the possible ways in which a ghost could enter a body. Ghosts were very sly and deceitful things; as soon as you discovered one of their tricks they were off to play another, and so you had to keep thinking about them day and night or you would never catch them in half their mischief. You had to have a wise old woman who could bow her head and perceive with a kind

93

of inner eye the hidden and mischievous tricks of spirits. Without such a woman any family would have been helpless.

It was little wonder, then, that the grandmothers were revered and held in awe, or that the members of this family now looked at the old woman with humble gratitude. She had made an astounding discovery. They understood that it was not enough to protect their mouth and nose and ears; there were other vents through which spirits could enter. As if reading their thoughts, the old woman went into the hut and returned with a piece of skin, and this she laid over the sick woman's pelvic area. After looking at it, she was not satisfied, and so she asked the woman to stand, whereupon, attaching a string to the piece of skin, she tied it around the woman's waist, letting it hang like an apron. At once the other women dashed away to find coverings for themselves, and presently all of them were wearing a piece of apron about the size of two open palms laid together.

Raven was looking down at his penis. With both hands he examined it; in his face was the look of one who had lost all his physical anchors. The other two men came up and stood by him and exchanged terrified glances.

"Look," said Raven, and the men bent forward to stare at what he was showing them.

Then they examined themselves; and when Spider realized that he could be invaded through his penis, he gave a howl of dismay. Rushing into the hut he seized a skin from his bed and hugged it against him. In a little while he came outside, wearing the skin; and when the other men saw what he had done, they grasped hides and held them like great aprons from their waist to their knees.

94

7

THE next morning the grandmother was unusually ener-
getic, and her disposition was ugly. After putting on a
protective apron and stirring the fire, she began to shout
at the members of her family, her voice shrill and abusive,
and Raven knew well what she was leading up to. There
was almost no food in the hut. As soon as she had worked
herself up to a fury she would scream at him and drive
him out to hunt. Her abusive tongue he did not mind as
long as she did not use her old-woman magic against him;
but he had learned that after her fury reached a certain
pitch she was never content merely to shout at him. She
would peer at him with sly and treacherous joy and mut-
ter to herself. She would ask invisible powers, with which
she was friendly, to single him out for special torments.

But he, too, was a cunning person; this morning, instead of waiting for her to make magic against him, he
hastened to his weapons as if he were eager to do her will.
She knew, of course, but in her rages forgot, that a man
could not hunt more than small and inoffensive creatures

without first preparing himself. He could search for nuts and fruits, or he could hunt for frogs and rabbits and timid birds; but if he set out to stalk snakes, or the wolf or tiger, or even the deer, he had to spend at least a day and a night to make himself invincible.

Nevertheless, Raven now seized his weapons as if he were ready, and indeed eager, to hunt any beast on earth; and while he pretended to be setting arrows in the quiver or testing the lance point or the blade of his stone knife, he slyly spied on the old woman. Almost at once her abusive howling dropped to a lower key. The two of them were furtively watching one another and matching their cunning, but it was the man who triumphed. The grandmother's tantrum fell to an angry cackle because she was deceived by his eagerness and by the bold way he dashed outside, as though there were nothing in the world of which he was afraid. When he was out of sight, the boldness slipped away from him and his manner changed.

This morning he was beset by more than his usual fearfulness. The old woman's amazing discovery had chastened all of them and added one more danger to the many among which they lived. Raven did not intend to go hunting. The moment he was over a hill and out of sight he sat down, his weapons at his side, and with both hands clasped his genitals to stare at them. As if he had been unfamiliar with this part of him, he slowly and painstakingly examined his penis, searching it for holes through which a ghost might enter. He could find only one hole, and it was very small, but he knew that the spirit of the largest animal in the world could creep through the eye in the grandmother's wooden needle.

After inspecting the penis, he took the scrotum in both hands; and with interest so intense that he slobbered, he pulled at the skin, this way and that, or picked at it with a fingernail to be sure that dirt spots were not holes, or rubbed an exploring finger over the part he was unable to see. He was worried by this invisible part, and so presently he arose and went to clear water and stood in it to his knees. After the disturbed surface had settled to perfect calm, he bent over, using the water as a mirror, and peered. Finding nothing to alarm him, he waded out and sat on the bank, and there, with a palm covering his genitals, he gave himself to thought.

Though she had, at least in the opinion of her family, great knowledge of magic, the grandmother had a very literal mind. To keep a ghost from entering a vent of any kind, she would apply an actual protective covering, and for her the covering would in no respect be a symbol. For all people, protective devices would become more and more symbolic, until various kinds of amulets would take the place of the apron or of the hand over the ear or nose. But on the day when Raven sat in thought, the grandmother had no knowledge of amulets. For that matter, none of her people had such knowledge, though in the more intuitive and reflective ones a kind of emotional alchemy was at work.

It was at work now in Raven. He was not wondering with what to cover his organ and protect it. If it had been as simple as that for him, he could have cupped it by using a large seed pod or half of a nut husk or the skin tip of a beast's tail after the bone and flesh were removed. There were many natural coverings he could have used—and which, in fact, men in other parts of the world were using

97

while he sat here on the bank; but Raven was thinking of objects that were imperishable.

He had been gazing at pebbles in the running water. Bending forward, he picked one up and turned it over and over in his palm; it was round, and it was as smooth as polished staghorn. Next, he reached for his lance and laid its point by the stone. The lance point was a piece of antler that he had polished and engraved. Like the pebble it was hard and changeless. From season to season there was change in all things that lived to die; but in things that never died there was never any change.

The Moon Woman changed, growing old and then renewing herself; but she changed because she was a woman. In things that were really eternal, like rock and bone and water and the sky-fire, there was never change but always that youngness which men envied and hungered for. Raven now recalled that the uncle, when alive, had often sprinkled himself with water in his old age, or, like a woman, had dashed about in falling rain, or when his swollen ankles pained him he had sat with his feet in running water. In a way that not even the grandmother could understand, fresh water was the essence of life. It fertilized living things because it was forever young and healthy and full of eagerness. The stones that lay in it were always more bright and attractive than those the water seldom touched.

Thinking of pebbles, Raven put a hand to his teeth and clasped two of them with a thumb and forefinger. Teeth never died. The bones in a man or a beast or a bird never died. The ghost left its home, the flesh wasted away, but the bones lay out in the light and the dark, season after season, and never changed. That, it seemed to him, was

98

because bones and stones were the same thing. There were parts in him that would never die.

This thought moved him to sudden thirst, to a kind of spiritual thirst; and so he lay on his belly and drank until his stomach was bloated with water. Water he loved because it was life; and after drinking his fill he rubbed his face in the running health and youth, or he dipped it by the handful and sprinkled himself. This simple ritual was the lowliest beginning of baptism.

All the while a persistent idea had been taking shape in his mind. To protect his penis against invasion by malicious spirits, it seemed to him it would be better to use a deathless object like a pebble, rather than to use, as the women were doing, a piece of skin that was no more eternal than the flesh itself; and with this notion in mind he searched along the stream for a stone that would be polished and attractive and to which he could attach a vine and so hang it from his waist. He found a stone that was shaped like two small eggs, connected by a short neck; at once he saw the resemblance between it and his testes. The likeness excited and pleased him, because this double pebble was a symbol of a part of himself.

Having no rawhide thong, he found a tough slender vine, and after attaching this to the stone, he tied it around his waist, letting the pebble hang close to his genitals. Then, standing, he looked down at it, his eyes shining with joy. No member of his family had ever used a charm to keep away evil things; and though this pebble was an amulet for him chiefly because of its eternal nature, it was also an ornament. It drew attention to his sexual organs. He was so delighted that he seized his weapons and has-

99

tened homeward, eager to have the members of his family look at him.

When his triumphant voice summoned them, the grandmother was the first to approach. He pointed proudly to his amulet, and she stared at it and then touched it with a dubious finger.

"What is it?" she asked, her old face puckering with a scowl of suspicion.

"It keeps ghosts away!" Raven said, his voice trembling with pride.

"How?" she demanded, observing that it dangled like a useless thing, covering nothing.

"Stone!" said Rose, and touched it. She knelt to examine it; and after a few moments she looked up at her mother and said scornfully, "Stone!"

"No!" Raven cried.

"Stone!" said Rose, and dismissed it as a piece of trivial foolishness.

Raven became almost frantic. For him it was much more than a stone; he tried to explain to them, not that it was a symbol and a charm—he had no words for these things —but that it was eternal like water, like bones, like the Moon Woman. The other men had come up and were staring enviously. Like small boys, they looked down at themselves and then at Raven's ornament, and found themselves barren and unattractive by comparison. When the old woman saw the envy and admiration in their faces, she examined the pebble more closely, touching it, turning it over, pressing it. Then she knelt by Rose, and Rose's daughter knelt also, and the three women touched the stone and clucked at one another.

Their exploring hands so excited Raven that he began

to tremble. He began to feel that they were interested not in the pebble but in his genitals and, unable at last to restrain his hunger, he seized the girl, intending to embrace her. This erotic move fetched the grandmother to her senses. She sprang up, shaking her gray mane and snarling; and a moment later she remembered that this lazy fellow had gone away to hunt.

"Food!" she cried angrily. "Where is food?"

The question was like frost on Raven's ardor. He picked up his weapons and backed away, his gaze fixed on the outraged eyes of the grandmother; and though he was showing himself to be humble and obedient to her will, something in his way of moving infuriated her. With the cry of one goaded beyond all control she grasped a club and ran toward him. But she was old and gnarled and crippled by pain, and her son was young and nimble. She ran as fast as she could, screaming at him and trying to get close enough to smite him, but in a few moments he vanished over a hill.

In his mind was a picture of such awful wrath that for a little while he forgot the charm that dangled from his waist. He was determined to find food and he went earnestly, with all his senses alert, until he heard a sibilant and scolding sound. It came from two large birds that were playing by the bower of their nest; but though they were in plain sight and within easy distance of his arrows, he did not dare attack, because he had not prepared himself with a propitiatory ritual. He would have to seek inoffensive and timid things whose ghosts would never molest him.

Coming to a sparse thicket, he entered it. The earth was covered with dead twigs and leaves and fallen limbs, but he moved with no sound at all. His trained eye could catch the slightest movement in bush or tree; his ear could detect sounds that were only soft whisperings; and his keen nose was able to pick out and distinguish the odors of animals and plants. From his dead uncle he had learned to study the habits of both beast and bird, to develop a remarkable sensory awareness, to stalk his prey with patience and cunning, and in moments of danger to hold every muscle of his body under control. But he was a lazy fellow who liked to lie in the sun and reflect on the world around him; besides, while now moving soundlessly with lance poised, as if approaching a large beast, he realized that he had not prepared himself for the hunt. With an audible sigh he straightened and left the thicket.

He came to a tree in the side of which a wound was exuding a thick sap. All saps and aromatic gums were regarded by his people with a feeling akin to reverence, because they were thought to be a vital fluid, like the menstrual blood of a woman. Raven dipped a finger in the sap and then spread the viscid juice on his forehead, cheeks, and nose; and on looking down and seeing the stone amulet, he smeared it also. Because he had not found a heart for the uncle's ghost, nor any blood but the rabbit's, he decided to take some of this vital sap to the grave.

Finding a large leaf, he thrust into the tree's wound with his stone knife and wiped the juice off on the leaf; and when the cupped leaf was half filled with a substance that looked like honey, he ran across the hills to the grave. It had not been disturbed. Either the uncle's ghost was happier now that its body had been carefully buried, or it had abandoned the grave in disgust to find a home elsewhere. Raven had forgotten that this ghost, at least in the grandmother's opinion, had entered the sick woman.

Kneeling, he peered into the hole down which he had poured the blood; after looking and listening, he thrust the leaf and its burden of sap deep into the hole. When he rose to his feet he felt pangs of hunger, and now, while roaming over the hills, out of sight of his family but within calling distance, he made a meal of edible roots, a frog, a few beetles, and the leaves of the rosebush. Now and then he hurled his lance at a small bird or chased a rabbit, but he was in no mood to hunt earnestly and with all his skill. He was too oppressed by dread. Unlike his dead uncle, he had never been a bold hunter; besides, he lived, as the uncle had not, under the constant scorn and disgust of an old woman.

He hated her because he was afraid of her magic. Sometimes he had wondered if he should not run away and seek a home with another family, but this impulse had always been restrained by fear. Interlopers were not welcome among his people. Each family was a unit that lived apart, seldom visiting another and tolerating no invasion of its orchards and hunting grounds. The families were friendly in an aloof and distant way; they had signs by which they recognized their group kinship; now and then, if the urgency was extreme, one could borrow fire from another; but they were suspicious, and their visits when these occurred, were brief. It was better, the grandmothers believed, to keep their families in their own small kingdoms.

But Raven was by nature a gregarious and friendly man, and today, without being aware of it, he pursued a direction toward a family he knew. He was impelled by a wish to find a more hospitable home. His approach was announced by a sudden bark, and he stopped, frightened, because the wolf-dogs kept by some families were savage beasts. He waved his lance and yelled, hoping the grandmother of the family would appear, but the sound of his voice aroused other dogs, and they set up a terrifying clamor. Undecided whether to flee or to stand his ground with lance poised, Raven howled like a man surrounded by enemies, but instead of quieting the beasts, his anxious wailing redoubled their frenzy. Three of them were rushing toward him when the grandmother, carrying a blazing torch, ran after the wolves, shouting and menacing them with fire; then behind her came other persons, also bearing torches. With fire they frightened the dogs and drove them slinking back to the hut.

Sweating and trembling, Raven advanced to the old woman, who stood, with eyes shaded, and waited for him; and when he came up to her he gave a sign by which the people of his group recognized one another. He opened his mouth wide as if to show that it was empty and said, "Man friend," using the word man in the sense of all human beings.

Though she recognized him, having seen him before, and though he was known personally to all the members of her family, the old woman nevertheless turned solemnly to those behind her and said:

"Man friend."

"Man friend," they repeated to one another.

But none of their faces was friendly. Like all other people, they were the constant prey of unreasoning fears that made life a burden. If a visitor came, he might come in friendliness, or he might be the tool of malicious spirits that had sent him on a mischievous errand. And so all of them looked gravely at Raven, their eyes asking the purpose of his visit, their minds suspicious; and Raven, who had wandered here like a naïve child, seeking a more friendly home, stared at them and felt more friendless than before.

"What you want?" the old woman asked.

The question confused him, and because he hesitated, having no glib answer, the woman was convinced that he had come for no good reason. Raven could hardly say that he had come to find a more friendly dwelling place. No man could have looked at this old woman's hard and doubting eyes and sensed in her stiff bearing an unwillingness to let him advance and been able to say a thing like that. And finally, because he could think of nothing else, he said:

"I want food."

That indiscreet and covetous remark brought a cry of anger from the old woman; but before she could speak or make a move to threaten him, a man behind her observed Raven's amulet. He came forward quickly and pointed to the stone.

"Look!" he cried.

Then they all looked at the stone. The man touched it with a tentative and nervous finger; Raven meanwhile stood like one who expected to be skinned alive.

"What is it?" asked the old woman.

"It keeps ghosts out," said Raven.

That statement made them exclaim with amazement.

"Out here?" asked the man, and pointed to his mouth. "No."

"Out here?" he asked, touching his nostrils. "No."

He touched an ear.

"No," Raven said.

They all drew close to bend forward and look at the pebble. Impatiently the old woman asked again:

"What is it?"

Raven tried to explain to them that in his home there was a woman with a malicious ghost in her, and that it had entered that part of her from which babies came. He had so few words to express the matter that he talked chiefly with gestures and exclamations; and when he saw in their faces only amazed incredulity, he grasped his penis and strove to make them understand that there was an opening in it through which a spirit could enter. The stone, which was eternal, would keep the ghosts away because they were afraid of it.

They did not realize that they were listening to the words of a genius. In comparison with Raven, they had dull and unimaginative minds; instead of sensing how remarkable he was to contrive such an ingenious protection, they backed away from him, more suspicious than ever.

"Go away!" the old woman cried.

"Look—" said Raven.

"Go away!"

When Raven did not move, two men, both larger than he, stepped forward and menaced him with their spears.

"Go away!" one of them said.

Raven slowly retreated but he did not raise his lance or bow or make any threatening gestures. He felt bewildered. He looked down at the stone and touched it and again tried to explain; but all of them began to shout at him, telling him to go away. One of the men advanced beyond the other and poised his lance.

"Go away!" the old woman screamed.

"Yes," Raven said, hoping they would not attack him.

Instead of placating the men, his submissive statement made them feel bolder, and both of them now rushed forward, waving their lances and shouting at him. Raven turned on his heels and ran, and the two men ran after him; but he was moved by terror, and the two men were moved only by anger that was half bluff. Raven was soon far ahead of them and out of sight. He did not stop running until he reached his home.

The sight of it filled him with the warm and surging thanksgiving that a hunted fox must feel when it reaches its burrow or a wounded bird that has winged safely home to its nest. Entering the hut and rushing over to the fireplace, he knelt there and seized a burning fagot and turned to face the entrance.

8

Standing in the doorway of her hut one evening, the grandmother looked up at the sky; and when she turned to her family and cried, "Come-look!" her thin voice quavered with joy. After the others left their beds and crowded in behind her, she went outside and they followed; then they all looked up at the slender shining crescent of a new moon. The periodic miracle of renewal and youth in the Moon Woman always filled them with deep happiness. With murmuring exclamations of delight they gazed at her, or turned, their eyes brimming with joy, to look at one another; because of all things in life nothing was so mysteriously wonderful as her power to become young again.

They had no belief that they themselves were also immortal. To be sure, their spirits would live after the death of their bodies; but if they had been questioned about the matter, they would have said that all spirits finally wasted away. Of all things in the world, only the Moon Woman possessed the secret of renewal; so she stood for all of them as a symbol of what they wished to be. Tonight she was young again and very serene. In the wide sky that was her home there was not a sign of anger, not a portent anywhere of malice or mischief; and now, while gazing at her and sensing her calm joy, they felt more secure than they had felt in many days.

The grandmother was thinking that tomorrow she would plant her barley and corn. She did not have much seed, and from what she harvested in any season she never ground more than a few quarts of meal; but for her and her people the grain had a value much greater than its nourishment. It, too, was a miraculous thing; they felt reverence for it because of its mysterious power of growth. They put it in the earth and fertilized it with water and blood, and it came out of the earth, frail and slender, and needing watchful care like a baby. Then it became tall and strong and multiplied itself.

They felt the same reverence toward all plants that bore flowers or fruit, especially the women, because it was the women who were devoted to birth. They loved wild violets and roses, jessamine and wisteria. They loved trees that produced nuts, plants that produced edible tubers, and all other things that nourished them or were friendly in their touch and smell. As the ones who planted and reaped, it was the women who perceived that plants gave birth, too, in their own strange way; and for all life-giving, no matter how lowly, they had a feeling of awe.

These people had learned never to plant seed when the Moon Woman was old and fretful; because she was the guardian of all life, it was much better to plant when she was young. After she had renewed herself and had come forth, youthful and radiant, to smile on the people, it was time to put the precious seed in the earth; and turning now to her daughter Rose, the grandmother said:

"Bring seed out."

Rose entered the hut and returned with two skin-pouches, each containing a double handful of barley or corn. These the old woman took to a tree and hung from a branch in full moonlight. If left in the full presence of the Moon Woman until morning, the seed would be more vigorous, more eager to grow.

The next morning at the break of day the grandmother left her bed and stirred the fire, but she did not go to her small hoard of food to give each his portion of breakfast. She was impatient to be at her work. Work, though, is hardly the word for it. The planting of seed or the harvesting of it or the grinding of the grain between stones was less a matter of labor than of ritual and magic. The women never dreamed that it lay in their hands to make the harvest more abundant. It is true that they had planting tools—a pointed stick to make holes in the soil, and a forked stick, one prong of which curved like a plow beam, to make lines—but the labor was wholly incidental for them. Of far greater importance was the kind of mood they felt, the joy that sang in them and was related to all that was joyful in life; the way they handled the kernels as if they were fondling babies; the magical things they did to make the seed grow.

When the grandmother went outside, she was followed by Rose and the girl, both of whom were healthy and fertile and therefore qualified to touch the seed; but when Barren came out to watch them like a timid and guilty creature who was spying, the old woman turned on her with a cry. She ran toward her, screaming and menacing with her arms, and Barren vanished into the hut. They might as well have thrown the seed away as to let a barren woman watch the planting; in the presence of such a woman nothing could be fertilized and nothing would grow. Nor would the grandmother let a menstruating or a sick woman look on, much less enter the garden plot or touch the grain. A woman in her menses was squandering her seed. A fine one she would be to put corn or barley in the ground! And as for a chronically sick person, she, like a barren one, was an enemy of all birth and life.

As if she were handling a small child, the grandmother took the pouches from the tree limb and carried them gently to her daughter. Rose had helped with the planting many times and knew what to do. She would keep the seed safe from all sick and sterile and destroying influences while her mother and daughter marked off the garden patch, dragged the forked stick to line up the rows, and brought water to fertilize the planting. While the two women labored, Rose kept a suspicious eye on the hut. If the barren or the sick woman had looked out, she would have screamed and stamped her feet, and if the offender had not disappeared after a moment, she would have called to her mother.

Raven did come out, smeared with red dyes and carrying his weapons, and at once his sister began to shout at him as if he were a blight.

"Go away!" she howled.

"Why?" asked Raven, staring at her.

"Go away quick!"

"No," he said, and his face darkened with pain and hate. Rose began to jump up and down in a wild tantrum.

When Raven did not go away, she called to her mother, and the old woman came charging like a furious beast.

"Go away!" she screamed.

Raven went away, hating both women with all his strength. In the kind of life he led, there was not much to feed a man's ego and give it meaning. He was only a serf who was expected to provide the food and eat without complaint what was given to him, and keep himself humble and out of the way when he was not needed. Perhaps once or twice in a year or in two years he found a woman receptive and was able to embrace her; but a woman did not suffer a man's embrace when she was pregnant or when she was nursing. Her period of nursing was always a long one.

Barren used to let him embrace her often; but despairing now of ever having a child, she had become sullen and spiteful and seemed to regard him as the cause of her misfortune.

Raven came back part way, a rather pathetic and very unhappy fellow who lived with five women and was scorned by all of them. He stared at Rose, a handsome woman, well built, healthy, and as attractive a mate as he had ever seen, but she looked at him as if he were repulsive.

"Go away!" she said.

"I will," said Raven, his voice humble and dispirited. "I will go far away."

"Yes," said his sister eagerly. "Go far away."

Then suddenly Raven hated her. If he had known any profane or obscene words he would have flung them at her. If he had lived in a more civilized time, he would have cursed her. But his ideas for which he had words were rather simple and inoffensive; and so he could only scowl at her and show his teeth like a baffled animal.

Observing his scowl, Rose said, "Go far away."

This so maddened him that he was thinking of rushing at her with his spear, but at this moment the grandmother came in sight, bringing a skin-pouch filled with water. Sensing that Raven was plotting mischief, she came up to her daughter and asked:

"What is trouble?"

"There!" cried Rose, pointing to him. "Tell him go away!"

"Go away," said the old woman.

Raven was nonplussed. He might have attacked his sister, but no provocation could be extreme enough to force him to attack the old woman. Such an affront was out of the question, and so, humiliated and angry, but still undecided, he looked at the women.

The grandmother did a strange and extraordinary thing. The people of this time often smiled but they seldom laughed, finding little that was funny in a dreadful and unpredictable world; but in some of the old women there was a touch of madness. For more than forty years this grandmother had lived in fear. Such a burden, so long endured, and so seldom relieved by lightness and gaiety, added year by year to an emotional tenseness that was almost frenzy. Now and then there was pressing need to release the tension in a wild outburst. Usually the old woman found relief in anger but once in a while she laughed.

She laughed now. While looking at her son she had noticed his phallic amulet, the stone dangling from his waist, and because of some dark incongruousness of ideas

113

in her unconscious mind she thought it was funny. She pointed to it and exploded with wild mirth, shaking her gray matted locks and looking like a convulsed witch. Her laughter was shrill and terrible. Her skinny frame shook with spasms of insane joy, and all the while her bony arm and extended forefinger pointed to the stone. Her daughter began to laugh, too, and after a few moments Barren and the two men came out of the hut.

Spider and Barren came over to see what the old woman was pointing to, and though at first they were more bewildered than amused, the laughter was contagious. Their faces broke in wide mirthful grins and they began to cackle. They also pointed to the stone, and as if they alone had discovered it they called it to the attention of the others. Laughing and pointing, they all went over to Raven and fenced him in, their fingers thrust at his amulet and their eyes swimming with mirth.

The anger died in him and he felt only galling humiliation. He paid no attention to the two men, though Spider was jumping up and down in frenzied glee; and he looked at none of the women except the grandmother. For him she was a symbol of knowledge and magic, and so he stared at her as he might have looked at the Moon Woman when the sky was dark with her disapproval and the earth was shaking with her wrath. He felt utterly helpless and debased. If the old woman had told the others to kill him, he would not have been surprised; his terror was so great that he probably would not have resisted at all. Sweating and trembling, he stood like a man condemned to death.

When at last he tore his gaze away from the old woman's convulsed and spiteful face, he saw an unbelievable image of friendliness. Rose's daughter, the girl, had come up with a pouch of water, having been out of sight by the stream when the laughter started; now she was standing back and looking at Raven's face. She was not laughing, nor even smiling. In her face, in her eyes, there was friendliness and compassion—because this girl was sexually receptive today and saw in Raven, smeared with his dyes and clutching his weapons, the only male in this family whom she could accept as a mate. She was not thinking that; she was feeling it. And with unerring instinct Raven sensed her friendliness and her hunger and moved toward her.

His sudden move fetched the old woman to herself. She had exhausted herself with laughter; remembering now the seed of corn and barley, and seeing the barren woman standing by, she swung from mirth to rage and ran for a club. Spider and Old Man vanished into the hut, swallowing, as they did so, their last guffaws of joy. An instant later Barren followed them. When the grandmother found a club and turned, Raven stopped in his eager rush toward the girl, and looking round now and seeing the old woman swinging the cudgel he took to his heels. He went like the wind until he reached the crest of a hill. There he paused to look back.

"Go away!" the grandmother was screaming.

And Rose echoed her, "Go far away!"

The girl came forward timidly, bearing her water. A girl—she was only eleven—when sexually approachable always felt timid and frightened, and struggled as much with an urge to resist as to yield. If she had dared to, she would have followed Raven into the hills.

Having emptied her weary old body of its pent-up and corroding anxieties and fret, the grandmother became very businesslike and turned to her task. Every step in her planting of the seed was part of a ritual. First, she took the hoelike instrument and marked a straight line across the garden plot. Then she grasped the planting stick and, with the girl at her side carrying a pouch of water, she made holes in which to drop the seed. She would thrust the stick into the pouch of water and then into the earth. These holes, about two feet apart, were for corn. After reaching the end of the line she straightened her aching body and turned. Her daughter knew that the moment had come for her to get a flint knife and open a vein.

Handing the pouch of corn to the girl, she entered the hut and returned with a sharp knife. After dipping the stone blade into water, she made an incision in her left arm, because she was the only woman pregnant and therefore her blood would be best for the seed. Now the three of them planted, walking together. The grandmother would take a kernel of corn and wet it in her daughter's blood and then kneel so that she could drop the seed into the hole with care. Next, she took a pouch of water and poured a little into the hole, filled the hole with earth, and pressed the earth to make it firm. Between the planting of every two seeds she would look up at the sky for signs of rain.

And so, slowly, devotedly, all afternoon, the three women planted a few handfuls of seed. Before the task was finished, Rose had probed the incision in her arm again and again to make the blood run. If Raven had been an able helper instead of a lazy philosopher wandering over the hills, he would have killed animals or birds and fetched their blood to the garden. In the grandmother's opinion, no seed would grow unless fertilized with both water and blood, and if there had been plenty of blood so that she did not have to be stingy with it, she could have felt more assured of a vigorous planting and an abundant harvest.

But Raven was a worthless fellow. From time to time while planting, the grandmother thought of him and grunted with disgust. The dead uncle had been a faithful provider; he had kept food in the house and at planting time he had brought rabbit blood to fertilize the seed. As for Raven—

"Where is he?" asked the old woman, looking at the hills.

"Far away," said her daughter.

The girl said nothing, but she hoped that Raven would come home.

After the seed was planted, it was the grandmother's task to persuade the Moon Woman to send rain. Her rain-making ritual was rather simple, though to this, as to other magical rites, she sometimes impulsively added details, especially when she felt certain of her power after she had worked herself into a kind of frenzied trance. With her, as with the other old women of her time, ritual developed under practice; and the daughters, learning from their mothers, inherited from each generation more inflexible customs. In this family the grandmother was the only one who could make rain; but Rose, who assisted her and studied her methods, would take over such functions after her mother was dead.

First, the three women went to the stream to get several pouches of water. Then, while Rose and her daughter held the pouches and stood back and waited, the old woman closed her eyes and stretched her arms to the sky.

It always took her a few minutes to shut out the world and place herself in harmony with the invisible powers. To get magically in touch with the Moon Woman, it was as if she had to push away, one by one, all the commonplaces of daily living. Inaudibly her lips moved over words, but these had not become an unvarying formula. They were such helpful words as came intuitively to her mind.

She would say, "Please make rain," or "Please make seed grow," repeating these entreaties over and over until other appropriate pleas grew out of her mood and declared their urgency on her tongue. When she sensed that the whole sky had become breathless and listening, that all unfriendly beings and forces had moved beyond hearing, and that she stood in deep and complete possession of her power, she would open her eyes; and then her daughter would hasten forward with a pouch of water.

The grandmother now took the pouch, and the two women walked along a row of seed, one sprinkling water over the other. "Please make rain!" the old woman kept whispering; and her daughter, bowed low and receiving the sprinkled water on her head, took up the words, and the two women chanted them together, their voices humble and pleading. Side by side, with a row of seed between them, they walked back and forth; and when this pouch of water was exhausted, the girl ran forward with another. From the hut, Barren and the two men were looking out, their faces holy with awe.

After the pregnant one had been sprinkled up and down all the rows, the rain-making ritual, as employed in former times, was completed; but today the grandmother felt impelled to improvise. It was as if she still had in her a fund of unused magic and was driven by a wish to enrich and invigorate her pleading. She knelt and bowed her head to her arms and told her daughter to sprinkle her; this Rose did, using the third pouch of water. When the old woman rose, her eyes were luminous with joy. Her impulsive kneeling had been a kind of gesture toward prayer. The water sprinkled on her had made her feel younger; there was something strangely girlish in her face when she turned to Rose and smiled. Rain would come soon; she had no doubt of that. The seed would be fertilized and would grow tall and strong. She felt happy because her task had been well done.

But the barren woman, watching from the doorway, was very unhappy. She would have suffered any abasement to have her mother sprinkle her with the fertilizing water and so make it possible for the seed of life to grow in her and, unable to restrain her intense hunger, she suddenly ran out to the garden and knelt before the old woman and begged her to make her fertile.

It was a dreadful thing to do. The presence of a barren one in the garden might offend the Moon Woman and wither the seed in the ground. For a moment the old woman was speechless; in the next she turned white with rage. Seizing a stick, she smote the kneeling woman on her skull and then, without giving her time to crawl away, she grasped her by the hair and dragged her from the planting like a dead thing. And all the while she screamed at her, calling her a fool, a barren fool, a worthless and empty woman.

When the clutch on her hair was loosened, the terrified woman crawled on hands and knees to the hut and went trembling to her bed. The grandmother looked up at the sky, but there was no joy in her eyes now. The whole task of making rain would have to be done again, and so she summoned Rose and the girl and they took the pouches and went to the stream. On her mattress of skins, the barren daughter buried her face and sobbed; and with no pity in their eyes, Spider and Old Man stood back by a wall and looked at her.

9

THE next morning, sensing that the grandmother was in an ugly mood, Raven slipped outside to sit by a tree. He was hungry, but he knew there was no food in the hut except some hard dry roots and some berries that had shrunk to nothing but skin and seeds. Glancing nervously round him at the planted garden or up at the pale tranquil sky or over at the doorway, he felt apprehensive because he knew very well that the old woman was disgusted with him. And while he sat like one determined to sulk in idleness and starve to death rather than face the hazards of hunting, she came outside. She walked over and looked down at her son.

Refusing to meet her eyes, he stared at her brown feet, at her brown hairy legs; and then, raising his eyes a little, he looked at her round sagging belly. No one, man or woman, liked to be fixed by an accusing stare, and least of all by the stare of one with knowledge of magic. Knowledge of magic was as much a part of a woman as knowledge of birth, and in the mind of Raven the two were inseparably related in a baffling and terrifying way. He did not think of this old woman as one in league with supernatural beings, such as gods and devils, and able, therefore, to pronounce destroying curses and cast spells, but he did know that she possessed mystifying powers. She could make rain. She could understand the moods and intentions of the Moon Woman. Sometimes she could drive ghosts away. And she could make life very miserable for a man when she wanted to.

He was determined not to meet her eyes. Without looking at them, he knew they were fixed on him with malicious unfriendliness. He knew that she was feeling contempt for him. And so, frightened but stubborn, he stared at her lean and calloused feet, knowing that her abusive words would come soon enough, after she was done with looking at him. He had no concept of a witch, or of evil as a force in life opposed to good; but nevertheless in his feeling for the woman she had the qualities of a witchlike and evil thing.

At last the old woman spoke, and her words were hard and rasping.

"Look up!" she said.

Raven did not look up. He turned a little, as if moved by sudden pain, but he kept his gaze on her feet.

"Look up!" she cried, speaking more sharply.

Oh, she knew, the cunning old tyrant, that nobody liked to look at her strange eyes. She knew that she had the power of magic.

"No," he said, speaking like a sulking child.

Instead of commanding him again, the grandmother sat on her heels and laid her thin arms across her knees. She shook her gray and shaggy mane. Her gaze now was level

122

with his, and she stared at him like a hypnotist whose victim would break and yield if given time. When Raven moved as if to crawl away, she cried:

"Be quiet!"

"No," he said, but he spoke as if his will were being sucked out of him.

"Look!"

"No."

But he had known from the beginning that he would have to look. Like an animal making a last despairing tremor toward escape, he shuddered and met her eyes. They were faded old eyes, rheumy and a little bloodshot, but they were full of disgust and subdued anger. His own eyes blinked swiftly, and spasms twitched his eyelids.

"What you want?" he asked helplessly.

"No food!"

"No food?" he asked innocently.

"Lazy, foolish man!"

Making an effort to tear his gaze away, he failed, and then his whole body turned limp, as if he were looking at a great snake and expected to be devoured.

"No food?" he asked, cunningly pretending to be innocent.

"No food—no meat—no nuts—no berries." She was cunning, too. "Are you hungry?" she asked.

"Yes!" he said eagerly, but realized that he had blundered. Her lips drew back in a cruel smile across the snags of her teeth.

"You eat what?"

"Nothing," he said, and opened his mouth to show that it was empty.

She rose to her feet. "Get up!" she cried.

He staggered up and then stood with arms hanging as if broken.

"Go hunt food!"

But now he thought of an excuse. It was more than an excuse, really, because when a man hunted the larger game he had to be fully prepared. He had to drink of fermented juices and add their courage to his courage. It was the woman's task to ferment the juices.

"No drink," he said, looking at her more boldly.

The change in her was remarkable. A man's preparation for the hunt was as fixed in ritual as the planting of corn, the making of rain, or the birth of a child. The grandmother knew that. She had forgotten to prepare the drink of courage for her man.

Looking crestfallen and bewildered, she turned and shuffled over to the hut, and a moment later Raven could hear her shouting inside. She was asking why there was no drink for Raven, though the gathering of the juices and the making of the drink were her own special tasks. She came out with Rose and the girl, all of them carrying pouches; and Raven knew they were going over the hills to find the magic that would make him brave.

After a little reflection he decided to go with them—not to help gather the juice of herbs and trees that would make a man's drink; he knew nothing of those things because they were part of a woman's magic. She was the botanist. It was she who knew which plants and fruits were poisonous and which were not; which herbs could cure physical ills; and which juices could make the courage that any man needed in the hunt. He was going not to assist but to follow the girl who had given him a look yesterday that still sang in him like bird music and who, on crossing the yard, now glanced at him again. Even a stupid man could have read the meaning in the girl's eyes. For Raven it was as clear and almost as urgent as his own hunger; and so, turning giddy with joy, he ran to get his weapons and follow.

The women went in single file up a path, with the girl in the rear; and when she saw Raven following she paused to look back at him. There was in her eyes the ecstatic promise of what he hungered for. But presently the grandmother also stopped and looked back, and when she saw that Raven was trailing them she gestured at him and told him to go away. Perhaps she did not want him spying on her gathering of magical herbs, or perhaps she had sensed the erotic hunger in the girl.

Old and barren women had little tolerance for the sexual embrace. With such hunger extinguished in them, with their bodies racked by pain, and with their minds and emotions dwelling on other matters, they looked on sexual mating with disgust and refused to allow it in their presence. Their disgust did not grow out of shame; they felt no shame. It did not grow out of envy. They felt that the act was meaningless. Around the tyrannical grandmothers, therefore, physical love-making had to be sly and concealed.

"Go away!" the old woman shouted. "Go back!"

The girl was not inviting Raven to sexual embrace; she had nothing like that in mind. But because of the wordless and persistent hunger in her she felt friendly toward him, and Raven could feel the friendliness. He did not go back home but he fell behind and out of sight of the two older women. The girl knew he was coming and from time to time she glanced back; and as Raven felt the moment of conquest approaching, he began to tremble with eagerness, and to plot to lure the girl away with all the guile he had.

His opportunity came when the two older women went out of sight over a hill and the girl paused on the crest. She looked back then, as Raven had hoped she would, and the moment she did so he made frantic gestures. His beckoning arms told her to come to him. With an anguished voice he called to her.

"Come!" he said.

But she did not come. She stood there against the sky, looking at him. He now behaved as if he were stalking a timid animal that would flee if he made an unfriendly move. Watching her intently, he advanced a little, beckoning all the while and making gestures intended to soothe and allay her fears. When she turned to look ahead, he thought she was about to follow the women and he jumped up and down in frantic indecision. Should he wait, lest she take alarm and run, or should he dash forward to clasp and hold her?

"Come!" he said in a loud anguished whisper. "Come here!"

Deciding that she would not come, he advanced, but not swiftly; he went as if he were sneaking up on a creature in a snare. His gestures were frantic but friendly; his whispering voice beseeched her not to run away. Like one rooted to the spot and unable to move, the girl waited. When he was within a few feet of her, Raven let his weapons fall and looked round him for a sign of the other women.

"Wait!" he whispered, though she had made no move to flee.

And now, with a ripe and receptive female almost within reach, he did not lay eager hands on her. Instead, he looked at her, and the girl looked at him, the eyes of both asking questions. She gazed at him as if he were a strange thing that had crept out of a thicket, and he looked at her as if, doubting his senses, he could not believe that she had waited for him and that they were now alone.

So it was for a long moment. Then hunger shone in his eyes, and she read the meaning of it and her eyes responded. The eyes of both were luminous and tender, not with affection, not even with companionship, but with that deep and ancient hunger of a male and a female, seeking their physical mate. Softly he went up to her and grasped an arm.

"Come," he said, and she went willingly. He led her into a thicket of thornless berry bushes. He wanted to hide, not because of shame, but because there were enemies around him, including the grandmother who might return and drive him away. When they were securely hidden and alone, he did not kiss her or hug her to him. There was not among these people, and there would not be among people for a long time to come, the kind of love-making that is today called romance. Because they lived in a world of enemies, their matings were brief, like the matings of all things that fled for their lives.

And as soon as the brief mating was finished, the girl broke away and ran, leaving him alone in the thicket; and for a little while he sat on his haunches, feeling overwhelming relief. His face and eyes were gentle. This was the first time in many weeks that he had embraced a woman. His sexual life, like that of nearly all men of his time, was pretty barren; sometimes there was no relief in a year or even in a longer while, and a man became morbidly restless. The women were pregnant or nursing their babies and they were content. A man wanted to wander over the earth in search of females, but fear restrained him, because all women lived in homes under the watchfulness of jealous men. A few moments of deep pleasure, of impassioned relief, came to a man so rarely that it is little wonder if he wanted to sit quietly, as Raven was sitting down, and strive to recapture it. His body felt relaxed and at peace. In his eyes there was the kind of tenderness that was in a mother's eyes when she looked at her child. He reached out and broke off a few berry leaves and thrust them into his mouth.

Taking up his weapons he went home, with joy singing in him as it had not sung in a long while. The sky and the earth both seemed more friendly now. But he was still an aroused and hungry male, and after he had laid his weapons aside he entered the hut and looked at the two women there. The sick one was lying on her bed; he was not interested in her because he knew she was possessed by ghosts. But the other one, only in middle age, and still healthy and firm, was a woman of another kind. Formerly he had embraced her, but now she was an unhappy and blighted creature who flew into a tantrum when a man approached.

When she saw Raven staring at her and saw the hunger in his eyes, she yelled at him and reached for a club. Drawing a deep breath, he made a movement like a shrug and went outside. Looking away at the hills, he wondered where the girl was and whether he might again lure her away from the avenging old woman. With hope beating in him like a pulse, he seized his weapons and set out.

The grandmother and her two companions returned late in the afternoon, each carrying an armful of herbs, some honey, and pouches containing the sap of the birch and other trees. Setting a big clay pot in full sunlight, the old woman placed the honey and sap in it and then crushed the herbs between stones and added their juice and pulp to the mixture. All this would ferment and make the potent courage a man needed to face his enemies in the hunt.

Meanwhile Raven, having missed the women when he trotted over the hills, had gone skulking through the thickets to spy on his nearest neighbors. In his mind was the thought that he might find a woman at some distance from her home and persuade her to yield. It was an unreasonable and obsessive notion, but reason has never been the companion of erotic hunger. Never before in his life had he gone prowling in search of a mate; so far as he knew, no man in his family, or in the whole world, had ever done so. But he was now driven by an urge that was stronger than fear. Then, and in all times since, sexual hunger has impelled men to the most foolhardy daring—to a recklessness even more extreme than that to which hunger for food has been able to drive them.

Raven was not a man in control of himself. To be sure, he was afraid because fear was always with him; he was anxious and stealthy but, nevertheless, he went like a man set on a path and stripped of all discretion and restraint. If a big cat had crossed his path he might have been restored to his senses. If the sky had darkened with the Moon Woman's anger, it is probable that he would have fled to his home. But the day was open and calm, with no sign of enemies anywhere, and he went trotting over the hills, his eyes shining with expectancy, his head thrust forward as if following a scent.

With him, as with all his people, an object and the idea

of it were the same thing. In his mind was the idea that a woman was waiting for him somewhere ahead, a girl on a hilltop, looking back. He was reliving his amorous chase of a few hours ago. He was not, of course, aware of that. He was lost in a kind of lunacy. When he saw no sign of the girl on the hill just beyond him, he expected to see her on the next hill, and he quickened his stride. And so he ran from hill to hill until, suddenly and unexpectedly, he came within sight of a hut.

Then he stopped, bewildered and confused, and looked round him. Realizing that he had entered a zone of danger, he stared on all sides of him, wondering where the girl could be; but when a dog barked, fear for the moment was stronger than the fixed idea, and he slunk into hiding. Then he crept forward until he could peer at the yard. A woman was there, a young and attractive woman, and Raven had no doubt that she was the girl whom he had been following. Remembering the friendly look in her eyes, he knew she would be glad to see him, and so he advanced to the edge of the thicket and stood in plain sight.

In a low hoarse whisper he cried, "Hooo-ohh!"

The woman heard the voice and turned and saw the man. For a long moment she looked at him; but when Raven beckoned to her she screamed, and out of the hut came several persons, angrily and wildly like huge wasps. Among them was a man who carried a spear. They all stared at Raven, their eyes questioning and suspicious; and then the man waved his spear and shouted a challenge and advanced.

Like one who had been walking in his sleep and was slowly and painfully awaking, Raven saw the man coming; and as the obsessive idea broke away like a fog, he realized

130

with a shudder of dismay where he was. Fear and guile possessed him now. He was not able to flee, at least not at once, and while his mind cleared in the cold and terrible light of his predicament, the man came up and faced him and bared his teeth.

"What you want?" he asked.

He was not by any means so intelligent as Raven; he did not have his nimbleness in subterfuge and trickery. As if he had come for this purpose—for so it seemed to him now —Raven pointed to the distant hills and said eagerly:

"Go hunt!"

"Hunt?" asked the man. He set his spear point on the earth. Most of the suspicion and anger faded from his eyes. "Hunt what?" he asked.

"Tiger," said Raven, improvising with glib genius, and having in mind, not the tiger, but any species of large cat.

The man shivered. He was an able hunter but he had never been bold enough to stalk the tiger. "When?" he asked.

"Now!"

The man scowled. "Dark comes soon now."

They had no word for tomorrow; and so Raven said: "When light comes again."

The man looked at Raven and considered. "Where is tiger?" he asked.

Raven had not seen a tiger's tracks in a long while, but he pointed to the sunset hills and said, "Out there."

The man was impressed. Never before had anyone been so bold as to come to him and propose a tiger hunt. He looked up at the sky to see if the Moon Woman was watching. He looked back at his family and called to the grandmother.

"Come!" he said.

She was a very old woman and almost blind, and she walked bent over with the aid of two sticks. She advanced and peered at Raven, looking up at him like a creature on four legs.

"He says hunt tiger."

"Ohhh!" said the old woman, breathing the word in soft amazement. "Brave man!"

Her praise made Raven feel as bold as the tiger itself. "Hunt now!" he said.

"Not now!" cried the man angrily. "Soon dark now."

"When light comes again."

"Yes."

"Brave man!" cooed the old woman, still peering at the bold stranger who wanted to hunt tigers. "You live where?"

"There," said Raven, pointing in the direction of his home.

"Far?"

"Yes, far."

Feeling more at ease, Raven looked beyond the man, eager to see the young woman, but, noting his glance and reading his mind, the big man scowled.

"Go home now," he said.

"Hunt tiger?" asked the wily Raven.

"Hunt tiger when light comes again."

"You come there?" asked Raven, pointing toward his home.

"Yes."

The man and the old woman turned away, and at once Raven felt an impulse to leap at the man and thrust a lance through his back; but in the next moment he looked over

132

at the girl. As if sensing the covetous stare, the man turned and looked at Raven and said angrily:

"Go home now!"

"Yes," Raven said.

On his way home, Raven went at full speed, feeling quite unconquerable. It seemed to him that he had gone over to propose a tiger hunt. He was proud of himself and he hoped his women would be.

At first they exclaimed with astonishment but after a few moments they were skeptical. In the grandmother's family there had never been a man with enough boldness to hunt tigers. The uncle had been a skillful hunter, the best she had known among men; he had killed wolves and deer and the bushbuck, but he had never tried to snare the larger killers. She gazed at her son with eyes that were cynically dubious, but the girl looked at him with eyes that were soft with admiration; and Raven, for whom the luxury of esteem was a rare thing, felt a little giddy with self-love and strutted before them, acting out some gestures of the hunt. While thrusting with his lance, or yelling, or skulking as if approaching an ambush, he saw the girl looking at him, her brown eyes aglow with wonder.

Yielding to a sudden impulse he ran over to embrace her. She was willing. Indeed, she made a warm and supple movement toward him; but the grandmother turned on him with a cry of fury.

"Stop!" she screamed. She ran to Raven and thrust at him with hard angry hands. "Go away!" she said.

Abashed, the girl turned and slipped into the hut. After staring for a moment at the scorn and contempt in the old woman's eyes, Raven went over and sat by a tree, feeling outraged and degraded. He still sat there after darkness came, his body sickened by frustrated hunger, his mind plotting the death of the grandmother. When at last he rose to seek his bed, he glanced up at the sky and saw there the clouds of anger and the Moon Woman hiding in the clouds; and he stole in softly on hands and knees, with only fear in his heart.

10

WHEN no man came the next morning to go hunting, Raven was not surprised; in fact, he had forgotten the matter. His proposal to hunt had been only a ruse to get himself out of a predicament. He was not aware that he had deceived his neighbor, nor was the neighbor aware that he had been tricked. Deceit and craftiness were not, for the most part, deliberate modes of behavior with these people; the world of cunning was the unconscious mind, and there, unperceived, it established through impulse and intuition its patterns of conduct.

The grandmother, for instance, was very cunning this morning, though neither she nor any of the others suspected it. On leaving the hut and seeing clouds in the sky, she remembered that she had planned to make rain-magic today. Actually, she had planned nothing of the kind. She did not know that sight of the clouds suggested rain. She could not have been aware of this because in her conscious mind there was no relationship between rain and clouds. Clouds for her were little more than visible evidence of the Moon Woman's anger.

But the unconscious mind was then and still is a store-house of knowledge, of subtle relationships, of logic and prophecy. It is the granary on which the conscious mind feeds. In very intuitive persons, there is often a remarkable partnership between the two minds, with the materials buried in the one guiding the behavior of the other. The grandmother was an intuitive person; otherwise she could never have been the successful physician, midwife, and seeress of her family.

The moment she saw the clouds, she recalled her plan to make rain-magic and, comforted by her foresight and wisdom, she called her daughter and granddaughter and went for pouches of water. A few minutes later she sprinkled the pregnant woman while the two of them walked up and down the planted rows; and she whispered little pleas for rain or paused to gesture at the sky.

Barren had left the hut and gone fifty yards away to sit by a bush. Ever since the old woman had begun to make magic to bring rain, the barren one had trembled with hope. Hers was a bleak and empty world, because a sterile woman was almost an outcast from her people. Other women, more fortunate, held her in contempt, and after a while the men shared this attitude.

They did not think of her as sinful; having no notion of gods and devils, or of forces that were constant in their goodness or their evil, they had no concept of sin. If they had had such a concept, they would have said that a barren woman was sinful, that she was barren because she had offended a benevolent power. Their attitude toward such a woman was instinctive rather than moral. If birth was the purpose of life, then a barren woman was an inexpli-

136

cable waste. She was meaningless and useless. And, being all these, she was an enemy of her people.

For such a woman life was an almost intolerable burden. Scorned and friendless, she lived like an impostor and an interloper day after day and year after year, abused, hated, and unwanted. She took such food as nobody else would eat. She made her bed of stiff old hides that nobody else would have. She seldom spoke, and was rarely spoken to save with angry or contemptuous cries.

This woman, in her early twenties, was Rose's full sister. The old woman was her mother, the dead uncle had been her father. Like most girls she had entered pubescence when about ten or eleven, and so for many years she had been childless. During the first of those years her suffering had not been so acute. While she was still a girl, the others had watched her for signs of pregnancy, content then to be patient and to wait; but as the childless years passed, one by one, the members of her family had drawn away from her as if she were leprous with disease. By the time she was twenty she had been given up as hopeless, and thereafter the grandmother had made it plain that she was only a burden on the others.

But Barren herself had never given up hope. She never would to the end of her life. It was her belief, as it was the common belief of her people, that a woman got a child, not by mating with a man, but by doing certain magical things. She had to fertilize herself, quite as seed in the garden had to be fertilized. She had to be looked on with favor by the Moon Woman. She had to drink warm blood and eat certain foods. All these this woman had done again and again.

Why she was sterile, none of them could have said. In

such matters the grandmother was wiser than the others, but much of her knowledge had never been formulated in concepts. Her wisdom was a kind of rag bag of intuitive hints. If she had been forced to explain, she might have said that her daughter was childless because her family or her people had in some way offended the Moon Woman; but of the nature of the offense she could have given no suggestion at all. If Raven had been asked, he might have given a more specific answer. His reflections were leading him to the belief that when the Moon Woman was offended, it was not by all people, or even by a family, but by some person. He had come closer to a concept of sin. He would have had no notion of what the barren one had done to offend, because such a sharp definition of purpose and morals was still far beyond his grasp.

As for the childless one, she never thought of herself as one who had offended. In her confused and tortured mind it seemed to her that she had no child because there was something she must do which she had not done. What this was she could not imagine. In times past she had slyly stolen barley and corn from her mother's hoard; she had drunk all the blood she could get, and sometimes had gone hunting alone to snare the fecund rabbit; and she never missed a chance to drench herself in fertilizing rains.

It was rain that she looked forward to now, with hope beating like a live bird in her breast. Hope was a light in her eyes while she watched the three women make rain-magic or looked up now and then at the sky for signs that rain was coming. She was so eager that she would shake terribly for a few moments; and then, after trying to hold herself taut and still, she would lose control and tremble with such violence that low cries would escape from her lips.

Life had closed in on her and become little more than an obsessed and sleepless wish for a child. Every night she dreamed of the things she must do to have a baby; and once in a while she dreamed that she had a baby, and then she would awaken with a cry and sit up, her empty arms hugging the darkness. She would feel all over her bed, or leave her bed and crawl over the floor, her frantic arms searching for the child she had never had.

While sitting down, watching and waiting, she pressed the palms of her hands to the earth. She did not think of it as Mother Earth; it was not a human being like the moon; but she knew that it was related to fertility and growth. The trees from which they gathered nuts or fruit, the shrubs from which they stripped berries, and the fragrant flowering things this woman loved—all these, like the corn and barley, stood in the earth and in a mysterious way drew their nourishment from it. For her and for her people, the earth was a kind and friendly thing. She liked to press her palms against it, or a cheek, or clasp a handful of it, or smell it, or lie on its goodness and strength.

She now clasped a handful, rich with centuries of decayed roots and leaves, and put a little of it on her tongue. This soil around her did not taste like some she had eaten. There was another kind, a fine heavy clay, that they sometimes carried to their house to lick when they felt need of salt. This kind the grandmother mixed in some of her remedies. Barren could taste no salt in this earth; it was more like old rotted wood that had become soft and spongy.

Looking at the sky again and seeing no sign of rain there, she went off by herself in the near-by hills, hoping to find the fragrant bloom of plants. The violets and all the other early flowers were gone now, but by a stream she found tall bushes laden with blossoms that smelled sweet, and she gathered an armful and hugged the mass to her breast. She had a greater love of such things than any other member of her family, for she had greater need to love. During the years of her womanhood there had never been a small child in her home; the only live baby she had ever seen was her niece, and she had been only a girl then. She knew there was a child in Rose, but after it came she would not be allowed to mother it. The old women of the families never allowed a barren one or a sick one to touch a child, or even its food or bed.

This woman was not looking forward to such privileges. She was resolved in spite of all her empty years to have a child of her own; to get one she would keep doing all the things it was wise to do. Above all else, she would have to be fertilized by the rains; but she would also rub herself with soil and sprinkle herself, as she had done so many times, with running water, or bury her face in bloom, as now, and breathe deeply of it. It was good for a woman to keep close to all the healthy and growing things. It was good to put arms round a tree and hug it and eat the bark and lick the sap. And of course it was good to drink the warm blood of such fertile creatures as the female rabbit.

She felt that all things that pleased her would help her. This feeling in her and in some of her people was the faint beginning of a sense of beauty—because human beings have found those things beautiful which have enhanced their sense of well-being. Flowers without fragrance she found attractive because of their color but she could not absorb them save by eating them. Fragrance she could draw in on her breath. While walking homeward she buried her face in the flowers and fed hungrily on the intoxicating odor that for her meant fertility and health. She was like a starved womb trying to absorb a child from all the sweet and vivid things of the earth.

Meanwhile, the grandmother was employing all the cunning she had. She never made rain-magic when there was little likelihood of success, but once she determined to make rain come, she persisted until it came. For four days, interrupted only by journeys in search of food, she performed her ritual in the garden. Each morning before stirring the fire she would go outside to stand in the yard; there her senses, unknown to her, would communicate to her unconscious mind certain subtle hints of what she was waiting for. Before going to bed she would stand in the doorway and look at the Moon Woman.

On the fifth morning the entire sky was overcast, but the old woman would not have said that the gloom foretold an approaching storm. She would have said, if pressed to an answer, that she sensed a coming of rain but saw no visible signs of it, having no need of such commonplace evidence as ordinary folk lived their lives by; and now, as if to impress her family with her mysterious powers, she summoned her helpers and devoted herself earnestly to magic.

The others were impressed. Even while the grandmother sprinkled water and uttered low pleas, the sky darkened and settled. The barren woman, trembling with joy and with her face upturned, waited for the precious drops to touch her, and the sick woman left her bed, looking happy and expectant, because rain not only fertilized the barren but often relieved the suffering as well.

Though awed by the old woman's wizardry, the men did not have a woman's interest in the things that promoted birth. For them rain could be an intolerable nuisance. Raven was reflecting that it would pour through the roof and soak his bed, and then the skins on which he slept would dry and stiffen into unusable shapes. The rain would drench him, too, and make him shiver with cold. It would soak the fuel and it might kill the fire.

While busy with these unhappy thoughts, he took his customary position by a tree and looked in turn at the lowering sky and at the old woman walking back and forth between rows of seed. For him she was a mysterious and dreadful person. Somehow, in ways and for reasons unknown to a man, she was in harmony with the Moon Woman, and the two of them, working together in baffling secrecy, could fill the world with rain. A man could do nothing like that. A man would not know what to say to the woman above, who, in this darkening time of magic, was somewhere out of sight but looking and listening nevertheless. What the grandmother was saying, Raven could not imagine. He could not hear her voice but he knew she was talking, because when she faced his way he could see her lips move.

For a man this power in a woman was the most frightening thing in life. Raven knew that it was related to her power to give birth, but that, too, was utterly mysterious. A woman fertilized herself with rain and flowers and blood, and out of the blood in her own body a child came. He had spent many hours thinking about it, but, instead of explaining the miracle, his reflections merely deepened his fear and his awe. They also intensified his hatred and distrust of women, because hate is a blind and unreasoning defense against a fearful object that is not understood.

He was a comically solemn fellow, sitting there by a tree, now staring at the old woman and hating her or now glancing expectantly at the sky. While racking his brain for a clue to a matter that wholly baffled him, he observed that Barren was standing off by herself with an armful of flowers. In the next moment he became conscious of rain. A few drops were falling—large soft drops that struck his arms and broke and splashed. The grandmother and the two women with her now left the garden and entered the hut. They were going to lay skins above the fire to protect it. Spider had come out and was looking up at the sky, with rain drops bursting against his face. But it was the one with the flowers who held Raven's attention. Many times he had seen women dance in the rain, but their wild behavior still fascinated him.

Barren was not dancing yet. She was walking in a slow graceful way, as if her body were filled with vibrant and waiting music. With a rhythmical gesture she moved the flowers up and down, lifting them to the sky and then gently drawing them down to her heart. When she lifted her arms, Raven could see her firm breasts pointing upward, but like all the men of his time he had no special interest in breasts. They were only the food pouches that a child suckled. He was more interested in her face which she turned upward to catch the rain. In her slow undulant movement she had drawn close to where he sat, and he stared with unwavering fascination at the intense passion in her face. He could see her eyes shining like two lights under the dark sky.

143

The rain now fell steadily, and Raven could hear it talking in the leaves above him. His hair was wet. Water ran from his hair down his face, clasping his eyelashes, gathering in lingering coolness in the depression of his closed lips, and dropping from his chin to cling like tiny pebbles to the hair on his chest. Like the feet of scurrying insects it tickled his back.

The woman was dancing now, but slowly, softly, as if these movements were only a kind of voluptuous overture. She lifted the flowers at arm's length and held them for a moment to catch the rain before hugging them to her. Tilting her head back, she opened her mouth wide to catch the rain and when she swallowed she closed her eyes and stood tiptoe, straining to the sky. The sick woman was not dancing; there was no feeling of ecstasy in her. She merely stood, with arms folded, to let the rain wash her like a healing salve. The other women stood by the hut. The fertilizing rain was a wonderful thing for all of them. It would help the pregnant one to have a strong and healthy child. It would add fertility to the young one so that she could become pregnant. And as for the old woman, it would soften the seams of age and soothe her aching joints. In all their faces there was a quiet joy that was almost holy, as if the Moon Woman had chosen them for a special kindness and were showering youth and health upon them. There was gentleness in the grandmother's eyes when she looked at her dancing daughter—because she was thinking of her now, not as a barren and disgusting creature but as one who would have a child and fulfill a woman's destiny.

The rain became a steady downpour, and Raven, looking up at its gray gloom, wondered what kind of vessels the Moon Woman used to gather so much water. Somewhere above him, but out of sight, she was pouring the rain. On all sides of him as far as he could see there was rain, but he could not see very far. He did not think it was raining over a large area. It was not raining on his neighbors. This was the rain that the grandmother had won with her magic, and it was falling only on her garden and the other things that belonged to her. . . .

The woman was dancing now and she was singing. Her movements had become swifter and more abandoned; she ran back and forth with quick light steps, pausing to spin round and round, and then dashing off, with the flowers lifted like a bird beginning its flight. Her singing would not have been tuneful to more civilized ears. It was a kind of lament, in one moment almost anguished in its pleading, in the next, punctuated by ecstatic cries. When she ran with long graceful strides, as if in haste to capture something, her voice was plaintive and beseeching, but when, on coming to the end of the run, she leapt skyward, with her arms seeking and the flowers spread like a host of butterflies, her cry was almost a scream. Still staring at her with solemn interest, Raven thought of her as something that was trying to fly.

The girl was the first to join her. She had been standing with her mother, intently watching, but all the while emotion had been welling up in her, and when it became an intolerable eagerness, she sped away through the lines of rain to gather flowers. Soon she returned and danced back and forth with the barren one. She, too, wanted a child, and dancing for her, as for her aunt, was a fertilizing ritual. But the girl did not imitate her companion. Obeying her own impulses, she improvised, the hunger in her body instructing her gestures and song. The singing of each stimulated the other, and soon their cries became a shrill melody, with the steady monotonous sound of the rain playing to them like a drum.

Though Rose was pregnant and knew she would have a child, she was unable to resist the wild and haunting music. When she hastened away through the gray wall of rain, the sick woman watched her go, but after hesitating for a long moment she uttered a cry that was like a choked sob and followed her. The two of them returned with flowers and began to dance. If anyone had been looking at the grandmother's wrinkled face, he would have seen it convulsed by an emotion close to anguish. She, too, wanted to dance but she was too old for that; her joints were stiff and her spine was bent with age. Nevertheless her whole body twitched as if the rhythms of dance and song were plucking at it. Leaving the doorway she approached the women, her body jerking with strange uncontrollable spasms, as if trying to respond to music and youth. But she made no effort to dance. She was content to walk back and forth in the rain, her eyes bright and happy in her old worn face under the gray wet mat of her hair.

Now the dancing, at least of two of them—the barren woman and the girl—was drawing to its climax. Directed only by the welling flood of their hunger, they were running and leaping and whirling, tossing their flowers like two creatures born of thunder and lightning, their drenched hair streaming like scarves and their open mouths feeding on the raindrops. Their voices were a shrill ringing call, wild with joy but touched by sadness, too, because they were suppliants, and no cry from them could be wholly free of fear. In their voices there was something so hauntingly asking, so persistent in its yearning, so sad

146

and lonely in its hunger and pain, that Raven was moved to his feet.

He went forward to stare at the women. He wanted to dance, too, and to cry and sing. He wanted to leap from the earth, as birds leapt, and deliver himself into the keeping of some vast and engulfing joy. The music of the rain and the women awakened dormant hungers in him that were deeper than his hunger for mating. But he was confused; and so he stood with arms hanging limply, and with water all over him like a cool sheath. Then he turned and went over to his weapons and looked at them, but they were not what he wanted. When he saw Spider watching him, he went close to the man and looked into his eyes. What he saw there troubled and excited him, but he did not understand its spiritual nakedness. He looked at Spider, and Spider looked at him, until both men felt embarrassed. Then Raven turned away. He was a man housed in a great hunger that had no windows and could open no doors.

II

MEANWHILE, the juices which the grandmother had gathered had been fermenting in a large clay vessel. During the hours of sunshine she had kept it outside but she had taken it in at night and set it by the fire; now and then she had stirred the mixture or licked the juice off a finger to learn if it was becoming potent. When she thought it was strong enough to give a man courage, she told Raven it was ready to drink and that he should now prepare for a big hunt.

Her words made him unhappy. As long as there was no fermented liquor to drink he had an excuse to hunt nothing more dangerous than rabbits, mice, squirrels, and the smaller birds. Going to the pot, he bent over and looked at its contents. There was about a gallon of the juice, mixed with leaves, bark, seeds, and beeswax. He thrust a finger into it and licked his finger; the stuff was as bitter as gall. With a stick he explored in the jug, turning up wax, leaves, shreds of bark, and sprigs of aromatic plants.

The grandmother came over with a wooden spoon and dipped up a spoonful and offered it to him; and like a small boy taking medicine, Raven shut his eyes and opened his mouth. She poured the bitter stuff into his mouth, and he swallowed it and shuddered; but after a few moments he could feel it burning down his throat and in his stomach and he knew it was full of courage.

"Good?" she asked.

He wanted to say no but he did not dare to. If he had said no, she would have abused him, saying that he was a disgusting and ungrateful fellow. Hunting, after all, was his chore and his duty, and it was out of the goodness of her heart that she fermented a drink to give him the boldness he lacked.

"You like it?"

"Yes," he said.

So pleased that her old face smiled, she ladled out another spoonful and poured it into his mouth. Then she fed him a third and a fourth, and as the alcohol warmed him he felt a little bolder; but this, he recalled, was not the proper time to drink the stuff. He had many preparations to make before he could drink a quart or two and go forth to the hunt.

First, he had to kill some fearless thing and mix its blood with his dyes to paint his face. A flesh-eating bird would do, or a weasel, or any small thing that killed its own food. But before slaying such a creature he had to placate its spirit. This ritual, like a woman's dancing in the rain, had not become fixed by habit, and so Raven, like his sister, improvised his supplication, obeying the impulses of the moment.

He went over and knelt by a tree like one in prayer—indeed, he was praying in his own way. He was beseeching the spirit of his victim not to be angry with him. He had to go forth now and kill something, and in a flash of inspiration he told the spirit that it was not his fault, that it was the old woman who was driving him to it, and that if anybody was to be punished, the ghost ought to punish her. This was the first time he had ever tried to place the responsibility on another. His brilliant notion, though born now like a flash of insight, had been taking shape in his unconscious mind for many weeks. Unlike the other members of his family, he had been formulating the idea that punishment—by the Moon Woman or by a spirit or any other invisible power—should be given, not to a whole family or group but to the particular person who was guilty of offending. The idea was not yet a conscious recognition, but the substance of it was in his mind, and out of it had come the sudden and inspiring thought that the grandmother ought to be punished. It was she who forced him to go out and kill things; and so, facing the tree, with his eyes closed, he whispered to the ghosts, asking them to understand that he was friendly and had no wish to destroy the house in which they lived. And when at last he took his weapons and went out to slay a hawk or a weasel, he went with a light step that was almost arrogant, because he felt that no malicious spirit would ever come to molest him.

About two hours later he returned, bringing with him a peregrine falcon. He was elated, and proudly he showed his trophy to the women. This bird was one of the most deadly of all things in the air—swift in flight, strong of beak and talon, and absolutely fearless. Raven had drunk a part of its blood; he now tore the breast open and ate the heart. Then he thrust a hand into the warm wet carcass and smeared blood over his face and body, his sexual amu-

150

let, and the skins of his bed. All the while he looked with sly triumph at the grandmother, knowing that if the hawk's ghost came seeking vengeance it would enter her. Because he hated his mother, he wanted to tell her that, but also, because this was his own precious secret, he wished to keep it. Caught between the two impulses, he behaved strangely, now staring boldly at the old woman and now turning away to gurgle with joy. Suddenly he shouted at her, and a moment later, observing her consternation, he chuckled with gloating delight. Wait, he told himself, until the falcon's spirit crept into her body; she would draw her skinny legs up against her stomach and moan all night with pain. . . .

"Go away!" he howled, with an excess of bravado.

"What?" she asked, startled.

"Go far away!"

The women hardly knew what to think of their man; but the grandmother remembered that she had fed him from the clay jug and she felt indulgent. He always behaved like a man in a tantrum when preparing for a big hunt. The uncle had done so, too. All men did so; a woman had to put up with their brashness in a time like this. It was the courage working in them. The more violent Raven became before going away to hunt, the more courageous he was likely to be.

After he had shoved his hand into the carcass many times, dragging out the vital organs and eating them and exhausting the blood, he tossed what was left to the women. Then he got his dyes and pigments, and, setting a jug of water in sunlight to use as a mirror, he proceeded to the delightful task of making himself look ferocious. Kneeling, he stared at the dim image of his face; then, using a finger as a brush, he put a streak of red dye down the bridge of his nose. Under either eye he smeared alternating arcs of red and green, and across his brow, from his eye ridges to his hair, he drew heavy red lines. Then for a long moment he peered at his reflection.

In smearing his face and body he followed no fixed habits but yielded in this, as in nearly all other matters, to sudden impulses. His only purpose was to make himself look so dreadful that he would frighten anything that crossed his path. He painted his front teeth, because when he faced an enemy he would snarl and show a red mouth. He daubed his ears, his throat, his chest, his arms and legs; whereupon, becoming intensely preoccupied, he took the sexual amulet and drew red and green rings around the stone.

Smearing himself with blood and pigments was only a small part of his preparations. When this was done he spent a long while examining his weapons to be sure they were sharp and fit. He had a handsome spear fitted with a flint point; a long flint dagger that was almost sharp enough to shave the hair on his arms; and a great bow and two dozen arrows, each with an obsidian head. No man in the area had weapons that were better or more carefully engraved.

Though he examined them one by one, solemnly, painstakingly, all this was only part of his ritual. The time a man spent preparing for a hunt depended on how timid or bold he was by nature, and how vain. A part of the ritual was intended to build up his courage; but a part of it—and with Raven a considerable part—was an effort to draw attention to himself. In such a time he became the center of the family group. If one of the men or women approached to see what he was doing, it was then that he pretended to be absorbed by his work. Preparations for the hunt were his special province and knowledge. Most of the time he was only a nobody, dependent on the old woman's indulgence, but now he was important, and all of them were aware of him and of what he was doing. His ego, usually repressed and ignored, now flowered in fine histrionic gestures, in sly acting, in impatience for their trivial spheres of life. He had taken the center of the stage and was resolved to make the most of it.

When, for instance, he was inspecting an arrow head, and one of them came up to see what he was doing, he would pretend to be unaware of the person. If it was a woman who watched him, he would pretend to do secret and mysterious things; but all the while he furtively watched the peering face to see if it was impressed. To startle, to arouse admiration, to become, at least for a little while, the most important member of his family, was the whole purpose of his cunning.

He was studying the engravings on his spear haft when the grandmother came up. He had been waiting for her. She was the one whom he wished above all others to impress. And now, vividly conscious of her presence and determined to confuse and astound her, he did absurd and baffling things. He drew the spear point close to him, concealing it in the hair on his belly; and then, without looking at the old woman, and pretending not to see her at all, he made swift cabalistic gestures, his hands darting out as if to capture strange emanations and then flashing in to touch the point, as if he were taking things from the atmosphere and adding them to his weapon. The grandmother had never seen a man behave so queerly. She was mystified.

She uttered a low indrawn "Ohhhh!" and Raven, hearing the awe and wonder in her cry, redoubled his efforts. But when the old woman asked, "What are you doing?" he was annoyed. When she made rain-magic he did not ask her what she was doing. Besides, her question assumed that he was aware of her presence, and of course he was not. He had given her no reason to think that he was.

"What are you doing?" she asked again.

He refused to answer. It almost seemed to him that he had not heard, so engrossed was he by his own secret magic. The grandmother called to her daughter. "Look!" she said.

Rose came over and looked. "What is it?"

"Look!"

Raven could hear the awe in her voice. He now took an arrow and thrust it between his legs, as if he were impaling a beast. Very slyly, so that they could not see what he did, he dipped a finger into red pigment, reached swiftly under his legs, and then held his finger up and looked at it. On it was a redness like blood. The old woman was so consumed by curiosity that she knelt, intending to peer under his legs to learn what was there; but Raven, sensing her purpose, shouted at her and leapt to his feet. He pretended to be angry. In fact, he was a little angry. The gestures he had made at first only to mystify had become meaningful for him—for it has always been the way of human beings to find meaning in everything they do, and even to transform the meaningless into elaborate rituals.

While improvising, Raven had been evolving a magic of his own; it was a part of his precious and secret knowledge and he did not intend to let an old tyrant spy on it.

"Go away!" he shouted; and when the grandmother did not move, he seized his spear and menaced her. She re-

154

treated hastily, her startled eyes searching his face. "Go away!" he cried, threatening both women.

They entered the hut, murmuring with astonishment. In the grandmother's mind was the notion that Raven had discovered some new magic of the hunt and would soon bring fresh meat. After a little while she looked out at him, her old eyes gentle and pleased.

During this night Raven was tormented by dreams, as a man always was when he planned to go far from the custody of his home fire and hunt the larger beasts. He moaned, or now and then he uttered a terrible scream and sat up, striking out violently with his hands. He had dreamed that he was stalking a big cat, but in the dream he had been neither vain nor bold enough to make himself triumphant. The cat had struck him and leapt on him and he had screamed.

In his dreams, and in the dreams of all of them, either the soul left its body and visited the objects that were remembered on awaking, or the soul of another crept into the sleeping body and told of what it had seen. Raven knew that his soul had left him and gone away to hunt. It was when the beast leapt on the soul that the body screamed and sat up; and then, of course, warned by the cry, the soul came swiftly and entered its home.

Afraid that it might be slain because of its foolhardy prowling, Raven, after being twice aroused, resolved to stay awake, and so he left his bed. The others had been awakened by his cries.

"What is wrong?" asked the grandmother, sitting up.

"Enemies!" he said angrily.

"Enemies where?"

"Out there," he said, and gestured at the world.

The thought of enemies closing in on them so terrified Spider that he burst with blubbering sobs. Even the sick one began to cry. Each seemed to be fed by the grief and terror of the others; in a few minutes the hut was filled with sounds of anguish. The grandmother rose and went to the doorway to look out. Seeing nothing alarming, she sniffed the air for the scent of beasts. Going over to stand by her, Raven also sniffed. Suddenly, with a cry that came out of him in a naked scream, he pointed to the darkness and in a voice of utter terror said, "Look!"

The grandmother looked just in time to see a pair of vanishing lights. They were two eyes glowing out in the darkness. She was so overcome that she grasped Raven's arm.

"What was it?" she whispered.

He did not know what it was, but he said, "Tiger!"

When the other men heard the word they came forward. They had not hunted in a long time, but they had their old weapons and they now advanced, clutching lances that shook in their hands. Raven rushed over to a wall to seize his spear, though he knew that it would be of little use against a tiger. All of them but the sick woman crowded to the doorway to look out.

"Tiger?" asked Old Man in a sick whisper.

"Yes," someone said.

"Out there?" he asked stupidly.

"There," said Raven, and pointed.

The first to recover from astonishment and fear was the old woman. Running to the hearth, she stirred the fire and laid wood on it; and while the others stood in the doorway, with none daring to step outside, the fire began to talk with cheerful boldness and to fill the room with light. It was a friendly thing. It was the friendliest of all things in their fear-ridden world. When it became a blazing and hungry life within its crib of stones, they all felt quite secure, knowing that no beast that roamed the earth would dare to enter their home now. Spider and Old Man and Barren returned to their beds.

After looking up at the dark sky and seeing no sign of the young Moon Woman, the grandmother took a flaming fagot and went outside. Raven stood in the doorway and watched her. With her crude lantern she went to the garden and back and forth in the yard, peering at the earth for animal footprints. Then she knelt and Raven could see her holding the flame close to the earth. After a long moment she called to him.

Poising his lance he went out, trembling with fear, and knelt by her.

"See there," she said.

"What is it?"

"Look."

Bending low, he sniffed and then rose slowly like an old man.

"Tiger," he said, meaning any large cat.

When he turned to the hut, with his back to the night and the unknown, he felt goose flesh in his scalp and down his spine, and after tiptoeing a little way, as if slinking from an enemy, he uttered a howl of terror and bolted headlong. Standing by the fire, he was unable to quiet the tremors in his frame for a long while.

When daylight came he ventured outside, and though he looked like a bold man, smeared as he was with blood and dyes, and with his muscles taut and bulging, he did not feel bold at all. He twitched and quaked as he walked

157

softly in the yard, looking for signs of a marauder. Sinking to hands and knees, he sniffed along the ground until he picked up the scent, and when he rose to his feet, he glanced anxiously at the hut like one measuring the distance to safety.

Believing that he was ready for the hunt, the grandmother came out, fetching his weapons.

"Go hunt now," she said, speaking in a calm and ageless voice, as if a man stalked the wolf or tiger as matter-of-factly as a woman laid wood on a fire.

"No!" he cried.

"Yes. We need food." She proffered his weapons.

Her insistence annoyed him. She knew very well, it seemed to him, that he had not completed his preparations. He would have to act out the hunt, as all men did, pretending that he was chasing his prey and overpowering it; and after he had killed the beasts in an imaginary drama of pursuit, he would have to propitiate the ghosts. And then, finally, he would have to go to the jug and drink deep of its courage.

"No," he said sullenly, but he accepted his weapons.

He felt enslaved by this tyrant's unreasonable whims. She wanted food, and little enough she cared what terrors a man faced or how often he risked his life. She lived safely, with fire to protect her, a home to sit in, and people to help her drive away dangers. But now, as if she coveted his death, she wanted him to go hunt, though his preparations were only half completed.

"Go find food!" she said sharply. "Go now."

Staring at her, he backed away. He went over and laid his weapons by a tree; then he went into the hut and came out with the jug of liquor. Setting it on the earth, he knelt

158

by it and poured one spoonful after another down his throat. It was so bitter that it was almost nauseating, but he knew that it was full of courage. He could feel the courage warming his stomach and spreading all through him, and after he had drunk about a pint of it, he felt encouraged to proceed to the next part of his ritual.

In this he would pretend that he was hunting a large and savage beast. This was a kind of rehearsal in which a man sharpened his senses, felt out the wiles of his enemy, summoned his own resourcefulness and cunning, and so convinced himself that he was the beast's master. For some men, another person acted the part of the animal, but no one in Raven's family would do that. The men were too old to skulk in the thickets or dart nimbly from tree to tree, and the women looked on such ritual as no part of their tasks. Indeed, they thought it a little ridiculous. As solemn as death itself, the grandmother would make rain-magic or exorcise ghosts or compound simples of herbs and sorcery, but Raven's preparations for a hunt seemed to her to be the antics of a foolish man.

And so he had to pretend that he was chasing a tiger. Having drunk a pint of alcoholic magic, and flushed by the courage that alcohol gives, he tied the quiver of arrows around his waist, grasped his bow with one hand and the spear with the other, and assumed the stealthy pose of the hunter. When the members of his family came out to watch him, he was delighted; the presence of spectators, even though some of them were amused and smiling, always impelled him to superhuman feats.

He struck an attitude of listening, his body bent forward, his ears cocked, his nostrils sniffing, and his gaze fixed on the tangled thicket. He knew a tiger was lurking there. He could smell the strong odor of the beast. In one moment he heard its low breathing, and in the next, the sound of its padded feet on old leaf depth. But he was unable to see it; the creature was concealed in the jungle, waiting for him to move.

Now, wholly possessed by his acting, Raven lifted his head and sniffed to get the direction of the breeze. He thrust his tongue out to feel its current; on the side from which the breeze came, his tongue felt cooler. Realizing that the air was moving from him toward his prey, he felt actual alarm, and swiftly he slunk back and to one side, describing a wide arc to approach against the wind. He could have moved no more noiselessly if his feet, like the tiger's, had been sheathed with fur and padded with sponges. His acting was so artful that the smiles left the faces of the women and they turned to look at one another. Spider and Old Man felt dismay. The grandmother wondered if the night prowler was still hiding there in the bushes and vines.

Quickly, but with no sound, Raven went to the leeward side, his left hand grasping both bow and lance, his right holding an arrow to the bowstring. Then, with extraordinary caution, he entered the jungle, his feet feeling their way and brushing aside, before accepting his weight, all twigs that might snap; his head and shoulders ducking sinuously under branches; his whole body lithe and poised and superbly controlled. Now and then he paused to sniff, to peer, to listen. A snake creeping up on an unwary bird could hardly have been more soundless.

An image of the beast was so bright and real in his mind that he thought he saw it, and in the next moment his right arm drew back the arrow, held it for a brief instant, and

160

let it go. Then, dropping his bow, he gave a dreadful yell and leapt forward with his lance, bringing it high above him with both hands and then driving it downward with all his power. He buried the head deep in the earth and held it firmly, waiting for the impaled beast to die. The struggle of the dying thing made the lance shake in his hands.

On hearing his cry, the men and women came running to the thicket, and presently Raven could see them parting branches to peer in. He heard one of them ask:

"Is it dead?"

"Yes," said Raven.

"Is it big?"

"Yes."

They all pushed forward. Then the women, recovering from the hypnosis which had made mock combat seem real, shrugged with disgust and went back to their home. But the men were not disappointed when they found nothing dead at Raven's feet. After all, they, too, had prepared for the hunt when younger and had slain many animals in the way this one had been slain. They did not look on this as pretense. In a strange world where so many things lived that were invisible, a man could never be sure what he killed, or whether the slain thing miraculously escaped when a lance was driven into the ground. They knew a tiger had been here because they had smelled it. While waiting for Raven to enter the jungle they had heard it. That it was not here now was nothing for any wise old hunter to marvel at.

Realizing that Raven must now propitiate the dead beast's spirit, they went away, leaving him alone; and Raven knelt on the earth where he had slain the tiger to make his peace with its ghost. In this part of his preparation, he would talk to it, not so much with words he customarily used as with humble and apologetic sounds. He explained that the killing was not his fault and that he was not to be blamed. It was the grandmother who forced him to go forth and slay things; if this homeless tiger ghost were to be restless and unhappy now, and were to come prowling in the dark, seeking a new home, then it should enter the old woman. For his part, he felt friendly toward it and wished to live in friendship.

He explained all this, murmuring like one in prayer. He humbled himself and offered sincere and childlike apology. Over and over he told the ghost the same story—that the grandmother was an old tyrant who drove him out to destroy the homes of spirits. "If," he said in effect, "you are unhappy and homeless and sad, if you feel vengeful, if you must enter a person to find a new home, then enter the old woman, because she is mean and malicious and noisy. She is the one who wants to eat your home. She is the one. . . ."

That is what he tried to make the spirit understand. And when he rose at last and turned to pick up his weapons, he looked like a sad and conscience-stricken man, a humble and dejected man who had made a prayer and was not sure it would be answered. He did not want to go hunting. He would have preferred to live all his days on roots and berries, and such small creatures as frogs and mice, whose spirits, though angry and invading, could never do a man great harm. He was foreseeing his own possible loss by sensing the loss and unhappiness of another; and in this power of projection and prophecy, compassion had its lowly beginning.

162

When he emerged from the thicket, the women paid no attention to him; and Raven, glad not to be fixed by the old woman's accusing stare or commanded to go hunting again before he was ready, sat by a tree and looked at the sky. Some men liked to stalk the larger beasts in spite of the hazards and the avenging spirits, but Raven was a timid man with a taste for the philosophic life. He liked to sit in relaxed indolence and reflect on himself and the baffling world around him. A woman spent most of her time within the circumference of fixed habits and rituals and the customary chores. A man like Raven felt an urge to alter and shape his environment; and this hunger led him to persistent efforts to revise the certainties and bring them into fuller harmony with his will.

During the past year he had done so in one significant matter. The desire to make himself more secure among the tyrannies of women had impelled him to the belief that a ghost could be persuaded to enter a chosen person instead of indiscriminately invading the first living object to which it came. In formulating this notion, Raven had come pretty close to a sense of good and evil, of human responsibility, and of benevolent and malign beings; and his vague idea of human responsibility was leading him in turn to a sense of sin.

But he was still far from it; and now, while sitting by a tree, he had so few ideas to think with, and those few were so burdened with superstition and error, that in looking at the sky or the earth he could feel little but its oppressiveness. Nevertheless he believed that the spirits of his victims would never molest him; he would urge them to enter the grandmother or the other women. The killing he must do was their fault and not his. This notion was so warm and comforting that he felt quite happy, and when, a few minutes later, the old woman came to the doorway and stared at him, he looked at her with eyes half lidded and flickering with triumph, knowing that she was doomed.

12

RAVEN's next and last step in his preparations was to drink deeply of the courage. It was not a habit with men to drink alcoholic liquors save in times when they needed great boldness, though they did crave condiments because of their unseasoned and flavorless diets. When they could find them, they liked to suck the juices of such aromatic plants as thyme, mint, and rosemary, or the pulp of the agave and other plants. Because they had no salt in mineral form, they licked clay banks or their own sweat, and if the beverage the women fermented had not been so chokingly bitter and astringent, they might have drunk it when there was no need of extraordinary courage.

How drunk a man became before venturing out to hunt the larger beasts depended on how timid he was. Raven was more neurotic and apprehensive than most men, and so this morning he drank the thick and bitter stuff in the jug until he was dizzy with intoxication. He did not pour it down in a hurry but sat by the pot and fed himself with a spoon, striving all the while to measure the growth of his boldness. His first imbibings merely warmed his stomach and flushed him with a sense of well-being. From time to time the grandmother came over to see how he was doing and to look at him with approval.

"Is it good?" she asked, meaning, "Will it give you courage?"

As if he had not settled the matter, he dipped a spoonful and poured it down his throat. Then he shut his eyes and shuddered. Guile told him not to admit that it was good, lest she become careless next time and prepare a drink even more bitter.

"No," he said, and shuddered again.

"Not good?" she asked, astonished.

"It tastes bad."

"Nooo!" she said, incredulously.

In concocting this beverage she had employed her most precious magic; he was an ungrateful man to say that it tasted bad. Bending over, she looked at the stuff and then knelt and sniffed it. He dipped in for a spoonful and offered it to her; with furious resentment she knocked the spoon from his hand. He knew very well that women, having no need of more courage, never drank such stuff. When ill, they drank magically steeped simples of herbs and juices, but never anything that was fermented.

"It is good," she said, sniffing.

"No!"

Firmly she answered him, "It is good."

To please her, he dutifully fed himself, choking and sputtering as he gulped the burning liquid. He was beginning to feel quite reckless. He was beginning to fancy himself as an indomitable hunter, able to face any beast without quaking.

166

"Go away!" he cried, waving to her with lordly contempt.

"What?" she asked, startled.

"Go far away!"

"Why?" she asked, staring at his flushed and arrogant face.

For a long moment he sat, comically solemn, trying to think of a reason why she ought to go far away, but, failing in that, he spooned the liquid, shuddered, and made faces to express his distaste.

After he had consumed a quart or more, all his senses were giddy and swimming; but he was not yet ready to take his weapons and leave. He had eaten little for days, and nothing at all during the last twenty-four hours, and so the drink seemed to rush all through him and fill his body with urgent and burning life. He could feel it down his arms and legs. It so stimulated his mind that fancies poured through in a bewildering pageant, as if all that he had ever thought and dreamed were passing in review.

Though he felt reckless and ready, he still sat by the jug and drank. He was so drunk now that he no longer minded the bitter taste and, instead of trying to dip only the clear dark liquid, he spooned the wax and leaves and shreds of bark along with the juice, and chewed and swallowed them. When the wax became imbedded in the cups of his teeth, he thrust in with a dirty finger to loosen it, his eyes meanwhile gazing with owlishly philosophic interest at the sky.

Never before in his life had he been so drunk. When at last he strove to rise, he staggered and almost fell over and then reached down to the earth with both hands; and there he stood on four legs like a man propped, his head turning from side to side as if it were trying to leave his helpless body. He stood in this position until two women came over and grasped his arms and lifted him to an upright position. Then the whole earth was a swimming thing of dancing lights and shadows. When he glanced up at the sun, it seemed to him to be jumping about wildly, and when he looked at trees, none of them was standing still.

"You go hunt now," the grandmother said.

He heard and understood the words. Yes, he would go hunting now. He turned to her, and the muscles of his face relaxed in a friendly grin of idiocy, but a sense of outrage still lived in his unconscious mind.

"Go away," he said, dismissing her with a drunken gesture.

"You find food now."

As far as she could tell, the man had all the courage he needed; and so one by one she picked up his weapons. She put the quiver of arrows around his waist and tied the buckskin thong. She put the bow in one of his hands and bent his nerveless fingers around it; she put the spear in his other hand. And there he stood, swaying like something in a wind, his arms outstretched, his fingers weakly clasping his weapons. When the grandmother said again that it was time to go hunting, he understood that it was time, and he staggered away, moving each leg as if it were half paralyzed. The other men stood by the hut and watched him. He was an absurd spectacle, this man going away to hunt dangerous beasts when he was so drunk he could hardly see the earth under his feet.

But he felt very bold. Nothing could frighten him now.

168

He was so reckless that he would have shot arrows at the Moon Woman. While he staggered off he grinned broadly, not with purpose, but because his facial muscles were so relaxed that he could not help it. Over his whole face was the wide and fixed and happy grin of a man who did not know what he was doing and did not care.

Still, that is not quite the truth. He did realize that he was going away to hunt. He knew he was moving, though he did not seem to be doing so by his own will; on the contrary, the earth seemed to be flowing under him, and on either side he saw trees and hills walking past. He even knew, in a vaguely blissful way, what direction he was taking. He was heading toward a broad bayou in a river.

Over one hill and another, up and down, he staggered along, his hands clutching his weapons, his face looking happy and expectant. It was good to feel so brave. It was good to know that all beasts fled in terror before him. After he had gone over several hills he uttered a sudden and triumphant shout that was both a challenge and a cry of joy. Then, pausing, he stood for a long moment, swaying unsteadily and looking round him. By force of habit he sniffed the breeze, but when he bent forward to search the earth for footprints, he fell over, not quickly, but in a drunken slow-motion descent, as if his muscles were made of stiff rubber. His hands touched the ground; his rump buckled and he collapsed; but almost at once he struggled and sat up. Then he tried to rise, and he did rise, first supporting himself on feet and hands and thrusting his hinder up like a cow, and then slowly drawing his torso to an erect position. He drew a deep sigh. Everything around him was still dancing in happy and wonderful bewilderment.

The still water to which he came at last was a bayou
in a river, perhaps two hundred yards wide and a little
longer than that. There were many fish in it, and in times
past he had fished here, wading along the shore and spearing the less wary creatures; but today he wanted a piece
of log on which to float. While searching in the woods
which stood against the bayou, quite by chance he came
on a fallen tree that had been struck by lightning. Most
of the tree had rotted and broken into segments; but one
of these, faced by a lightning scar, and about twelve feet
in length, was well preserved. Lightning had gutted it,
burning deep into the wood. Any modern man, looking
at this segment of tree, would have noticed its resemblance
to a canoe, but Raven knew nothing of canoes and boats.
For him this was only something that would float and
carry him out to deeper water. By lifting one end over
and then the other, by rolling it across bushes and around
trees, he got it to the beach; whereupon, leaving bow
and arrows behind and taking only his lance, he pushed off.

His labor had sobered him a little, but he was still very
dizzy, and a moment after straddling the log he rolled
over, his legs and arms turning like spokes. His head and
body went under and his legs pointed to the sky. He
splashed and flailed like a water beast, with no part of
him showing except his legs; and when at last his head
emerged, he was almost strangled and half-drowned. His
legs still clasped the log, and in the next moment he rolled
and went under again. When his head came up this time,
his wild eyes looked ready to burst from his skull, and
his mouth spouted water. One hand still grasped his spear.
The other made frantic gestures, as if searching for an
anchor in the air above him. A third time he rolled under,

and a fourth, before he was persuaded to push the log to the land and have a look at his problem.

Most of the alcoholic dizziness had left him now, and so had most of his boldness. After reaching water shallow enough to stand in, he thrust the log shoreward and then looked around him and up at the sky like one who had been attacked and was seeking his enemy. Seeing nothing unfriendly, he stared at the log.

Laying his spear on the bank, he drew the log out in water waist-deep and studied it; and presently he realized that when afloat it seemed to prefer one position. It lay with the depression above water. When he rolled it half over, it hesitated for a moment and completed the turn and again lay with the gutted part up. Rolling it over and over and studying its behavior, Raven became excited; for this man, standing to his navel in water and experimenting with a log, was discovering the principle of the canoe.

Letting the log lie against him in the position it favored, he dipped water with his cupped hands and filled the depression; and when it was level with the bayou, still the log did not roll over or sink. Wading ashore and dragging the log with him, Raven sat on the bank. He was a pretty sober man now and he was pressing forward to a great discovery. If a hollowed-out log would carry a burden of water, then it might also carry a man. Finding this thought logical, he accepted it as a truth and proceeded to the next. The larger the basin in the log, the more water it would hold; if it held more water, would it not then be supporting more weight? This notion was rather complex for one who had lived his life chiefly by impulse and magic; but nevertheless Raven resolved to excavate the log and test it.

Taking the long flint knife from the quiver, he gouged at the burnt wood and learned that it chipped off easily. By jabbing and digging and then thrusting the blade under to pry, he was able to break off pieces as thick as his wrist; and so he labored here most of the afternoon, enlarging the chamber or dashing out to the water to experiment. On discovering that the log would float after he was able to put more and more water in it, he worked feverishly, and presently he had a canoe that would support his weight; but it was, he soon learned, a treacherous and un-friendly thing. While he was sitting in it, proudly reflect-ing on his ingenuity, it suddenly turned, for no reason clear to him, and pitched him head over heels. Then it floated away, arrogantly graceful as a duck, and he had to rush frantically for a long stick to reach out and capture it.

When he felt the coming of night he beached his canoe and took his weapons and ran homeward, uttering triumphant cries and eager to tell the women about his invention. The women were not interested. The grandmother was angry because she had waited all day and he had come home with no food in his hands. She had used her magic to make courage for him, and he had spent a long time preparing for the hunt; now he came home with nothing at all. He came with blood and dyes washed over him, with his hair in a wet tangle, with his mouth babbling of some strange thing he had made.

"Where is food?" she demanded.

"Ahhh!" said Raven. He had forgotten about food. "Come look," he said, and pointed to the distant river.

"No!"

"I am hungry," he said.

That indiscreet statement made the old woman sputter with fury. This disgusting and lazy man had gone away to hunt and now had the impudence to come home with empty hands and ask for food. She had no interest in philosophers and inventors. What he had been doing all this while she could not imagine; if he had not been hunting for food, then he had been wasting his time.

Though all the women but the sick one had spent the day hunting for such food as women could find, Raven was given nothing to eat and went to bed hungry; and the next morning, after a night of drowning dreams, he got no breakfast. But like a boy breathlessly agog over a new toy, he did not mind. Leaping from his bed, he seized his weapons, rushed to the bayou, and, after spearing a fish and eating it, he spent all the day perfecting his canoe. He spent the next day there, too, and the next; and at last he was able to sit in his boat without spilling, a proud and triumphant man. He could lie in it and peer over the edge and watch the fish in deep, still water. Not for some time was he able to sit or lie in the canoe and thrust with his lance without capsizing; but after patient and persistent practice, he learned to do this, and then his joy was complete.

Lying on his belly, with his feet thrust across to keep the canoe balanced, he would look over the edge and poise his lance. Then he would slowly lower the lance into the water and wait for a fish to swim under the point; whereupon, with a short swift jab, he would impale it.

The fish he speared were sluggish and witless. He saw trout deep in the water, but they were fast and wary; besides, for him a fish was food, and little he cared what

173

kind it was. He toiled earnestly, spearing one after another and interrupting his labor to take each to the bank, lest he tip over and spill his cargo; and when at last he went home, walking like one who had breached the last barriers between his family and starvation, he took about thirty pounds of fish. He carried them on a large forked stick, with one prong thrust through the gill opening and the mouth.

The women were speechless with amazement. For one thing, they were fond of fish, and of all other creatures, like frogs and tadpoles and crabs, that made their home in the fertilizing waters. For another thing, they had decided that as a hunter their man was no good. The grandmother hastened over and took the fish. If she had been an effusive and affectionate woman, she might have given him a smile or a kind word; but for her he was only a servant, and a lazy and unpredictable one at that. She did not speak to him. As if she were tearing a tuber from the earth or a cluster of fruit from a tree, she wrenched the stick from his grasp and hurried away.

During this evening they all feasted. The grandmother would cut a sucker into three or four segments and hand the pieces to those who made the hungriest clamor. They ate everything, including the fins, heads, and intestines. After their ravenous appetites were appeased, they impaled their segments with green sticks and roasted them in the fire, turning a piece over and over and bending low to sniff its hot odors. When the old woman was not looking, Raven stole a smaller fish for himself and, after it was hot and brown, he took it in his hands and licked the juices off it and off his fingers. First he bit off the tail, crunched it two or three times and swallowed it. Then he

174

bit off the head. Thereafter he took alternating bits off either end, choking and gulping and staring greedily at the portion in his hands.

The others were also choking. Spider had been eating a half-cooked segment cut from the middle of a large sucker, and a big tough bone had lodged in his throat. His first sound of distress was a violent sneeze that blew almost a handful of fish out of his mouth. The next sound was a terrible groan. When the others turned to him, he was sitting on his haunches, looking strangled and undone, his eyes rolling in his skull, his nostrils twitching. His Adam's apple moved up and down as he swallowed again and again, trying to dislodge the thing in his throat. His whole body was convulsed. Then he staggered to his feet and, like a doomed man who was renouncing all pleasures, he let the uneaten portion fall from his hands.

When he choked again and gave a violent snort that shook him like a blow, the others stopped eating and looked at him with terror in their eyes.

13

THEY all knew that the sneezing meant only one thing, that a ghost was trying to enter Spider's nostrils; and the grandmother, in spite of all her ageless wisdom and magic, was completely nonplussed. Like the others, she stood too frightened to move. Her first thought was that the uncle's ghost was present; but Raven, feeling a sly guiltiness, remembered that he had forgotten to apologize to the fish. He had been so proud of his catch and so eager to get home that he had taken no time to propitiate the spirits; and now he suspected that all the ghosts of the captured fish had followed him home. Unwilling to confess his dereliction, he stepped back from the others and waited to see what the old woman would do.

The first thing she did was impulsively to seize Spider by his nose and milk it with thumb and finger, hoping to draw out the ghost. This only made him sneeze all the more violently. He seemed to tighten in a momentary and rigid paralysis, with his eyes, full of wonder and horror, almost popping from his skull, and then the paralysis dissolved in a spasm that rocked him from head to feet. All the air in his lungs burst in one furious and maddened snort, spraying the grandmother with mucus and particles of fish. In the next moment he gasped and wildly sucked air into his mouth and down his throat like a man coming to the surface after being too long under water. As if he had set up a headlong air current in through his mouth and out through his nose, he sneezed again, and this time the blast was so desperate that he almost fell over. He reached out with frenzied hands and clasped the old woman and tried to lean on her; and while she struggled to loosen his grasp, he suddenly hunched his back, like a dog retching, and sneezed again. This blast of air and frenzy was followed by another and still another; all the while he hugged the grandmother as he might have clung to a tree.

She was bewildered and frightened. She wanted to be rid of his clinging arms but the more she struggled, the more desperately he hugged her. His nostrils were full of excruciating torture. His throat was convulsed with pain. With all her strength she threw him off and leapt away from him; and now, like a man thrown from his last anchor, he fell to hands and knees and began to crawl. After going a little way he would pause. His body would stiffen, with his back arching, his head going down between his arms, and his knees coming up against his belly; and then, with violence that threatened to rend him apart, he would sneeze again. He crawled out of the hut and entered the yard, and there, like a strange nocturnal creature seeking its burrow, he went round and round aimlessly, sneezing as he went.

Except for Raven, all the others were frantic. Crying and gesturing, the grandmother followed the man, now dashing forward as if to head him off, or looking up wildly to see if the Moon Woman was in sight, or dropping to her knees, with sudden desperation, to clutch Spider's nose. Ghosts had invaded her home many times, but none had ever been so bold and persistent in trying to enter a person. Usually loud outcry would frighten spirits away, at least for a while; but this one, sinister and stubborn and unafraid, kept following the tortured man and creeping into his nostrils. She knew that was so because Spider continued to sneeze.

Raven was frightened but he was also slyly amused. He had withdrawn to sit by a tree, with one arm and hand protecting his ears and the other hand cupping his mouth and nose. His sexual amulet protected his genitals. And so, presenting no opening that a spirit could enter, he felt safe. But more than that he felt again, with greater certainty, that spirits chose a victim for reasons of their own instead of invading the first home to which they came. In all his life no ghost had ever entered him, nor tried to; and this was so, it seemed to him, either because he was too bold and dangerous or too inoffensive.

Spider, on the other hand, was weak and helpless. He was not able to frighten the ghosts away. Nor was the sick woman, who spent most of her time in bed, groaning and fretting, with a malicious spirit housed in her belly. Like the predatory beasts, ghosts chose as their victims those who were too feeble to resist—the old, the sick, or the very young. Or they entered those who offended them. Raven wished this spirit of a fish would leave Spider and enter the old woman. He would have been delighted to see her crawling around and sneezing, with her eyes rolling in terror.

At this moment she was shouting for help. Convinced that Spider was determined to crawl away into the forest, she was trying to herd him into the hut, and in a few moments she was assisted by the other women. Like persons trying to drive a pig, they were yelling and gesturing at him, but like a pig he ignored them. Then the grandmother seized him by a foot, Rose grasped the other foot, and Barren and the girl took Spider's hands. The four of them half dragged and half carried him, belly up, into the house and laid him on his bed. Old Man followed them in.

Darkness had come, and Raven looked up to see the Moon Woman, neither young nor old now but in middle age. He could see her eyes, her nose and mouth, and the dark shadow of one cheek, and while studying her features he realized that they were unfriendly. Beyond her, as if she had thrown off her garments, were dark clouds, and Raven became aware next of a strong wind, moving across the earth. Leaves above him were dancing and whispering, and around him the trees swayed as if trying to walk. They bent forward and then straightened, with their arms striking out at invisible things. He rose softly and entered the hut.

All the women but the sick one were sitting or kneeling by Spider's bed. The sound of the wind was outside, and in the walls and roof, and the unrest of it was tormenting the fire. Raven stared at the dim figures in firelight and was afraid. He went to his bed and sat on it and covered his ears and nose and mouth; then he looked at the kneeling women and listened to the growing menace of the wind.

Spider was the only one who really knew what had happened to him. A ghost had entered his throat and was stuck there, unable to get out or to move on in. He could feel the sharp pain of it, especially when he swallowed or opened his mouth wide. It was as if the ghost had lodged crosswise, with the nails of its fingers and toes gouging at the walls of his throat. Meanwhile another spirit kept entering his nose like a thing creeping in and finding its way barred. After sneezing he would have to swallow, and then the pain in his throat was so intense, and the sickness in him so deep, that he would moan and reach up with both hands to clutch his neck.

"Listen!" the girl said.

They listened and heard the sound of the wind, but for them it was not a wind. It was the pain and unrest and seeking of all the lonely and homeless beings of the invisible world. Rising, the grandmother went to the door to look out, and when she saw the darkened and scowling face of the Moon Woman she began to tremble, knowing well that this would be another night of terror. The sick woman was crying on her bed; and Raven, sitting up and still covering his mouth and nose and ears, did not look like a bold and dangerous man. He looked like one who expected calamities against which he had no defense.

Across the sky the clouds were scurrying as if in haste to hide; and down below, the trees bent forward as if eager to run and then rose like great waves of deeper darkness in a wild, dark night. With her old bones quaking, the grandmother returned and sat by Spider's bed; after a few moments her eyes met the anxious gaze of her daughter. Rose's eyes were wide and staring, as if they were looking out of the memory of countless centuries of struggle and pain and heartbreak—out of a heritage of fear and desperation.

"Listen!" she said.

All the terrors of the past were being heaped upon this night. Above her in the dried vines of the roof the wind whispered and cried; its agony sobbed in the walls and moaned around the corners; it blew down in sudden fretful spite against the fire. The flames leapt like angry tongues and went out and then suddenly were there again, striking like tormented things. After a moment of quiet under the driven winds, one of the women would say, "Listen!"

They used this word because more than any other it expressed the haunted quality of their lives. For centuries their people had cried "Look!" or "Listen!" but always in the dreadful blackness of the nights it had been "Listen!" because there had been little to see then and much to hear. The word united them in a kind of fellowship. It drew them closer in moments of danger, making them forget self in the larger security of the group. When the word was uttered, they felt an impulse to move closer to one another, as if, with their several bodies, they could build a house of refuge that would stand against the mystery and menace of the world. And when they looked at one another in a time like this, there was a warmth in their eyes that was akin to affection. "Listen!" Rose said; and her daughter, the girl, moved close to her, with their hair mingling and their faces almost cheek to cheek for a moment.

As the night deepened and the winds became more frenzied in their loneliness and seeking, at last the four women sat shoulder to shoulder by the bed of the tortured man. Then Old Man came over to be close to them, and Raven did so, too, and the six of them sat as one person. They did not put arms around shoulders or clasp one another's hands; such gestures of affection were unknown to them. Affection is not what they felt. They were six frightened animals, huddled together and feeding on one another's warmth and strength.

Because the others sat so close to him and thereby hushed his fear, Spider suffered for a little while in silence. He had learned that if he did not move his tongue or lips, or if he did not swallow, the ghost would lie still in his throat; but if he swallowed, then it gouged him as if trying to get out. His mouth was open to allow the saliva to drool. But now and then, because suffocation grew in the back of his mouth and almost shut off his breath, he had to clench his hands and swallow; then the ghost stabbed him, and he felt such sharp pain that he would gasp and sneeze. For a while he had been too terrified to think; but now, sensing the friendliness of those sitting by him, he had enough courage to realize his misfortune. It was as if his mind stood off and peered fearfully at his body. He reasoned that if he were to lie quietly, perhaps the ghost would crawl back out; to encourage its withdrawal he kept his mouth wide open. Surely if it were too large to enter him and had got stuck, it would come out after a while and try to enter somebody else.

"Listen!" said Rose, speaking in a sad whisper. She bowed low, and her hair fell in a shower to her knees. With her face hidden by the dark mass of it, she began to make a sound—a kind of murmuring lamentation, sad and ageless, like the wordless blend of a psalm and a prayer. The barren one also bowed her head, and her

182

voice joined the lament; then the girl did likewise, and at last the grandmother; and the four women rocked gently back and forth, their faces hidden by the foliage of their hair. Their voices were low and hauntingly mournful. They did not utter words; their lips were closed. It was a sad and nasal murmuring, full of loneliness, of yearning, of all the emotion in them that had no altars, no shrines, no gods before which to kneel. It was the sound of women lost to humility and grief.

The mournful quality of it was more than Raven could endure. It aroused in him a wild, blind emotion that could see nothing, that could think of nothing, on which to vent itself; and so he got to his feet, but with no purpose in mind, and went over to his bed. And in Spider, too, the lamenting voices became an intolerable ache. He recalled that the women had made this kind of sound after the uncle died. It seemed to him that they believed he was dead and were lamenting over his body. For a little while he listened without moving, but then he began to twitch and writhe, and when he could stand it no longer he sat up suddenly and screamed. He staggered to his feet, choking with terror, his eyes rolling wildly and his hands striking out as if he were escaping from the enveloping coils of a huge snake.

The women did not stir. They were only dimly aware, if at all, of the man's scream and hasty departure. They were sunk deep in the hypnosis of their own melancholy music. They were striving in the only way they knew for some kind of emotional catharsis, for a cleansing of their minds and souls of their great burden of loneliness and fear. With their faces lost in the bower of their hair, they continued to rock gently back and forth, their voices lamenting under the frenzied clamor of the winds.

Spider looked down at them as if they were loathsome. He looked over at Raven, and at the sick woman who was moaning on her bed; then, with a choked gasp of terror, he ran to the doorway and bolted outside.

His were insane eyes when they looked up at the sky. They saw tumultuous masses of darkness, rolling in a vast and heaving anarchy across the face of the Moon Woman. For a long moment she was swallowed and lost but then she came out, as if pushing her way through the wilderness, and he saw her scowling face fleeing across the night. Beyond the garden he saw trees flinging their arms and trying to run; bushes leaping back and forth in awful frenzy; the dim shadows of ghosts racing across the yard and the sky; and everywhere he heard the shrieking anguish of the tormented and the driven.

His terror was now so great that his hands, moving like things seeking a refuge, came up to his chest and trembled against him. His whole body shook. Though his feet did not move, his knees kept smiting one another, and he could feel the pain as bone struck bone. His mouth was wide open; his tongue came out and lay across his lip. And when he swallowed and had realization of the ghost driven like a knife into his consciousness, he uttered a wild scream and then reached out into the darkness. Finding nothing to grasp, his hands moved round and round him and downward, and slowly, like one stricken, he sank to his knees.

He began to crawl, his tongue hanging out, his wide eyes staring at the dim and convulsed shapes of the night. There was no plan in his mind, no purpose, and almost

184

no sense of his own movement. He was a creature completely possessed by terror. In what he felt, and in his total unawareness of what he was doing, he was little more than a moving organism, devoid of mind, with all its senses so confused and darkened that there was no consciousness of sight or of sound or of smell, and almost none of touch.

In such fashion, in a long-ago time, jelly-like organisms in the sea aimlessly moved away from danger, striving blindly to escape their enemies, guided not by eyes or ears or mind but only by instinct that impelled them to roll, to turn, or to float in the currents. As such organisms moved with the tides, this man now moved with the wind; but he was not aware of the pressure of the wind against him. When his face thrust against a bush, he was like a senseless creature drifting in the deep; there was only movement in him; he turned to one side in an effort to pass, and then to the other; and after he passed and came to another bush or tree, he repeated the blind trial-and-error behavior, moving like something the wind was blowing across the earth. His eyes were still wide and staring, his mouth was open, and his tongue hung like a dead thing from his mouth.

Terror had stripped him of all human qualities, even of all animal qualities except movement. Terror had blotted out his mind. He was not thinking. He was not conscious of where he was or what he was or what he was doing. All that human beings had become through centuries of struggle had been stripped from him, and he was only an organism that lived, that moved, that was lost in its small dark prison of fear.

Using his head as an antenna, he crawled around or

through the bushes and entered the jungle. It was a dense growth of hanging vines that were stout and supple like suspended ropes; and now, like a thing trapped and seeking a way out, he turned round and round, crawling, thrusting with his head, backing up, going forward, but never once pausing. Little by little he became entangled. The vines coiled round his legs, his arms, his body and neck; the more he turned and struggled and fought against them, the more hopelessly he became enmeshed. All these clutching and imprisoning things aroused fresh terror in him—not in his mind, which was still blacked out, but in his body, in the moving organism that, like a lowly and barely sensate form of life, was striving to find a refuge. As if it had drifted into the clutch of an octopus, the organism fought to throw off the enveloping arms or to turn and roll away from them; but all its efforts only seemed to multiply their number and make their grasp more secure.

After a while it was so completely captured and held that it could not move forward or backward; it could only rest on the earth and throb like a huge heart. For a few minutes it could draw its feet up or shove them back; or turn its head or move it up and down; or wiggle its arms like things enveloped by heavy blankets; but there were so many vines around its throat that at last the head ceased to struggle. In its entangling prison, the whole organism throbbed like a great pulse. Then it sank slowly to the earth, with the legs doubled up under the belly and the arms tied across the chest. The open mouth rested on a depth of old leaves, and the tongue protruded like a naked thing hanging from its sheath. The eyes were still open and staring. It was as if, knowing that it had been cap-

186

tured and that all further effort would be useless, it waited, with its terror hushed, to be absorbed by a stronger power.

And now there came to it something that was like deep peace. There was no struggle. The flesh twitched, there were hot spasms in the throat, and the whole body throbbed through and through like a single great heart. A finger would move a little and then be still. At long intervals, the lids would slowly shutter the eyes. When the organism swallowed, the tongue would draw up, and there would be a sharp stab of pain in the throat. A thumb moved over to a finger and touched it and drew gently along half its length. A big toe rubbed slowly back and forth across the toe next to it. And at last, under the wild winds and the night, the lids came down softly like drawn curtains and covered the eyes.

14

THE wind left with the coming of dawn, and everything was so quiet that not even a leaf stirred. In the great blue roof of the sky there was no sign of a cloud. There was only the sun like a golden eye looking across the treetops.

The grandmother went out first to search for Spider, and when she was unable to find him anywhere in the yard or garden, or by the tree where it had been his habit to sit, she called to the others. Rose came out.

"He has gone!"

Rose looked round her. "Where?" she asked.

With an impatient gesture the old woman cried, "He went away!"

Going to the hut, Rose looked in and announced, "He went away."

Raven stood up in his bed, but before speaking he looked down to see if the sexual amulet was in place. Then he asked, "Where?"

With the same impatient gesture her mother had used, Rose answered sharply, "He went away!"

188

"Ahhh!" said Old Man.

"Far away?" asked the girl.

Rose supposed he had gone far because she had seen no sign of him. "Far away," she said.

Raven went over to his sister in the doorway, and their eyes met. Never before, in their experience, had a person left his family and fire and gone far away on a wild night. It was very strange.

"Which way?" Raven asked, thinking of his canoe.

Rose turned to look at the earth and the sky. Raven went out to the yard. After a few moments he saw signs on the ground where Spider had crawled. He went down to his knees and sniffed; he looked round him for other signs; and when he stood up he turned to the grandmother and asked:

"Which way?"

She did not know, but it was not a habit with her to admit her ignorance. She pointed impulsively and said, "That way."

"Far?" asked Raven.

She was troubled by another moment of indecision. "No," she said.

"Not far?"

Well, if that were so, perhaps Spider could be found; and while the women roasted fish for breakfast Raven began to search. After a few minutes he saw the dead man back in the thicket, so trussed with vines that it looked as if he had been bound by human hands. But no such thought as that occurred to Raven. He knew that Spider had been trapped and slain by ghosts, and the recognition that spirits were not only entering his people, but were also ambushing and killing them, was so terrifying that he

189

yelled. And still shouting as if pursued by enemies, he rushed to the hut.

"Come-see!" he yelled, thrusting a white face inside.

The grandmother came quickly, knowing by the way Raven trembled that he had seen something dreadful.

"What is wrong?" she asked in a choked whisper.

Raven was unable to speak. It had taken him a few moments to realize the full and horrifying significance of what he had seen; now he could only babble and point. All the women but the sick one hastened to the jungle. When they saw the dead man, bound with vines, they uttered cries of lamentation and terror.

"He is dead!" the girl whispered. "Look, he is dead!"

She did not speak the man's name. Nobody would ever speak his name again because a spirit was summoned by the name of its dead body or by any sound similar to it. Ghosts were always lurking and spying and waiting for clues that would betray the whereabouts of their home.

"He is dead!" said the grandmother, speaking as if she alone had the power to settle such matters. She turned and saw Raven and beckoned to him. He came up, shaking with fright. The old woman wanted him to enter the thicket and bring the body out. It would have to be buried, and the sooner, the better.

"Bring him out!" she commanded.

But Raven made a sound of terror and fled.

They all knew that this was no ordinary death, and that it would be difficult to placate the ghost. During his life Spider had been a man given to violent tantrums, to spells of malicious fury and vengeful loathing; but, even worse than that, he had been allowed to crawl away in the darkness, friendless and tormented. Without any help from

190

his family, he had been attacked and bound and killed. His spirit would never forgive that.

And because he had died neglected by his family, he would need an extraordinary burial. They would have to use extreme care in handling the body, and they would have to be more than usually cunning in hiding from the ghost. These were the thoughts in the old woman's mind. But also in her mind was the notion that the ghost would be resentful if its body were not removed at once, and when Raven showed plainly that he was too fearful to venture in, she boldly entered the jungle. She grasped a foot, intending to drag the body out, but the strength of ten women like her would have been unavailing. It was so securely bound that she could barely move it. The body was roped to the earth and the trees; and when she perceived what a thorough job had been done and realized that several ghosts must have labored here to bind a man so securely, she raised a shaking hand to her face. Never before in her life had the powers of the invisible world done anything like this.

In a quavering voice she called to Rose, and Rose went to her side, but the two women, using all their strength, could do no more than to wiggle the body a little.

"Bring knife!" she said.

Rose went to Raven and asked for his knife and, after returning with it, she knelt and began to hack at the vines. They were tough, and she had to saw back and forth with the stone blade to sever them. The vines around the throat were so tightly drawn that she was barely able to thrust the blade between them and the flesh. While working, she observed that the tongue was hanging out, and she knew then that Spider had been choked to death. This evidence of such physical strength in ghosts was a dreadful thing.

"Look!" she said in an awed whisper, and pointed to the tongue. Turning to her mother, she met her eyes and added, "They choked him!"

"Yes."

Exhausted after a while more by fear than labor, she stepped back and handed the knife to her mother; and the old woman knelt and sawed at the green ropes. When all the vines had been severed and the corpse was free, one grasped the feet and the other the hands and they carried the body out and laid it in sunlight on the earth. Raven and Old Man stood fearfully a little distance away, but the four women, bolder in these matters than any man dared be, looked at the dead face.

"He was choked!" Rose whispered again.

This truth, so unmistakably plain to all of them, was a revelation of what ghosts were able to do. They had known that malicious spirits could enter a person and torment him, and sometimes, but only after long and persistent effort, kill him. They could convulse the world, as they had done last night, with wild unrest. They could do many sly and terrible things. But they had never known that ghosts had the power to seize the living and bind and strangle them. Realizing this, the world they lived in became a more dreadful thing, and they looked anxiously at one another.

Spider had been a strange and malicious man. This meant that the spirit in him had been sly and treacherous —and that spirit still lived. Even now it was lurking close by and spying on them and waiting to see what they would do with its home; and the grandmother was thinking of all this when she said that they would have to hide from it. They would have to disguise themselves so that it would not recognize them; they would have to be silent or talk only in whispers so that it would not overhear their plans. For even in this moment, of course, the unhappy thing was listening, as well as looking. It might be hiding in a tree or stone, or it might be in a hole in the earth, peering out at them. You never could tell where a ghost was or what it was plotting to do.

But there were ways to outwit spirits. They could be tricked and deceived. Though they were able to cause thunder, nevertheless they could sometimes be frightened by human sounds. Though they wandered through rainstorms, they did not dare to cross rivers. The grandmother reflected that if this spirit persisted in molesting her, she would move her home across a stream, or in some other way escape from it.

But now their task was to disguise themselves, and for this purpose she went to the fire and returned with a double handful of charcoal. Then she began to smear the black over her body, and the other women did so, and Old Man, too, after a few moments; but Raven did not. He might have done so formerly, but thinking during the past weeks had convinced him that ghosts singled out certain persons to torment. He had always been kind to Spider, and he saw no reason why the man's ghost should bother him.

And besides, while the grandmother explained to the women that they must disguise themselves, Raven's mind had been busy. He had stood back, looking at them and thinking; and he understood at last that the women, with their terrible lamentations during the night, had driven

Spider out of the home. He even suspected that the old woman had summoned the spirits to choke him. If he had lived in a later time, he would have said that she was a witch in league with devils, but in this hour his philosophic reflections had not led him to such a definite concept. He did not think of her as a witch, nor did he have any word to express such a meaning. He had no words to express what he felt, but nevertheless he did think of her as one who had a mysterious relationship with the invisible world. She had knowledge of simples. She could make courage by gathering herbs and seeds, sap and honey. She could summon rain. It was an easy and logical step to the notion that she could also summon spirits. He believed now that she had done so, and that they had lured Spider into the jungle and strangled him; and so it seemed to Raven that if the ghost were to choose anyone for torment, it would be the old woman.

That is what he was thinking as he stood back and watched the women and Old Man rub charcoal over their faces and bodies. They had reason to be frightened. They had need to disguise themselves. But he was sure that Spider's ghost would never bother him; in any case, if he were to protect himself he would do it by wearing more amulets, in which, during recent days, he had learned to place a great deal of faith. He glanced down at the stone by his genitals. Then he decided to go away and get some fresh blood to rub around his ears and nose and mouth.

When he returned, after a considerable while, he was protected, not with blood but with several handsome stones. Around two of them he had tied a vine and then tangled the vine in his hair, allowing a suspended stone to hang down by either ear. He had thrust smaller stones into

194

his nostrils, and he carried still another between his teeth. And thus, with the vents in his body protected, he felt secure.

The women meanwhile had been busy. Not having enough charcoal on hand to blacken themselves, they had built a large fire outside; and now, assisting one another, they were smearing their backs. By the time they had finished their labor, they were as black as coal from head to feet, save only their hair and eyes. The grandmother's hair was gray, and Rose suggested that it ought to be blackened, too, lest it betray her presence; and so she knelt, with her face to the earth and her hair spread like a carpet while the other women rubbed charcoal on her hair. They still whispered when they talked. The girl remembered the sick one in the hut and pointed in her direction, but the old woman did not care about her. She was already infested, and it little mattered what happened to her.

"No," she whispered, and shook her head.

"See him!" whispered the girl, and pointed to Raven.

When the women moved toward Raven, intending to blacken him, he shouted at them, and his voice, after so many hours of whispering, sounded terrifying. He pointed to his stones and told them that he was protected, and again he set the pebble between his teeth. Curiously they advanced and stared at the pebbles in his mouth and nose and hanging by his ears. Having little of his faith in the magic of amulets, they wanted to smear him with charcoal, but when they moved to do so, he ran away. Then he turned and shouted at them with such angry contempt that the grandmother was afraid he would betray their presence; and so, with a shrug, she dismissed him. If he wanted to stand conspicuously naked, that was all right with her, because he was only a lazy fellow at best.

Their task now was to bury the body and in doing this they would have to be very sly. The ghost would follow its body, of course, to learn what they did with it, but it would not be able to see them because they were black as the night and nothing could see a black night. They would take such tools and trinkets as Spider had claimed as his own; they would bury the body deep; and they would leave a small hole so that the ghost, when weary of wandering, could descend to the heart. These were the thoughts in the grandmother's mind.

Entering the hut, she found some of Spider's old trinkets and weapons, and she gave these to Old Man to carry. She also handed him a flint knife and a stone spade for digging. Then the four women lifted the body, each grasping a foot or a hand, and carried it toward the hills. After they had gone about a hundred yards, the grandmother whispered an order to halt. They would rest here a little while because the ghost might not have been watching them when they left; they would go slowly and pause from time to time so that it would be sure to see its body moving and follow. The old woman felt so secure in her disguise that she looked at the black faces of the others and smiled. Nothing could see them standing here on the hill. Not even the beasts and birds could see them, save those nocturnal ones that hunted in the dark. It did not seem strange to her that they could see one another. She did not think about that. With these people, a piece of logic that was urgent and self-evident always obscured any logic that contradicted it. Standing here on a hill and calmly gazing round her, the grandmother thought of herself as invisible as pitch darkness.

"Go now!" she whispered, and grasped a hand.

And again, after carrying their burden to another hill, they halted and stood for several minutes, giving the ghost every chance in the world to explore its surroundings and learn where its body was. They paused many times; dusk was coming before the grandmother came to a spot she found suitable. The earth was moist and tender and would be easy to dig. Kneeling, she took the spade, and Rose took the knife; but after a few moments of digging, the grandmother arose and whispered to the girl. She told her to go away and find four sticks as large as her wrist and about as long as her height. Then she dug rapidly, because night was settling on the hills, and when she grew weary, her barren daughter took the spade and dug.

In a little while she thought the hole was deep enough and she touched Barren's arm and told her to climb out; then they took the corpse and lowered it into the grave. They placed it in a sitting posture because the grandmother believed that Spider would like to sit up. They laid the trinkets in the lap and the weapons by the legs; and the grandmother knelt and reached down and placed the handle of the flint knife within the palm of a hand. Then, at the head of the grave, she set the four short poles upright by the torso, standing them in a four-square position; in this way they formed a kind of tunnel that could not be filled with earth, and this tunnel could be used by the ghost to descend to its home. And then the four of them scooped the earth in with their hands. There was no food for the ghost to eat, but if it molested them, the grandmother intended to bring food.

She did not believe that this ghost would ever bother her family. No matter how malicious and unhappy it might feel, it could never know the persons who had carried its body away and buried it here. Lurking somewhere near, it had been watching its body, of course, but it had not been able to see those who dug the grave; and this was such a comforting thought that the old woman clucked with gentle triumph when she turned away. She felt that this task had been well done.

After they had gone a little distance, she stopped to look back; she wanted to spy on the grave and see if the ghost would enter. There was nothing for the others to see, but an old and wise woman, enriched by experience and with knowledge of many strange things, would be able to tell. While the others waited they stared, not back at the grave, but at the old woman's blackened face; and when they saw her eyes open wide and heard her draw a sharp breath, they knew that the ghost had come. The grandmother saw it descend to the grave and enter. Perhaps what she really saw was some faint shadow, some darkening in the gloom, but for her, who usually saw what she wanted to see, it was the dead man's spirit, coming swiftly out of the night and slipping into the tunnel formed by the poles.

"Did ghost come?" Rose whispered.

"Yes."

"Did ghost enter grave?"

"Yes."

"Ahhh!"

And the girl whispered, "Is ghost happy?"

Because she always resented too many questions in a brief time, the grandmother hesitated for a long moment and meanwhile gazed at the grave, as if she were watching something there. Then, in a low quiet voice, she said:

"Ghost is happy."

"Ahhh!" said Old Man, the breath coming out of him in a long sigh of relief.

That was enough. They all felt secure now because they had done their duty by the body and at the same time had outwitted its spirit. They could go home, knowing that all was well.

Darkness had come, and the five persons looked like deep and moving shadows in it. They did not speak again, and they walked as softly as they could, realizing that the ghost might come out of the grave and listen for sounds. If it could hear them, it might follow the sound of their feet and trail them home. The grandmother was cannily aware of that, and so, from time to time, she touched their arms, and they stopped and waited. If the spirit was following them, it would wander away after losing the sound, and then they could proceed. The grandmother also took a roundabout course homeward because ghosts were sly things that could not easily be tricked.

They were very hungry when they reached the hut, but the fish, to which they had been looking forward, had all been eaten. Happy to have the women out of his sight, Raven had roasted the fish, giving a little of it to the sick woman but eating most of it himself. When the five black shadows came in he was lying on his bed. The grandmother went to a corner where she had hidden the fish under a pile of skins and, on finding none there, she turned with a shrill cry of anger. She marched over and looked down at Raven like a black and terrible avenger.

"Where is food?" she demanded.

Raven sat up and pointed an innocent finger to the distant bayou. "Out there," he said. He was a sly rascal. He pretended not to know what the old woman meant.

"You lazy man!" she cried.

"Out there," he said. "Fish out there."

Blind with rage, she rushed to the fireplace and seized a stick; but Raven had anticipated her move and before she could strike he leapt up and fled. Screaming abuse at him, she followed him outside, but because he had hidden behind a tree she could only stand in frustrated rage, grasping her cudgel and peering into the darkness. She commanded him to go and find food; and Raven, craftily watching her and listening to her frenzied commands, felt so triumphant that his face broke into a sly grin. He would let the old tyrant rant and threaten; after a little while she would exhaust herself and go to bed. He was not so afraid of her as he had been. She could cry her abuse and summon all the ghosts of the earth, but nothing could harm him because he was protected by his amulets.

Her tired old voice had fallen to a thin rasping lament. Presently she entered the hut, and then Raven left his hiding place and went softly to the doorway. He sat by it on his heels, well-fed, philosophic, and full of mischievous designs, and waited for the sounds of sleep.

15

AMONG the people of his time Raven was a genius. To be sure, by later standards, he was a very ignorant man who lived in superstition and fear; but in the light of intelligence, even superstitions develop and more fully serve human needs. For many months some of his notions had been growing under persistent thought, and he was now convinced that neither the Moon Woman nor ghosts molested anyone without reason. Their malice was not aimless and unpredictable. When a person became angry it was because he had been offended; and it was so, Raven believed, with all the spirits of the invisible world.

But he did not know for what reasons these beings were offended; that was a matter for further thought. He did perceive that they had not been offended by him. He was healthy, he suffered no pains, and he had no spirit in him save his own. So far as he could tell, it was women who were the principal offenders. One of them in his family was sick because she was tormented by alien ghosts; another was barren; and the grandmother herself was constantly racked by aches and pains. As for Spider, he had been a strange and unhappy man, but Raven believed that he had been strangled by ghosts whom the old woman had summoned. He did not think she had cast a spell on the man but he had come pretty close to such a thought. He did not think of her as one deliberately in league with evil powers, but nevertheless in his opinion of her and her doings, and in his emotional attitude toward her, she had the qualities of a witch.

What he felt about her was this: that she had mysterious powers which she did not always employ for the welfare of her family. In this respect he was a moralist; he had come to the hazy notion that some human acts led to happiness and some to misfortune. The women, for instance, had frightened Spider out into the dark with their wild lamenting, and there unfriendly spirits had killed him. If they could do that with Spider, they might do it with any man unless he were constantly on guard.

Raven intended to be on guard. He distrusted the old woman and he had cause. She could make rain; she had a dreadful intimacy with the Moon Woman; and by rocking back and forth and moaning she could drive a man into the grasp of his enemies. In short, she was a terrible creature. He would have to protect himself against her. How to do that he did not know, because he did not understand her powers and how she used them. While waiting for sounds of sleep he thought of the problem and, after crawling to his bed, he dreamed that he was fleeing for his life, with the old woman in furious pursuit. On awaking and recalling the dream, he knew that his spirit had left his body during the night and that the grandmother had risen from her bed to chase it. Such evidence of her unfriendliness supported all his earlier suspicions and made him twice as wary.

Now realizing beyond all question that she wished to destroy him, he left his bed and stood by his weapons and wondered what he should do. Not to feel safe in his own home placed a man in an awful predicament. If, in the deep of night, the grandmother left her bed to chase his wandering soul, then there was no malice to which she might not resort. Staring at her blackened face and body and watching her deft hands build the fire, he understood that she was more dangerous than he had ever supposed.

After she had stirred the fire and realized again that there was no food in the house, she turned to Raven as if her anger of the previous evening had not died but had only waited and grown stronger. Her countenance alone was enough to terrify him. During the night, tears had run from her rheumy eyes to her cheeks, and, in wiping them away, she had made hideous charcoal patterns all over her face. Part of her cheeks and nose had been washed clean; other parts were still as black as midnight. Charcoal hung in small wet pieces to her eyelashes and half obscured her eyes, and when she bawled at him, her tongue looked blood-red in her black mouth.

Raven had expected the outburst. After staring at her a few moments with horrified amazement, he seized his weapons and ran outside. When she followed him to the yard, shouting abuse at him, he hastened over to the pot of courage, a part of whose juices still remained. Seeing him take the spoon and begin to drink, the old woman stopped shouting and looked at him.

"Go find food!" she cried.

"Yes," he said, eager to quiet her.

The fermented juices were covered with drowned spiders and beetles and many small insects, and these Raven chewed while sipping the liquor. Indeed, he skimmed them off and made a breakfast of them. Mixed with the bitter juice, they seemed to him to have a more agreeable taste. His eyes winked thoughtfully while he crunched beetle armor and then washed the mouthful down with a spoonful of juice. After he had skimmed off and eaten all the dead creatures, he tipped the jug to his mouth and drank deeply; whereupon he arose and picked up his weapons and felt round his skull to learn if the amulets were hanging by his ears. The old woman was still watching him.

"We want food," she said, as if many iterations were necessary to lodge a thought in this man's mind.

"Yes," he said, fumbling with his charms.

"Go find food!"

"Yes," he said, and drew a deep sigh.

Day in and day out, season after season, he heard this cry for food. But the alcohol had warmed and encouraged him, and he felt quite happy; the day was serene, without a hint of threat or menace; and when he turned away, he was singing a kind of song. It was a wordless but tuneful humming in his throat.

On reaching the bayou where he had anchored his boat, he stopped in amazement. The canoe was gone. He knew it had not drifted away, because on the sand before him were a man's footprints. With anger rising from his bowels in a warm flood that poured through his heart and beat in his throat and temples, he went down on hands and knees to examine the tracks. Then he searched the beach in both directions and found incoming tracks but none that led away; and he knew that the stranger had stolen his log and floated off. He was drunk now with both alcohol and rage. Jumping up and down in a tantrum of frustration, he shook his lance at the sky, while his eyes, darkened by pain and wrath, searched the water for a sign of the man.

He intended to kill him. He had never killed a man in his life, not because of scruples but because there had been no need. There were no moral taboos in him against murder. Though there was a strong sense of property rights among his people, the taboos against theft had not become strong enough to make such rights inviolable; a man sometimes stole the belongings of another when he could safely do so. It did not occur to Raven that this man might have thought the canoe was only a log, beached by the waves. He had spent so many hours excavating and perfecting his boat that it had become a part of him, like his bow and lance and knife, and the feeling in him now was that of a person who had been robbed of a part of his meaning. If he had been sober, no doubt he would have looked at the matter more sensibly and he might have reasoned that the stranger had made a mistake. But he was full of alcohol and rage, and he felt extraordinarily vengeful. In a way so deeply buried that he was hardly aware of it, he liked this challenge to his manhood and the murderous lusting it aroused in him.

In turn he ran up the beach to the right and the left and looked across the prairie of water, and when at last he espied the thief, far out, riding the canoe and fishing, Raven slunk back into hiding and became very stealthy in his movements. He was now a hunter, stalking his prey. After disappearing into dense timber, he peered out to take his bearings and to note carefully the man's position. The·stranger was perhaps a hundred and fifty yards away

205

but not far from the circling beach, and Raven perceived that he could slip through the jungle and come close to him.

He went quietly, his left hand grasping the bow and his right the lance, and when he thought he had covered the distance and was abreast of the man, he moved toward the water's edge as stealthily as a cat. He was trembling, not with fear, but with the excitement of the hunter drawing close to his prey. Hardly a leaf rustled as he slipped through the heavy growth of bush and vine.

Because of the overhanging foliage he could not see the man but he could hear him. He could see small ripples moving shoreward from the canoe. Withdrawing to the jungle, Raven went forward again, pausing from time to time to listen; and when at last he crept to the edge and peered out, the man was in plain view. He was only a few yards off shore. Lying crosswise in the canoe, as Raven had done, he was reaching down with his lance. Raven could not see his face; he could see only part of one leg, the broad hairy shoulders, the arms and the back of the skull.

Raising his bow behind a screen of leaves, he set an arrow to the bowstring and sighted. Resolved to take his time, and to kill with one arrow if he could, he aimed in turn at the shoulders and head, wondering which part would be more vulnerable. Not the skull, he decided; it was too small a target and, besides, it was all bone. There was also tough bone in the shoulders and back. Lowering the bow, he examined the arrowhead to see if it was sharp and attached well to the shaft. He examined all his arrows and chose the one that seemed to be the straightest, heaviest, and sharpest. Then he sighted again.

206

Now he perceived that the canoe was slowly turning and drifting gently toward the shore. The man was half facing him. While Raven hesitated, wondering whether to shoot now or to wait, the man speared a fish and, before drawing the lance from the water, he moved carefully to sit up. His free hand grasped the far side of the canoe to steady him; he rose slowly to his knees; and then he drew the lance toward him, with a fish wriggling on the point. He was not more than thirty feet away now, and the canoe had turned so that Raven looked at the stranger face to face. The man seemed to sense that danger lurked near him. He glanced quickly at the jungle in which Raven was hidden and sniffed the air, lifting his muzzle like a wolf.

Raven had never seen this man before.

Without disturbing a twig or a leaf, he drew the bow-string far back, sighted at the man's throat just above the collarbone, and released the string. But he was trembling so with eagerness that the arrow missed. It grazed the man's neck and sped out and struck the water with a hiss and a sound of choking. Knowing that he had been shot at, the man gave a bellow of rage; then, forgetting that he was kneeling precariously in a canoe, he stood up. In the next moment the canoe turned under him and he was pitched head over heels, with his lance, grasped in one hand, flashing as it wheeled downward and went under. Shaking like a naked man standing in zero weather, Raven set another arrow to the string, sighted for a brief moment, and let it go. It struck the man in a floundering shoulder.

With a cry more of amazement than of pain or rage, the man beat the water with flat palms as if trying to lift himself above the surface. The waves that rolled away from

207

him sent the canoe close to the shore. Raven had fixed a third arrow, but he became aware now that the man was struggling toward him like an enraged water beast. He was neither swimming nor wading; he was beating the water with flat hands. Then, as if only now conscious of the arrow in his shoulder, he reached up with a hand and grasped it and tried to tear it from his flesh. In the next moment he sank; and when he came up, spouting water and bellowing with fury, Raven sped the third arrow. Driven at close range with all the power in his shoulder, it struck the man in his soft throat and so nearly passed through that it hung by its tip. Blood gushed out and dyed the water. Then the man sank backward, as if sitting down. He sank slowly, and in the long moment of sinking, Raven saw something in the man's eyes that he would never forget. The eyes opened wide with incredulity and horror, and then closed, as if in resignation and peace. Then the water rushed over them, and for a little while there was nothing to see but the churned and bloody surface.

Laying his weapons aside, Raven slipped quickly to the shore and found his canoe. He pulled it in and beached it, and the recovering of his property filled him with such joy that he forgot the man. Even when the canoe was safely beached, he clutched it with both hands, as if afraid some malicious power would snatch it away. He sat in it, remembering with delight how it had carried him over deep water, and like a mother caressing a child he rubbed his hands over the wood. It was a priceless part of him. As long as it remained with him he would never hunger again, because he could ride it out in the bayou and catch fish. It was for him what a garden or a pantry was for women.

After his senses had feasted on its presence he remembered the enemy, and with an exclamation of alarm he ran blindly to find his weapons. When he came down to the shore, he advanced with an arrow set to his bow, ready to shoot; but his enemy was dead and afloat only a few feet away. Putting aside the bow and arrow, Raven found a long stick and reached out to the body and drew it toward him. It lay in shallow water at his feet. He stared at it, but not with remorse or regret. He was looking at a thief who had stolen his canoe, and even in death he hated the man.

Where to bury him he did not know. The jungle along the water was so bedded with roots that he could never dig a grave there, nor could he carry so heavy a burden through the forest to open ground. While considering the matter he looked out at the bayou, and the thought came to him that perhaps he could bury the man in water. He knew that dead bodies floated; but now, bending forward and pressing down with his hands, he perceived that this body would sink under a little weight. Then he realized that if he buried the man in water, the ghost would never be able to find its home, and he sat on his heels to ponder the dilemma.

He began to feel lonely and afraid. Little by little there was borne in on him the almost crushing realization that he had killed a man, and that the ghost, lurking somewhere near, must be very angry. In a panic he arose and gazed anxiously round him, listening and sniffing. Here in a jungle, far from his home, he was surrounded by enemies; the courage he had drunk was all spent, and he felt weak and unprotected and helpless. If there had not been deep jungle walling him in, he might have fled, leaving the man unburied and the canoe for anybody to claim; for he was now overcome by that timidity which always possessed a man after his alcoholic courage was exhausted. He was afraid to enter the jungle. And so, apprehensive and non-plussed, he stood like a man suddenly imprisoned and wondered what he should do.

In casting about him for a plan he thought of the boat, and with frantic haste, as if his life depended on speed, he gathered his weapons and ran to it. He laid in it the bow and lance. Then he dragged it off the beach and shoved it out to deeper water, wading behind it, and carefully crawled into it and lay on his belly, reaching over a side to paddle with one hand. After a few strokes on one side, he would reach across to stroke on the other. When he was fifty yards from the shore he felt safer, though he knew that the ghost was following him. It might even be riding with him in the canoe. Nevertheless, he felt bolder —so bold, indeed, that when he had pushed far out into the bayou he reached over to spear a fish. He caught a two-pound sucker and ate all of it, including the head and guts; whereupon, feeling strengthened, he paddled to the shore that lay closest to his home.

He was back in familiar surroundings and had a path that led to his family, but he knew that if he went home the ghost would follow him. He would not have cared about that if he could have been sure that the spirit would enter one of the women and, while thinking of the grandmother, there came to him, in a flash of insight, a plot so craftily perfect that he shouted with joy.

He would build a fire here and make enough charcoal to blacken his body; then, as invisible as darkness itself, he would go home, and the ghost would not be able to follow him. But that was only part of his plot. Meanwhile the bewildered and frustrated ghost would be lurking in the area of its dead body; and so he would lure the old woman out here. The spirit would see her and it would think she was the one who had destroyed its home. It would follow her. It would torment her sleep, fill her with pain and sickness, bloat her with swellings, poison her food and drink, and perhaps goad her into divulging her strange secrets.

His plan was such a sly piece of genius that he snorted with delight and was content for a little while to gloat over the old woman and imagine her agonies. He hoped she would suffer terribly. He hoped that this would be a malicious and tireless spirit that would be extraordinarily resourceful in devising torments. Crying with joy, he danced up and down and waved at the sky, as if to invite all living things to observe what a clever man he was; and then, his face a picture of malice and mirth, he hastened away to find fire sticks and dry grass and wood.

16

WHEN Raven appeared late in the afternoon, it would be an understatement to say that the grandmother was startled. He came up, grinning and capering and as black as midnight; if the old woman had not recognized his walk and grin, she would have thought he was a stranger. She had expected him to come with another burden of fish; and instead he appeared empty-handed, except for his weapons, and smeared with charcoal and impish with mischief.

She was so astonished that her mouth fell open, showing the snags of her teeth. For a little while she was unable to speak, or to believe that this clowning fellow was her son. During the day she and the other women had gone to a stream to wash the black off themselves, and they had sat in water to their waists, laughing and splashing like small girls. They were not clean now by any means, though they had used earth and fine sand as an abrasive and had scrubbed themselves and one another. Mixed with the grease and sweat of their bodies, the charcoal had been difficult to remove. They were now streaked with stains browner than their skins. There were dark spots in their ears, under their jowls, behind their knees; but the fertilizing water had refreshed and invigorated them and they had been in a gay mood. They had looked forward to another supper of roasted fish.

Now the old woman approached close to Raven and peered at him. She was half blind, but even when younger and with good vision she had never been quick to read the meanings in human eyes. Nevertheless, Raven's eyes were so alive and dancing that she saw enough to awaken her suspicions, and she demanded sternly:

"Where is food?"

No question could have been better suited to his purpose. He turned and pointed to the bayou; and when he turned, the grandmother, and the other women standing back a little, gasped with astonishment. Raven's back high between the shoulders had not been covered with charcoal. By contrast, this part of him looked glaringly white. He appealed to their sense of the ridiculous; because there he stood, the silly fellow, imagining that he was hidden to all but human eyes, yet with his back advertising his presence wherever he went. Rose snorted with mirth and smiled at her daughter. Then the women smiled at one another in turn, knowingly, like persons who shared a very funny secret.

When Raven faced them, the white patch on his back was hidden. He saw their sly smiles but he had no notion why they were smiling. The grandmother clucked with malicious delight. Then she asked:

"Where is food?"

Raven turned again and with a lordly gesture pointed to the distant bayou. "There!"

"Plenty food?"

"Yes. Plenty fish."

"Ahhh!" said the old woman. She supposed he had caught many fish and was too lazy to carry them home. "Go bring fish," she said.

"No," said Raven, shaking his head stubbornly. "You come." He started off then, indicating that he would gladly lead the way; and the four women followed him, turning now and then to smile at one another. The grandmother was thinking that he was a very ignorant man. Why he had blackened himself she could not imagine, unless he was imitating her and trying to fathom her precious secrets; but didn't the simpleton realize that he must cover his whole body if he wished to be hidden? While he walked ahead, the women stared, fascinated, at the irregular pale brown patch on his back, and from time to time one of them would whisper, "Look!" and point to him and giggle. They were like four mischievous girls, laughing at a dull-witted bumpkin. "Look!" said Rose's daughter, and snickered with joy.

Raven, in the secrecy of his plotting mind, was also delighted. Unsuspecting, and as obedient as slaves, the women were following him. He was glad there were four, because now the ghost could take its choice. Strutting ahead of them, and gesturing aimlessly, he felt like one who was leading four tyrants to their doom. Blissfully invisible, he could caper and shout at the sky and show off to his heart's content. The ghost would hear him but it would not be able to see him; his cries would only bring it to the scene. Afraid that it might have wandered away during his absence, he began to yell like a crazy man when he drew close to the bayou, and the women exchanged startled glances and wondered why he was behaving in this way. The grandmother thought perhaps he was exulting because he had speared many fish, but when she came to the beach she looked round her and saw only the dead embers of a fire.

"Look!" Raven cried, and pointed to his canoe, and like a vain man eager to show off he ran to it and climbed in. He lay down in it and reached over with his lance to thrust at the sand, showing them how he speared fish. But the women were not interested in his antics. Even the canoe, which for him was the most wonderful thing in the world, they dismissed with a shrug.

"Where is food?" the old woman asked. Her voice was vexed and impatient.

Forgetting for the moment why he had led them here, Raven was intent on shoving the canoe out to let them see how he could ride in it and fish, but the grandmother had no time for that. She marched over and cried at him with a voice so menacing that he hastily left the canoe and looked at her. Staring at the impatience and anger in her face, he remembered the ghost, and at once his manner changed. His eyes turned cold and crafty. He glanced across the water at the jungle where the dead man was lying. He listened. He walked slowly across the sand to higher ground and then, with no warning at all, he gave way to such strange behavior that the women could only stare at him, bewildered and amazed.

He began to howl; he ran back and forth, waving his arms and baying at the jungle and the sky. He seized stones and hurled them at trees or out to the water. After a few moments of frenzied leaping and calling, he would pause to listen. Then he began to hurry around at a fast trot as if searching for something; and the women, staring at him, saw that his lips were moving. He was whispering, but they could not hear what he said. He was saying, "Ghost, enter old woman!"—repeating it over and over. Suddenly he almost startled the grandmother out of her wits by pointing to her. Twenty yards away he was dashing back and forth, pointing to her and whispering. He had forgotten that his extended arm was invisible. So eager was he to direct the ghost to the home he wanted it to enter that he was pointing to it.

The matter became so weirdly unpleasant that the old woman lost her temper. She ran at him, shrieking, with bony fingers half bent and ready to clutch, but she was old, and Raven was young and nimble. Staying well beyond her menacing hands, he faced her, pointing and whispering. She chased him until she was exhausted; she picked up stones and hurled them at him; and then, as if deciding to use reason instead of threats, she demanded:

"Where is food?"

Raven was too overjoyed to stop and listen. For one thing, he had the center of the stage and he was making the most of it. For another, he saw the grandmother trembling, and he thought the ghost was probably trying to enter her. Dashing up close to peer at her, he saw that she was sweating and shaking; whereupon, standing only a few feet away, he pointed impudently to her and whispered in a voice that only he and the ghost could hear, "Please enter old woman. . . ."

The grandmother looked stricken. Never before had she allowed herself to be led away by a man on a fool's

216

errand; but worse than that was this arrogant fellow who kept pointing to her and moving his lips as if he were talking. If she could have invoked a supernatural power she would have killed him on the spot.

"Stop!" she screamed; but Raven continued to dance round her and to point and whisper. The other women, standing some distance away, were watching him with horrified eyes. They thought he was possessed by a malicious spirit. Spider had indulged in such inexplicable tantrums, but he had never been so bold as to point an accusing finger at the grandmother or to grin at her with such gloating delight.

"Stop!" the old woman yelled.

Again, desperate with rage, she pursued him, hurling at him anything she could find. But she was famished and weak and presently she collapsed, as if all the life had run out of her. Her legs simply gave way and she dropped. Then the other women ran up and knelt by her and looked anxiously at her face. It was a face drained of blood and deathly white—a face in which anger twitched at the lips and looked out with bleak despair from the eyes.

Raven now stopped his leaping and pointing and whispering. He was satisfied. He knew that the ghost had attacked and knocked her down; he could hear her moaning; he could see her hands clutching the earth. He felt so triumphant that he wanted to sing, but instead he went over and sat on the canoe. He urged the ghost to follow her home.

After a few minutes the women helped the grandmother to rise, but she was so weak and spent that her skinny legs shook and she would have collapsed again if Rose and the girl had not held her. These two supported her and they turned homeward. Barren turned to look at Raven, sitting on the log; and though impartial eyes would have seen only disgust and contempt in her face, Raven saw nothing but fear. He waited until they were almost out of sight and then he arose and followed, and all the way home he kept whispering to the ghost to encourage it. From time to time he looked down across his blackened body and smiled. Now he had a way to protect himself against the tyrannies of women. Now, any time he wished, he could summon ghosts to torment them and drive them to their death.

17

FOR two or three days Raven lived in his sheath of charcoal, and during this while he fished and hunted small game, and his family had plenty to eat. He was generous because he felt that his station in life had improved. After her humiliating experience on the beach the grandmother was chastened and unhappy; instead of treating Raven as a servant who must be tolerated because he was useful, she looked at him with troubled eyes; and to Rose she confessed that he had discovered some kind of magic. This suspicion disturbed her notion of the world and of her function in it. Men, it is true, had a simple magic of their own when preparing for the hunt, but even then it was the old women who gathered the juices and herbs and fermented the courage. In the more important matters relating to the Moon Woman, birth, growth, health, and all the dreadful and invisible powers, men had no magic. At least, that had been this grandmother's belief. But now, looking back to her humiliating experience and trying to recall exactly what had happened, she could not escape the feeling that her son had used magic against her.

For one thing, a woman did not collapse, exhausted and trembling, merely because a man danced around her and pointed an impudent finger; and for another thing, since that hour she had been racked by pains. She had cramps in her belly and a heavy choked feeling in her heart. She did not think that a ghost had entered her. She had no knowledge of casting spells and therefore she could not believe that the man had bewitched her. Nevertheless, she did not feel good, and she suspected that her trouble was the result of something mysterious he had done.

Raven had no doubt of it. Instead of feeling compassion for the old woman when she shuffled around, bent over and suffering abdominal pains, the rascal looked at her with a sly and knowing grin; and with all the cunning he had he plotted to make her life thoroughly miserable. Repeatedly he whispered to all the invisible things, beseeching them to enter her. Long ago she had laid aside her protective apron; and now, when carrying water to her garden or busying herself with other chores outside, she often walked with her mouth open. He perceived that she was vulnerable to invasion and he hoped that very malicious spirits would possess her.

He became so arrogant that the women hated him. It was not uncommon for him to leap around, as he had done on the beach, and whisper and point; and when he realized that the younger women, too, were afraid of him, he included them in his capers. He pointed to them also and, grinning and whispering, asked spirits to enter them. Old Man and the sick woman were the only ones he ignored.

He was motivated by more than resentment of an old woman's tyranny and envy of her powers. He was an erotically hungry man. There were wild fruits now, as well as an abundance of fish and rabbits and small birds. He spurned the rabbits for his own use, but he ate the organs of all the birds he shot or snared, as well as fish and berries and certain roots, and such a diet made him feel vigorous and lustful. But he had no mate. His sister Rose was big with pregnancy, and her daughter had not been receptive since those blissful moments in the thicket. His barren sister would not suffer his advances. And so, in his unconscious mind, Raven was trying not so much to destroy them as to make them yield to his embrace.

And, besides, his ego was thriving on the rare luxury of feeling important. The women sometimes yelled at him and told him to go away; they menaced him when his arrogance became extreme; but all the while he sensed that they were afraid of him. In his efforts to push his advantage to a complete usurpation of all power in the home, he went too far one evening and lost a good part of the prestige he had won.

Of such food as was brought in, it had always been the grandmother's habit to give those portions that were less choice to the men. This evening she picked out the skinniest fish of the lot and handed it to Raven, and with a furious cry he struck it from her hand. He was done with eating what no one else wanted. After all, he was the one who labored to get the food and bring it home, and it seemed to him that he ought to have the best of it. So he knocked the fish to the floor and went to the pile to choose one; and the old woman, as if accepting the rebuke, did not argue with him. She was cunning, too, and she intended to chasten him in her own way.

Among the dried herbs that she gathered and stored to

be used as curatives, she had a very powerful emetic. Now, unobserved by Raven, she took a big handful of the leaves and steeped them in a natural stone urn which she set by the flames. Then she took an especially choice fish and carefully roasted it and while it was hot she immersed it in the potent juice of the herb. She roasted and immersed and roasted until the fish was saturated with the juice; whereupon, with an innocent smile that masked her spite, she went over to Raven and offered it to him.

He was astonished. Never before in his life had a woman taken such pains to prepare a delicious meal for him, and, least of all, this old woman. He was astonished and he was also deeply flattered; her gesture, and the friendly smile on her face, were evidence of the growing respect in which he was held. He took the hot and dripping fish, never for a moment suspecting the malice behind it, and thrust the tail end into his mouth. It had been so carefully cooked and was so enriched by warm juice that he found it extraordinarily savory and devoured it with greedy gulps. He licked his fingers and looked round him like a man who had become an esteemed and privileged person. He asked the old woman to roast another fish for him, and with a smile that was all motherly innocence she said that she would. She asked him to choose one.

Aware of what the old woman was doing, Rose and her daughter looked at one another and exchanged smiles of malicious joy, and his sister asked Raven:

"Was it good?"

"Good!" he said, and smacked his lips. Again he licked his fingers, and down his wrists where the juice had run.

"You want more?" asked Rose innocently.

"Yes!" he said, nodding vigorously.

"More fish?"

"Cooked fish?"

"Yes."

"More!" said Raven, and looked hungrily at the grand-mother, standing by the fire.

But suddenly there was a change in him. As if someone had slipped up unexpectedly and struck a heavy blow on his back, he hunched forward, rounding his shoulders and bringing his hands protectively to his belly. He stood thus, solemnly anxious, like a man who expected to explode. A tremor ran up his frame, paused for an instant in his stomach, and then gurgled in his throat. It was followed by a hot and sickening flood of emotion that relaxed his body and opened his mouth. His eyelids fluttered, lifted, and slowly fell, as if to shut out a dreadful vision. He now stood like a man who had unwittingly swallowed a live thing and was waiting for it to crawl out.

Rose and her mother were slyly watching him, though they pretended to be busy. They exchanged smiles. The old woman was unable to restrain a chuckle of delight.

Like a man waiting to explode from a convulsion in his belly slowly gathering its forces, Raven stood humped over, hands clutching his stomach, his eyes closed, his mouth wide open, and his legs spread and braced. The awful sickness in him had clouded his senses. When the eruption came it was overwhelming in its violence. His stomach caved in under a spasm; his shoulders shot up to his ears; his head sank as if his neck had been broken; and then out of his wide mouth poured a torrent of fish and juices. Mixed in the outpouring was a sound that began as a gurgle and ended in an anguished shriek.

The grandmother chuckled. Rose laid arms across her plump breasts and bent over in hysterical laughter.

But Raven did not hear the mirth; he was lost in a tiny dark world no larger than himself and his sickness. Hardly aware of what he did, he sank, stricken, to hands and knees, his whole body convulsed and tortured. After he had completely emptied his stomach he continued to puke and gasp, with each seizure so desperate that it moved him as if he were shoved from behind. His eyes were still closed. The cramps were so excruciating that after a few moments he rested his chin on the earth and clasped his belly with both hands. The next seizure flattened him out; he fell to his stomach and lay face downward, groaning and twitching.

Rose was so overcome by laughter that she sank to the earth and rocked back and forth, tears streaming down her face. The grandmother chuckled and prepared another fish.

When his pain eased a little, Raven struggled to his hands and knees again and began to crawl. He opened his eyes now; they were swimming in tears of agony that so blurred his vision that he could not see where he was going. But he did not care; he felt gutted and dying and he wanted to be alone. Crossing the yard, and pausing now and then to gasp and strain, he came to a tree, and he stood on hands and knees by the tree and waited. He felt a little better. There was a gurgling sound in his stomach and a deathly sickness all through him, but by pressing hands against his stomach and remaining very quiet he was able to keep from retching. He wondered vaguely, dully, unhappily why he was sick, but he did not suspect the grandmother of trickery. Though he had seen persons vomit in an effort to expel a ghost, he had never vomited before or been sickened by anything he ate.

After a few minutes he felt well enough to turn gently on his haunches and sit up. He blinked his wet eyes and looked at the world. Darkness had come. Beyond the sky line of far trees he could see a luminous area, but this did not tell him that the Moon Woman was rising. The rest of the sky was full of night. There was no wind, nor any hint of enemies and terrors.

The grandmother came over, carrying a roasted fish. Resolved to chasten him thoroughly, she had also soaked this one in the juice of the emetic. She hoped he would eat it.

"You feel good?" she asked.

Raven groaned miserably and shook his head.

"You hungry?"

"No," he said, feeling as if he would never eat again.

"Not hungry?"

"No."

The sly and calculating gammer knelt by him and with solicitous concern proffered the fish. She moved it back and forth under his nose to let him breathe the appetizing odors, but the smell of it sickened him and convulsed his stomach. Angrily, he struck it from her hands.

She picked it up and brushed off the twigs and leaves. She sniffed it, her eyes watching his face. She even pretended to take a bite of it.

"You not hungry?"

"No!"

"It is good," she said gently, patiently, and smacked her lips as if chewing.

With a shudder of distaste he turned away.

225

"Smell," she said.

"No."

"I cooked it." Again she put it under his nose, and again he struck it from her hands. "Ahhh!" she cried, picking it up and brushing it.

"Go away!" said Raven.

"Are you hungry?"

"No!" he cried, and shuddered.

"It is good."

"Go away!"

As if moved by a power stronger than his will, Raven met her eyes. What he saw in them he did not like and did not trust; and what she saw in his eyes made her understand that it was useless to urge him. She found some green leaves and laid the fish on them.

"You will be hungry," she said.

"No!"

"You will be hungry soon."

She arose and straightened. Raven had turned away.

"Look!" he cried suddenly, and pointed.

The Moon Woman had risen above the trees. She was old tonight, and round and full, and as Raven gazed at her face he could clearly see the features of a human being. She seemed to be looking down at him and scowling, with one eye distorted and half shut, as if by an old scar.

"Look!" he said.

The grandmother stared for a long while and then went to her garden. When the Moon Woman was old it was time for matured growth and ripening, but on examining her grain she saw that the stalks were only knee high. There were no heads on them. She went to the hut for a jug of water and fed a spoonful to each plant.

Raven looked down at the fish. He picked it up and sniffed it. Then he bit off a piece and began to chew it, slowly, experimentally, as if he expected a return of his sickness. He thought it tasted bitter. With his mouth full of it he opened his mouth wide, and his tongue, acting as a shovel, thrust the fish out. It fell in wet morsels down his black chest, and after staring at it with distaste he brushed it off. Then he threw the remainder of the fish away.

He was now in a philosophic mood. Clasping his arms round his knees and pressing his belly hard against his legs, he looked at the Moon Woman and began to think about himself and the world.

18

Like all his people, Raven humanized the sounds of nature; as he perceived the world, it was filled with unrest and unhappiness and pain. He could see, merely by glancing at them, that some trees were young but others were old and sick. Whether trees suffered pain, or whether the sounds they made were of ghosts hiding in them, he did not know; but he knew that the sap in plants was their blood and that there was no blood left in them after they died. Sometimes there was none left in those still standing.

But chiefly he lived in a world of spirits, and these, as far as he knew, never died. He did not have a sense of the remote past, but he was aware that many people and animals had died and that all their spirits still lived. There was no evidence that the ghosts were ever happy; on the contrary, they could never be happy because their bodies had died and they were homeless. They hungered day and night for the things they had lost. The human ghosts wanted the food, the beds, and the other joys they had once had, and all these they strove ceaselessly to recover;

and because their own bodies were dead, they tried, quite naturally, to enter and usurp those of the living.

That much he understood. That much for him and his people was unmistakably plain. And he knew also that the spirits could be very sly and treacherous in their attempts to enter the living. Sometimes they came up boldly and slipped in by way of your mouth or nostrils or ears; but if you were always on guard against them, they disguised themselves. They might take the form of a serpent or an insect; or they might hide in your food and try to enter you that way.

He knew now, after pondering the matter, that a ghost had hidden in the fish he had eaten and the ghost had slipped down to his stomach. He had vomited it out. He knew that the ghost was not in him now because he felt no distress; if there had been one in him, he would have been sick and tormented like the woman inside. Furthermore, he knew that this spirit had not singled him out as the one it had wished to enter. It could not have done so because he was still black and invisible. It had entered the fish because the old woman had had the fish in her hands. It had intended to steal into her. Realizing this, Raven decided that it had been the ghost of the slain man. He knew now that the ghost had followed the grandmother home, as he had hoped it would, and it had supposed that she would eat the fish in which it was concealed. Hereafter he would accept no more food from her hands.

Having figured out the matter with extraordinary logic, and having realized that the invasion of him had been a mistake on the ghost's part, Raven drew a sigh of relief and looked at the Moon Woman. He did not like her face tonight; it was reddish and inflamed with anger. Whether

229

she could see him in his black disguise he did not know, but he thought she was looking at him and he felt uneasy. Save in her face, there was no sign of anger; there was no dark wrath around her and she was making no sounds. But he felt a sense of impending trouble nevertheless. Once or twice before he had seen her face flushed and red like a woman in bad temper; and now, after staring at her anxiously for several minutes, he went softly to the hut.

They were lying on their beds, but he could see them in the dancing firelight. He knew that the grandmother was not asleep.

"Come-look!" he whispered.

The grandmother lifted herself to an elbow. "What is wrong?"

"Her," said Raven, and pointed to the sky.

"Is she angry?"

"Yes."

"Ahhh!" said the old woman, and left the bed. She went to the doorway, followed by Rose and Barren and the girl. She looked up at the Moon Woman. The others did so, too; then they stared at the grandmother's face, trying to read her thoughts. She knew the Moon Woman and her moods and whims much better than the others.

"Is she angry?" Rose whispered.

The grandmother was not to be hurried; in a moment like this she felt her power and knowledge, and the dependence of the others on her. She would take her time, as if she were consulting a hidden wisdom.

"Is she?"

Still the old woman would not answer. She folded her arms across her flat chest, lifted her face to the sky, and stood like one who was smelling out a riddle. Her rheumy

eyes were wide and intent. Though half blind, she could
see the distemper in the Woman's face, but she could see
no other sign of anger. There was no dark wrath, no sound
of fury.

Now Raven spoke. "What is wrong?" he asked.

"Ahhh!" said the old woman, and her eyelids fell. She
had explored her almost boundless knowledge of secret
and magical things and she had found the answer. Unknown to her, it had come as an intuitive recognition out
of her unconscious mind. It had been born out of something the girl had said the day before, but the old woman
thought she had discovered it by looking deeply into her
hoarded wisdom. Slowly, impressively, she turned to the
girl and fixed her with a hypnotic stare.

"You will have baby," she said.

The other women gasped with astonishment and delight. Barren looked at the girl, her eyes desperate with her
own hunger, and gently she reached out to touch her. The
girl's healthy face broke into a smile of joy.

"I will have baby?"

The question pained the old woman. The pain was a
convulsive grimace in her wrinkled features. If she had
been less cunning, she might have looked again at the
Moon Woman to confirm her judgment, but she was never
foolish enough to awaken doubt of her power. When she
said a thing would happen, then, of course, it would happen. It bored and pained her to have her pronouncements
questioned.

The girl's question had been rhetorical. She knew it was
true when the grandmother spoke, and her question had
been only a cry of joy, only an effort to realize the wonder
of what had happened to her. Smiling now like a small

231

sunrise, she trembled with delight and looked in turn at those around her. Her mother beamed happily. Barren's face was a picture of joy, too, but behind the joy was intense longing. Raven's face was glum.

He was thinking that if the girl was pregnant, then he would have no sexual mate at all. Two women were pregnant, one was old, one was sick, and the other scorned him. He withdrew a little, sulking and spiteful, and looked up at the Moon Woman, daring to hope that the grandmother was wrong. How did she know these things? What was the mysterious relationship between her and this woman in the sky? Fearful of her, he slipped away and when he was out of hearing he began to whisper to ghosts, beseeching them to attack the old woman. It would have delighted him to see her fall to the earth in agony and puke and scream.

But a little arrogantly, like one in possession of all knowledge, the grandmother, without looking at the sky again, entered her home. The other women followed her. Happy in the realization that another child was coming, they went to their beds; and Raven stole to the door to listen and heard the girl chanting a wordless song. Frustrated and vengeful, he returned to his tree to sit by it and think.

He gazed earnestly at the Moon Woman, wondering how she communicated with the grandmother; and while he stared at her, one question among the many in his mind stood out with greater urgency: who was this woman and where had she come from? He knew, to be sure, that she was the woman in the sky, that she was eternal, that she had been there before he was born and would be there after his body died. For reasons completely dark to him

232

she was the guardian of rain, of fertility, of birth; these were certainties that nobody questioned, but they did not explain her. She favored the nighttime, coming out then to spy on people; and, save rarely, she hid during the time of light—but why? She connived secretly with old women and shared her extraordinary knowledge with them. She chose among women those to have children. But why did she favor the girl and deny a child to the barren one? For what mysterious reasons did she determine these things?

While staring at her and lifting questions one by one from his troubled mind, Raven was startled by a thought that was pure logic. It could have occurred only to a man endowed with the capacity for brilliant speculation. The thought said: "Maybe she is the first woman." Was there a first woman? he asked himself; and after pondering the matter he decided that there must have been. The thought was so bold and revolutionary that he got to his feet, trembling with excitement, and he was about to run to the hut and tell the others this new truth when something in the Moon Woman's countenance stopped him. A fearful change had come over it. The face seemed to be burning with light, very golden and lucent, with a horrifying darkness on one edge; and while he stared at it, something happened that was stranger still. The edge of one cheek seemed to be disappearing. He gave a cry of astonishment and looked at the sky roundabout for signs of an obscuring wrath. But there was none. The entire sky was as clear as quiet water. Fascinated and horrified, he gazed at the Woman, and he saw beyond any doubt at all that one cheek was disappearing. With a yell of terror he ran to the hut, making such wild outcry that everyone inside, including the sick woman, came to the doorway. Raven

233

pointed to the Moon Woman and told them that she was being swallowed. That was the way it seemed to him. A segment of her face had vanished as if it had been bitten off.

In the grandmother's mind there was no doubt of what was happening; one anxious glance told her that the Moon Woman was being swallowed by a monster. She began to scream and wave her arms. Then the other women joined her, and together they made the most dreadful clamor Raven had ever heard.

"Scare it away!" the old woman shrieked.

They all took up the cry. The women dashed back and forth, as if out of their minds, waving their arms and screaming; and Old Man, aroused to frenzied action, seized sticks and hurled them. Raven stood like a man rooted; but presently the screaming was more than he could resist, and he bolted into the hut, returning with his bow and arrows. The Moon Woman was half engulfed now. An arc like a scar lay across the visible part of her face. The monster was not visible, but by studying the face and realizing which part of it had been engorged, Raven could tell where the monster was, and he shot an arrow at it and watched the arrow speed away out of sight. He waited a moment to learn if he had hit the creature and, deciding that he had not, he shot one arrow after another until his quiver was empty. Then, beside himself with rage and terror, he ran for his lance.

The women, too, were so beside themselves that they were hardly aware of what they were doing. They continued to scream without letup and to rush back and forth, menacing with their arms. The old woman was hurling sticks and stones and handfuls of earth at the sky. The women all kept their gaze on the Moon Woman while they

234

ran; sometimes they stumbled and fell, but they got up, their shrieking frenzy redoubled. When the grandmother's eyes, wide with horror, saw that the Woman was almost swallowed, with only a slice of one cheek now visible, she stopped running. She was shaking with fear and exhaustion, but there was a thought in her mind. Clearly enough, wild sounds and gestures were not enough to frighten the monster; something else would have to be done.

She would have to use magic, but because she had no magic for such a disaster as this, she obeyed her first impulse. She dashed into the hut and got Raven's knife.

"Be still!" she shouted.

The other women, observing that she stood apart with a knife in her hand, paused in their shrieking and running and looked at her. With one firm stroke, the old woman made an incision in her left arm. She let the knife fall. Then she caught the gushing blood in her right palm and tossed it in a thin mist toward the monster. Her lips were moving, but nobody could hear what she said. In turn they looked at her and up at the sky; again and again she caught her own blood and hurled it at the Moon Woman.

For a long and terrible moment the Woman was completely swallowed. There was no sign of her, and there was only a luminous darkness where she had been. But with her lips whispering frantically, and her hand catching every drop of blood that ran from her arm, the grandmother worked her magic; and the others, hardly breathing, watched her and waited.

It was Raven who gave the first shout. He saw a very thin slice of face appear, and with another cry, poured out of the deepest emotion in him, he pointed.

"Look!" he yelled.

The others saw the slender rind of face and, even while they stared at it and held their breath, it grew in size. Instead of releasing its victim with one despairing and defeated belch, the monster seemed to be trying to hang on; and after perceiving that this was so, the grandmother renewed her efforts. Her lips moved faster. She summoned Rose and asked her to squeeze the arm to force out more blood. She caught the blood and tossed it again and again.

Now, beyond all question, the monster was releasing its victim. Nearly half of her face was in sight. The younger women would have cried with joy if they had not been so amazed and awed by the grandmother's magic. They had never realized that she was endowed with such power. They stared at her, wide-eyed, their mouths open, their breathing slow and deep; or they glanced up at the sky. While they watched and waited for what seemed to them a long time, the Moon Woman came out of the engulfing throat, and her face was round and whole, with no sign of a wound. A part of it was darkened and most of it had a reddish cast, but it was unscarred and untroubled, and they knew that she was unharmed.

When she perceived that the Moon Woman was safe, the grandmother uttered a low moan and collapsed. The others rushed to her and knelt, thinking she was dead, but she had only fainted. Though her eyes were closed and her mouth was a sickly white, they saw that she still breathed. Rose put an ear to her thin chest and heard the feeble beating of her heart.

"Help me," she said, and they carried the old woman into the hut. They laid her on a bed and sat by her.

Raven stood in the yard and looked at the sky. He was so overwhelmed by wonder and awe that he could not

236

think. He could not move. For several minutes he could only stare at the Moon Woman and tell himself over and over that she was unharmed and safe. When there was no longer a golden radiance about her, but only the calm dignity which she always wore in her periods of untroubled age, he went stiffly to the hut and peered in. The grandmother was awake. From her assortment of herbs she had chosen some leaves to chew, and she now bent over her arm, sucking the wound and applying the mouthful of juice as a salve.

Softly Raven entered and went over and stood by the women. They were looking at the grandmother. Like Raven, they were awed and curious; they wanted her to explain what the dreadful enemy was and from where it had come. But the old woman was too sick and spent to talk. After salving her arm, she lay down and closed her eyes, and those gazing at her saw that her face was very white.

Rose looked up at her brother and asked, "Is she well?"

Knowing what she meant, Raven went to the doorway. The Moon Woman was calm and untroubled. There was not a hint of wrath or impending danger anywhere in the sky.

"She is well," he said.

The grandmother now spoke. "Water," she said.

Rose fetched a jug of water. After drinking deeply, the old woman lay on one side, with a palm under her cheek, and closed her weary eyes. The others laid a skin over her for covering and went to their beds. For a little while Raven stood in the doorway, studying the Moon Woman's countenance and assuring himself that she was all right.

His world had become more mysterious and dreadful;

there were destroying things in it that he had not known about; and there was such magic in old women as he had never dreamed of. On going to his bed, he tiptoed past the grandmother with humble respect and, instead of lying down to sleep, he sat on his skin mattress, with arms clasped round his knees, and looked over at her. All that he had knowledge of, all that he was able to do in this world, was very trivial, he realized now, in comparison with the power in old women.

19

WHEN, a little after daylight, the grandmother arose to
stir the fire, she moved with feeble and faltering steps,
like one who had aged many years in a few hours. In
frightening the enemy away she had been aroused to such
frenzy that waste poisons had poured into her blood
stream, and now she felt sharp pains in her joints and a
nauseous sickness in her stomach. But in spite of this, there
was a sense of joy and triumph in her. Though she would
never have confessed it—for she was too cunning to destroy her own prestige—she had not realized that she had
such power with magic. Nor had she known that there
were invisible enemies in the world that could attack and
swallow the Moon Woman.

During the night she had considered the matter and she
had come to the conclusion that the Moon Woman was
not so supreme a being as she had imagined her to be. Even
she had enemies and could be attacked. This would have
been a terrifying truth if the grandmother had not also
realized, with a pride that warmed her like a fire, that she,

the grandmother, was able to protect her. She understood now that the Moon Woman had less power, and that she herself had more, than she had ever suspected.

This recognition of the other's frailty and of her own strength was in her bearing and in her eyes when, having stirred the fire, she went to the doorway to look out. She saw what she had expected to see—a calm world without any visible sign of unfriendliness or menace. She looked at it with something in her eyes that was close to contempt. After all, if she could frighten the dreadful creatures that lurked in the sky, what was there to be afraid of?

When she turned to her family her manner was arrogant. She told them to get up, and all but the sick woman left their beds with haste. The grandmother went over to the sick one and looked down at her. If, she was thinking, she had power to frighten sky monsters, then surely she could drive the ghosts out of this woman.

"Are you sick?" she asked, and her voice was harsh and unfriendly.

Even a half-blind person like the grandmother could tell that the woman was sick. Her belly was swollen. The flesh was wasting away from her bones. Her face was drawn and bloodless, and in her eyes was the utter hopelessness of one who felt herself doomed.

"Are you sick?"

Receiving no answer, the grandmother knelt by her and pressed the swollen groin with rough unsympathetic hands. The woman gave a low scream.

"Ghost in you?" the old woman asked.

"Yes!" the sick one whispered.

Ah, well, the grandmother reflected, she would think

about the matter for a while and then she would contrive some magic to force the ghost out. There was nothing she could not do now—nothing, she decided, recalling her amazing triumph. She was more arrogant, and the others, in the same measure, were more humble. They had stood back like mute servants, watching her and expecting another miracle. If they had had a concept of supernatural beings, they might have imagined that the grandmother was one, or that the soul of one had entered her.

Old Man felt the deepest awe. He was this woman's brother and had lived with her all his life, but he had never known that she was endowed with such power. The one who was least awed was Rose. She would be a grandmother some day; on the death of her mother's body, all the old woman's powers would be left in her. One among them, the girl, was awed, too, but she was also full of joy and song. She had been told that she would have a child. This knowledge filled her with such happiness that she wanted to be away; there were things she must do to prepare herself for the growth in her body and for a healthy birth. Without waiting for breakfast she went outside.

Raven slyly followed her. Out in the yard, the girl was standing tiptoe, her firm breasts pointing upward, her eager face lifted to the morning sun. She was a picture of youth and happiness. Her face was so radiant and her eyes so bright that Raven gazed at her with wonder. He had never before seen a young woman dreaming of her first child. He had never seen such joy in a human face. He thought that perhaps she was receptive and waiting for him, and with hunger turning hope into belief he softly approached her. When he was almost close enough to touch her arm, the girl turned and saw him, trembling with

241

eagerness, and, instantly reading the meaning in his eyes, she came down on her heels and scowled.

"What you want?" she asked.

He felt rather foolish. There was nothing inviting in the girl now. She was looking at him with scorn and after a moment she gestured impudently at the distant hills and said:

"Go far away!"

"No," he said. He was crestfallen and a little angry.

"Don't bother me," she said, still eyeing him with girlish impertinence. Then, as if he were a stupid fellow who needed to have all things explained to him, she added, "I will have baby."

"Ahhh!" he said, his voice sinking to a ridiculous whisper. He had forgotten that the grandmother had told her she would have a child. He had come out with the foolish hope that the girl was luring him away to the hills and to a hidden spot, and the hope had been so strong in him that it still shone in his eyes.

Reading in his eyes the hope in his mind, the girl became angry. Her sudden movement was that of an animal preparing to strike.

"Go away!" she yelled.

Raven was backing off when the grandmother appeared. She had heard the girl's cry.

"What is wrong?" she demanded. Her voice was that of one who expected a quick answer.

The girl pointed to Raven. "Make him go away."

Slowly advancing, with menace in every movement and feature, the old woman came up to Raven and fixed him with an accusing stare. "She will have child," she said.

Raven nodded vigorous assent.

242

"She has baby."

"Yes!" said Raven, hoping to be able to slip away.

Thrusting an arm at him like the tongue of a snake, the grandmother said sharply, "Go find food!"

"Yes!" he said eagerly, and ran to get his weapons.

The girl wandered away to be alone, though she had only vague notions of what she ought to do. Preparations for the growth of a child had not been fixed in rituals; for the most part they were still impulsive and spontaneous, guided chiefly by the woman's intelligence and resourcefulness. A pregnant woman usually sprinkled herself with running water and with fresh blood, and the girl had these in mind; but she was too happy for purposive behavior. She wanted to be alone more fully to realize the wonder of what had happened to her; and so she went aimlessly, with a song in her heart that bubbled and escaped at her lips.

Unknown to her, Raven stealthily followed.

Even for the wise old women, birth was still a mysterious thing. A child started to grow in a woman; its body was formed of the menstrual blood; but nobody knew how the baby started to grow. The Moon Woman had something to do with it. She decided that some women would have babies and some would not, but nobody knew why. Sometimes, to be sure, a barren woman could become fertile by dancing in the rain, by bathing in running water, by eating certain foods, and by drinking the blood of those creatures that had many babies. All these things helped, but these were not always enough. The barren aunt in the girl's home had done all these many times but she was still childless.

No, it was really a miracle, as the girl told herself while

243

wandering idly over the hills. The Moon Woman had chosen her as a favored one; and the grandmother, who was wise in these matters, had known that she had been chosen. If the girl had been told that her baby had begun its life when she had hidden in the thicket with Raven, she would have been incredulous. The miracle of birth had nothing to do with a man. It was a precious happiness that the Moon Woman gave to those who pleased her.

That, at least, is all this girl knew about it; thinking of herself now, and of the child that would be hers, she hummed a kind of simple song and looked with glad eyes at everything around her. When she heard running water she hastened to the stream and, after assuring herself that this water was also happy and singing its own song, she waded into the stream and sat, with water to her waist. For a little while she played in it with her hands. Then with both hands she began to toss water above her head to let it descend on her in cooling rain. Water, like blood, gave strength to things and made them grow. She would have preferred to dance in a rainstorm; since there was none, she made her own rain. With hands cupped together, she would fill them and hurl the water above her, turning her face upward to let the falling drops strike it. When lifting her face, she closed her eyes but opened her mouth, and she swallowed the water that fell into her mouth.

After making a lot of rain she lay in the water on her back, with only her head out. She liked the music of this stream, singing a glad song as it ran. Reaching a hand out into the swifter current, she felt the vivid life of it pouring against her arm and rushing between her fingers. Water like this was a living thing for her; it moved, it made sounds, it could feel. She did not know whether it could see and hear; unlike Raven, she was not a philosophic person and she did not trouble her mind with what she could not understand. It was enough to know that she would have a child, and that this water was friendly to it and would help to make it strong. She resolved to come here every day and sit in rain which she would make.

From a thicket, Raven had been peering out to watch her. Months ago, when his sister was first pregnant, he had seen her sit in this stream. He knew that running water gave babies a more vigorous life, but he did not understand why and he did not care. Babies were a small part of a man's life. He was so hungry for this girl that he was unable to think of anything else; and he was foolish enough to hope that she had lured him to this spot and was waiting for him.

Leaving the thicket, he stood in full view and called. The girl turned to look at him but there was neither surprise nor resentment in her face; she was too lost in her own blissful dreaming. Raven waited, and when she did not cry sharply or tell him to go away, he went toward her, approaching like one whose hope looked over a precipice. But even when he stood on the bank, almost within reach, the girl paid no attention to him; she was murmuring a song and splashing water over her body. Nonplussed because she sat deep in the water, but encouraged because she seemed friendly, he stared at her with covetous eyes; and after a moment of indecision he sank to his heels and reached out to touch her.

As if she had been trained to simulate haughty amazement, the girl looked at his hand, and in the voice of one who was not thinking of him at all, she said:

"Go away."

"No!" he cried. Rising quickly, he looked at her and beckoned. "Come!" he said.

It was what she saw in his eyes that brought her out of cloudy reveries. A woman always reads unerringly that look in a man's eyes. Her face changed. Her eyes turned hard and cold. She arose, shaking with anger; and when Raven saw that she was angry, he backed away. But he had not given up all hope.

"Come," he said, but his voice was quavering and weak.

Drawing herself to her full height and looking at him with disdain, the girl spoke in a voice that was sharp and final. "Go away!"

When he did not move, she was filled with sudden fury. Stooping swiftly, she picked up a stone and hurled it at him. She missed, but she hurled other stones; and when one of them struck him with a stinging blow, Raven's hunger was absorbed by a flood of wrath. He grasped his lance, intending to attack her, but the girl read his mind and rushed at him, screaming. Her cry was so wild and animal-like that it shattered his will, and with the picture of an avenging grandmother in his mind he turned and fled. Fifty yards away he stopped and looked back, hoping that the girl might change her mind; but when he saw her hurling pebbles and shouting at him, he shrugged like a man misunderstood and abused and went out of sight.

After he vanished, it took the girl a little while to recover her mood of joy. She sat in the water again, but her face was dark and scowling, and her eyes were suspicious. For her, nothing could be more unfriendly, more unreasonable or senseless than a man with that look in his eyes when a woman was dreaming of a child. If this girl had been questioned, she would have said that she had never been able to see much meaning in a man. The only sensible thing men ever did was to bring food home. The grandmother, who knew all things, had little respect for them.

And so, thinking of Raven with disgust, she splashed angrily and scowled at the world; but when, after glancing at the hill where he had disappeared, she saw no sign of him, she felt better and began to make rain. The falling drops brought her back to her reverie, and after a while, feeling refreshed and happy, she arose and wondered what else she should do.

She wanted a rabbit. Her grandmother said that rabbits were best for a woman with child because they were both gentle and fertile. Birds without talons or flesh-tearing beaks were also good. She had no way to capture birds but she had watched the grandmother snare rabbits, and she now searched for a rabbit warren in the growth along the stream. She made snares of long slender vines, tying one end to a bush or tree and suspending the loop in a rabbit run. After she had prepared several of these, she ran back and forth through the thickets, beating with a stick and shouting to flush the creatures out of hiding.

She was not successful today but she came out the next day and the next, a patient and determined woman; and when at last a rabbit was caught and held until she could grasp it, she hugged it to her breast and headed for home. In her arms it seemed to be nothing but soft fur and a wildly beating heart. Its heart pounded so violently that she could feel the throb of it in her own body, and from time to time it struggled so desperately to be free that she almost crushed it. It was half dead when she reached the hut.

Still hugging it fiercely, she asked her mother for a

247

knife and a vessel in which to catch the blood; when these were brought to her, she laid the creature on the earth and placed a knee across its flanks.

"Is it woman rabbit?" asked her mother.

"Ahhh!" said the girl.

It had not occurred to her to examine it. Recalling now that the blood of a man rabbit would not be good for her child, she spread the hind legs apart and inspected the creature, looking at it and probing with a finger.

"It is woman rabbit," she said, glancing up.

To make sure, her mother knelt and examined it. "Yes," she said.

Rose now grasped the big ears and held the clay vessel, and with a flint knife the girl cut the throat. She shoved the blade into the throat just under the neck bone and with a powerful stroke cut through the flesh and fur. The blood poured out in a vivid stream. When it no longer ran but only dripped, the girl held the creature up by its hind legs, and while she held it, her mother massaged it downward to force out all the blood.

Then, laying the beast aside, the girl drank about half the blood. It was warm and thick and tasted of salt. With the remainder of the blood, she sat by a tree to complete this part of her preparation. Dipping a finger into the vessel, she rubbed blood on each nipple; her child would take its food from them and they should be healthy and strong. After repeatedly bathing each one, she poured a little blood into a cupped palm and massaged her breasts. She rubbed blood over her belly within which the child would live and grow and then, looking at the other parts of her body, she tried to remember what else she should do. Unable to think of anything else, she called to her mother, but it was the wise grandmother who came over to her.

"See—" the girl said, and pointed to her breasts and belly.

Instead of explaining what should be done, the grandmother knelt to do it for her. With a forefinger she dipped into the blood and smeared the girl's mouth, nostrils, and ears; and the girl remembered then that blood repelled malicious ghosts. With what was left of the blood, the old woman vigorously massaged the girl's abdomen and breasts.

Arising, she said, "Come!" and went over to the rabbit.

With the knife she ripped the belly open and peeled the skin back. She pulled the bowels out and searched them until she found the uterus. This she cut away and handed to the girl.

"Eat it," she said.

It was good for a pregnant woman to eat the uterus of a female rabbit because it had been the home of many babies. The girl took the warm tough sac and ate it, biting off pieces and gulping them without chewing. Her eyes shone with happiness. She was an intelligent girl who was making thorough preparations and would have a healthy child. Then the grandmother gave her the vital organs to eat, including the heart, liver, lungs, and kidneys. The remainder of the carcass she took into the hut to use as a part of their supper.

Raven, meanwhile, had been standing back at a respectful distance and watching them. Once before he had seen a woman prepare herself for pregnancy but he did not understand why it was necessary to do these things. Of some creatures, the blood and the organs, especially the heart, were good for a man—but not those of rabbits.

249

These were the most slinking and timid of all the beasts he knew, and the ones he held in the greatest contempt. He thought it would be much better for a woman to eat the blood and heart of a wolf, a tiger, a weasel, or a hawk; and the next day, having made some arrows, he went forth to shoot a falcon.

He brought it home and squeezed a part of its blood into a clay pot; whereupon, moved only by friendliness and good will, he took the blood to the girl.

"Rabbit?" she asked.

"No!" he cried, and made a face of disgust.

"What is it?"

"Look!" he said, and ran proudly to get the falcon.

When the girl saw what he had she stiffened with horror and struck the pot of blood from his hands. She ran screaming to the grandmother and told her what Raven had done, and the old woman came rushing at him, shouting violent abuse. She would have been no more angry if he had tried to poison the girl. No pregnant woman in her right senses would ever touch the blood or flesh of a hawk. It was a savage and destroying thing; the growing child, and the mother who housed it, needed gentleness and peace.

"Go away!" she howled. When Raven did not move, she rushed to him and seized the falcon and hurled it from her.

Abashed, Raven went away, feeling very vengeful. He had been moved by an instinctive devotion to the welfare of the group, and especially of its young. The paternal feeling in him was so weak that it can hardly be said to have lived at all; but nevertheless, in a generous moment, he had gone to get the kind of food he thought would make a baby strong and bold—and he had been dismissed with contempt. Now, feeling debased, he turned away, his eyes clouded with pain.

So it was then, and so it has always been: some of the deepest interests and emotional hungers of men and of women have been in ceaseless conflict. Women have sought the ways of peace and gentleness, and to nourish and protect their children they have turned to such symbols as the dove; but the men have been lured to the adventurous paths, to the hazards, to the frontiers—and to such symbols as the eagle, the falcon, and the wolf.

Outraged by what she took to be a man's wish to destroy a child, the grandmother went into her home, and this for her was another symbol, though for the man it was only a bed and a fire; and Raven, unable to understand the woman's way, took his weapons and strode about, enlivened by vengeful thoughts. He plotted against the old woman. He whispered to ghosts, beseeching them to enter her and torment her. Some day he might become bold enough to strike her down. With this hope refreshing him, he went to the falcon and tore out its heart and ate it. If he could have eaten the heart of a tiger he would have been almost as happy as the girl.

And so another night found them, the girl feeling as soft and gentle as the creature she had eaten, and the man hungering for conquests, kingdoms, and the heart of the wild.

20

DURING those recent days, the grandmother had looked at Rose's huge belly from time to time, and in these moments her eyes had been very gentle. There would soon be a baby in her home, and babies were the meaning of life for her. Or she would ask Rose to lie down, and then she would kneel by her and put an ear to her belly and listen; or she would press gently to feel the child's movements. In doing this she wished to assure herself that the baby was alive. "Soon," she would say, hoping the child would be born when the Moon Woman was young. Things born when she was young lived longer than those born when she was old.

Having no knowledge of the week or even of the month in which a baby began its life, or of the length of time spent growing in its mother, a woman did not know when to expect birth. When her belly became very large and her breasts filled with milk, she knew the birth would be "soon"—but for these people soon could mean a few days or a few weeks. When the time of birth was soon, the mother had to make preparations for it; and one morning the grandmother, who was wiser in these matters than younger women, put an ear to her daughter's belly and said the time would be very soon. Those were the words that Rose had been waiting for.

With her barren sister and her daughter helping her, she went to the hills to gather wood. For most of two days they labored at this task, adding stick by stick to their pile until the old woman said they had enough. Preparations for birth, like those for pregnancy, had not been fixed in inflexible ritual but were determined largely by the imagination and the impulses of those who participated. Such preparations had to take place under the light of the Moon Woman because she was the giver of life; and there had to be a huge fire outside the hut so that the Moon Woman could clearly see in its light what her people did. There was dancing. Though the dancing was a part of the ritual, it was chiefly an expression of joy.

When the pile of wood was ready, the women fetched water in skin pouches and clay vessels; and the grandmother meanwhile searched her knowledge of things to choose the night. Above all else, the Moon Woman should be calm and happy, with no signs anywhere of distress or anger, and there should be little or no wind. It would also be better if the Moon Woman had renewed herself and was slender and young.

And so the grandmother waited until the Woman changed from age to youth, and then told her daughter that the time was right. Before dusk, the women gathered armfuls of dead grass and stuffed it under the pile of wood; they set the vessels of water safely by trees; and then they waited for the Moon Woman to come in sight.

She was a long while in coming, and though for Rose this seemed to be an omen of misfortune, her mother was unperturbed. After all, the Moon Woman had a lot of people to watch and care for, and sometimes she was delayed. Or perhaps she was out of sight somewhere, making rain and refreshing herself. Or possibly she had hidden to peer out at them to see if the wood was abundant, the vessels filled with water, and everything ready. Whatever the reason, the grandmother knew, after waiting two or three hours in darkness, that the Moon Woman would come, and so, sitting by the hut, a picture of ageless patience and wisdom, she calmly waited, now and then glancing up at the sky.

Feeling more and more apprehensive, Rose went over to her, and at last she asked:

"Will she come?"

"Yes."

"Tonight?"

"Yes."

Raven was sitting by his tree, watching and waiting. In the darkness he could barely see the women and he was too far from them to hear what was said. He had never seen preparations for birth, or at least none that he remembered. When the girl was born to Rose he had been only a boy and had had no interest in such things. Three or four years after that she had given birth to another child but it had been born dead. He did not remember it. Now he was curious and excited. He was thinking of the Moon Woman and looking up at the sky—because it was easier to keep her in mind and think about her if you looked at her home.

In some mysterious way she gave babies to women;

254

and he was thinking now, as he had reflected many times before, that she denied babies to some of them. That fact troubled him. He wondered why she chose some and ignored others; and again, as before, he decided that women were favored or not favored because of the way they behaved. But what had the barren one done to offend the Moon Woman? That was a riddle. So far as he could see, she was as worthy as any other to have a child. Thinking of the matter with all the intelligence he had, he again came close to a concept of sin, but now, as formerly, the notion eluded him and was only a persistent and baffling intimation among his confused and amorphous thoughts. Try as he might, he could think of nothing the barren one had done to offend the Moon Woman. If he had known of something, he might have associated a fact with a conjecture and come to the notion that this woman was guilty.

While Raven struggled with his baffling problem, the grandmother thought an intuitive impulse from her unconscious mind was a conclusion she had deliberately arrived at. Because the night was very dark, she thought a fire ought to be made so that the Moon Woman could tell where they were. She was not aware that she had seen a very faint suggestion of light in the far sky. Entering the hut, she came out with a blazing fagot and ran to the pile of wood.

Again, as in so many former times, she astonished the others with her knowledge of matters inscrutable to them. Soon after the fire became a room of light, the Moon Woman came out of hiding, a slender and radiant girl peeking above the treetops. Raven was so impressed that he went over to the old woman.

"Look!" he cried, and pointed.

The grandmother shrugged. She was secretly pleased by his astonishment but she pretended to be bored. She had known all the while that the Moon Woman was there, hiding and waiting for a light.

"Look!" cried Raven again.

"She can see us now," said the old woman.

As if this miracle needed explaining, Raven turned to the other women. "She can see us now!" he told them.

He had always supposed that the Moon Woman could see in pitch dark. Realizing now that he had been mistaken, he looked at the grandmother, wondering how she knew all these things.

"Can she hear us?" he asked.

She hesitated in the annoying way she had and then said gravely, "Yes."

Raven considered that. If the Moon Woman could hear what was said, then perhaps she had heard him urging ghosts to enter the old woman. He wondered if she also knew what a person was thinking. He asked the grandmother if that was so; and when, after a long moment, as if she were consulting an invisible oracle, she said yes, it was so, Raven was dismayed. If a man had no privacy, even in his thoughts, then the hazards of life were greater than he had suspected. Staring up at the Moon Woman, he wondered what she thought about him.

When the pile of wood became a great light, Rose began to dance. Because of her huge belly she looked grotesquely awkward, but she was nimble on her feet and she was graceful in the movement of her head and arms. Dancing close by the fire so that she could be clearly seen, she would take several quick steps toward the Moon Woman and then pause and bring herself tiptoe to her fullest height and make a kind of embracing and fondling gesture with her arms. In this moment she would lift her face to the Woman's light and kindness and whisper words which only the Woman could hear. She was asking for a child that would be healthy and strong. After another series of dance steps, she would repeat the supplication, asking this time for an abundance of milk. Having danced along one side of the fire, she would cross to the other side and repeat her gestures, seeking to keep herself in brilliant light all the while.

The others stood back and watched her. Now and then one of them would look at the grandmother's face to read there the measure of success or failure. If the old woman's face smiled, they watched the dancing with rapt interest, but if she scowled they felt apprehensive.

The few dance steps and the supplication Rose had learned by observing other pregnant women in times past. Some women did no more than they had seen others do; but some, of livelier fancy, improvised, especially after they had become emotionally entranced. Rose was an imaginative woman. Suddenly she walked away, clear beyond the firelight; and when the others glanced at the grandmother's face they saw that she was alarmed. She was on the point of crying out, because darkness, in such a time as this, was not good for a pregnant woman; but before she could speak, Rose came dancing gaily toward the fire, extending her arms in a beseeching gesture. Realizing then that her daughter was coming in from darkness to attract attention to herself, to be sure that the Moon Woman would see her, the grandmother relaxed and smiled. She knew a smart woman when she saw one, and she perceived now that Rose was no fool. On glancing up, she was sure that the Moon Woman had seen the gesture and approved. Clucking with satisfaction, she folded her arms and waited to see what else her extraordinary daughter would do.

Several times Rose went off into darkness and then danced swiftly toward the fire; but before withdrawing again to the gloom, she would dance back and forth by the fire and whisper her requests. Her face was so enraptured that it shone like the one above her. Her eyes danced like the dancing fire. After studying the Moon Woman's face, the grandmother knew that she was watching Rose, and she felt deeply happy. This would be a strong child.

For perhaps half an hour Rose danced; whereupon, like a girl looking with complete faith at her mother, she gazed at the Moon Woman. Then she smiled at her. The grandmother pointed to the Moon Woman and said, "Look, she smiles."

The other women saw clearly that the Moon Woman was smiling, but Raven was dubious. He was something of a skeptic at heart. He saw that the Woman was calm and untroubled, and that she had risen above the trees for a better view; but on the slender curve of face that was visible, he could see no smile.

"She smiles!" Barren said.

And the girl cried, "Look, she smiles!"

"She is pleased," said the old woman.

Raven turned a solemn and searching stare on the faces around him. He looked up at the Moon Woman and was still unconvinced.

Rose went over and picked up a pouch of water and dipped her fingers in it; now while she danced she flung bright drops of rain above her. She danced at a little distance from the fire. For reasons mysterious even to the grandmother, a fire did not like the fertilizing rain but hissed with suffering protest and sometimes died when rain fell on it. And so Rose danced many feet away, taking a few quick steps and then pausing; and while looking at the face watching her, she would toss water above her head. When the pouch was emptied she picked up another and danced and sprinkled herself until all the water was gone.

She now began the third part of the ritual. Entering the hut, she returned with a large wolfskin, and this she spread on the ground, with the fur side up, a few feet from the fire. Then she lay on her back on the skin and took the position of giving birth. Because the grandmother acted as midwife in child-giving, she went over and sat by Rose. The girl went, too, and after some moments of indecision, the barren one followed her. When she saw the barren woman standing close by, the grandmother leapt up with an angry howl and rushed at her, beating at her with both hands.

"Go away!" she screamed, and her barren daughter turned and fled.

The sick and the barren were not allowed to stand near a woman when she was preparing for birth. Their presence was offensive. If the grandmother had not driven the lonely and childless one away, the Moon Woman would have been so outraged that she might have gone off to hide, or she might have killed the child before it was born.

Peering into the darkness, the old woman shouted, "Go far away!"

Barren felt so degraded and shut out that she went over

and sat by Raven, and when his gaze met hers, he misunderstood the hunger and loneliness in her eyes. Thinking she was receptive, he made a move to embrace her, and the barren one cried with disgust and struck him.

"Be quiet!" she said.

"Why?" he asked.

"Look!" said Barren, and pointed to the sky.

"Why?" he asked again.

"She is watching."

"We will hide," Raven said.

"She sees us."

"There," he said, and pointed to a thicket.

"Be quiet."

It had been a long time since he had embraced this woman. He thought her coming over to him meant that she was friendly and willing. "We will hide," he persisted. He had always hidden when embracing a woman.

"Look," she said, and pointed to the group.

Raven glanced at those by the fire, but hunger was stronger in him than curiosity; and while Barren stared out of darkness at the woman, with her body yearning toward the child, Raven looked boldly at her.

Rose was now simulating the pains of birth. Her body had become tense and twitching. She was moaning. The grandmother watched the Moon Woman, seeking in her calm face some sign that she understood. The purpose now was to convince her that a child would be born soon, and to solicit her protection and guidance. The dancing had told her a story of youth and health. The making of rain had indicated to her that this woman was fertile, that her body was an acceptable home for a baby. Now it had to be made plain to her that there was a child in this woman

260

and that it would need her personal devotion if it was to be born alive and well.

To assist in all this, the grandmother sat back from the fire so that nothing would obstruct the Moon Woman's view. Rose had presented her swollen belly, but lest this sign might not be enough, she affected all the pains and movements of birth-giving. Her eyes were closed, and her extended hands were clenched. Her legs were spread far apart. And in her body were convulsive movements of the kind a woman made to force a child out.

She persisted for several minutes; whereupon, pausing to rest, she opened her eyes and asked softly:

"Does she see?"

The grandmother was not sure. Because she was half blind, she did not read the face above her as unerringly as she used to. Besides, she had been waiting for some intuitive hint. In all such matters as this, she was guided by intuition rather than by her senses.

"Make more birth," she said, and Rose resumed the struggle. The grandmother stared intently at the high and inscrutable face. At last, for a reason she never could have defined, but which nevertheless for her was certain, she perceived that the Moon Woman understood. "Now she sees you!" she cried happily, and Rose rested in her labors.

In a little while the three women left the fire, which had sunk to a bed of embers, and entered the hut. The night was quite dark now. Raven had hoped the barren one would remain with him and be persuaded to enter the thicket, but she left him hastily, as if afraid, and ran to the house. Then he was alone. Feeling unhappy, he looked over at the glowing embers or up at the Moon Woman.

In the wonder of birth there was no place for a man.

261

In the miracle of creation he was a useless spectator, an outcast, a starved and frustrated creature who was driven by his own restless hunger to try to build a creative life. He could carve images on staghorn handles or draw them on tablets of stone. He could turn in loneliness to ideas, to reverie, to philosophy, and in a later time he would turn to tyranny and enslavement and murder. He would turn to organized war and strive to make himself supreme within his artificial kingdoms.

But in the time when Raven lived, he could only sit as Raven sat now, baffled and resentful, and strive to understand his place in life. He could hatch vengeful plots and designs. In such ways as he had, he could try to alter his environment and so find in it a fuller image of himself and a deeper sense of his own meaning. A woman's way was the way of birth and peace; but a man's way, by an inexorable design not of his own making, was the way of war and plunder, of tyrannical usurpations, of compensatory metaphysical systems and ideologies, and of the ingenious imitations of creation and growth that were to become known as art.

21

Knowing that the child would come soon, the grandmother was worried by the presence of two persons, a sick
one and a barren one, both of whom were a menace. She
wanted them to go away. Sterility and sickness were enemies of life. They were offensive to the Moon Woman.
Sickness was offensive to her because she had overcome
age; she had learned how to renew her youth and make
herself eternal. Sterility was no less offensive because she
was the giver of new life. To suffer the presence of such
women during a time of birth was to invite disaster; it
was hard to tell what the Moon Woman might do. She
might not appear at all, or she might be so outraged that
she would shout at her people in a voice of thunder and
hurl the lightning of her wrath across the world. Or to
show her utter disgust she might send a dead child. She
had done so once before, and the grandmother remembered the wild night in which that dead child had been
born.

But the sick one was too feeble to go away, even if she

263

could have been persuaded to do so. So many ghosts had housed themselves in her that she was like a corpse possessed by an invisible and parasitic life. For days she had not left her bed. Hoping that she would be able to rise and walk, the grandmother went over and knelt by her; and she was appalled by the woman's condition. The poor sick creature was barely able to speak. Her groin did not seem to be more swollen, but her face was bloodless and her eyes were sunken.

Deciding to place her bed at some distance from the hut and have her carried to it, the grandmother rolled her over and off the skins and took these to a thicket and made a bed there. Then she asked Raven and the girl to carry the woman away; they did so, one grasping her hands and the other her feet. In the jungle the sick one would be hidden. By her bed the grandmother set a pouch of water, and once a day she intended to take the woman some food.

After she had been laid on the bed the sick woman tried to sit up and look round her. She was frightened but she was too weak to protest. Like one who had been laid out for burial, with an open grave within plain sight, she shuddered and lay back. Slowly her eyelids closed.

The grandmother went next to her barren daughter and looked at her with eyes in which there was no compassion or friendliness. She said:

"You go away."

"No," she said.

"Baby will come soon. You go away."

Barren stared at the old woman. For many weeks she had looked forward to the coming of this child. She had hoped that she would be allowed to touch it, to hold it, and perhaps even to nurse it. Empty and starved and lonely, she had been waiting for it. She knew, as a matter of bitter truth, that her presence was not good for a baby, but emotionally she did not feel that way at all. Looking steadily at her mother's unpitying eyes, she said stubbornly:

"I will not go away."

"You must go away."

"No!"

Mother and daughter looked at one another and in neither was there any sign of yielding.

Raven had been watching them and had heard what was said. His sly mind perceived an opportunity. If the younger woman would go hunting with him. . . .

"Go with me," he said.

His sister looked at him scornfully. "Be quiet!"

"We will find food."

"No."

"We will eat fruit."

The sister was cunning too. She guessed what was in his mind—she had only to look at his eyes to know what the rascal was plotting; besides, she recognized this as a move to get rid of her. They wanted her to be far away when the child was born so that she could not touch it, or even see it. She backed off, looking in turn from the old woman to the man, and distrusting both of them.

Raven ran to get his weapons; and then, as if she were an animal to be coaxed, as well as a stupid thing that needed pantomime to make it understand, he dashed away from her, looking back and pointing. He set an arrow to his bow and made a gesture of shooting. He threatened imaginary foes with his lance.

"Come!" he cried.

His sister looked at him, and the disgust in her face was softened a little by amusement. He was a fool to think she could be tricked so easily. From the beginning she had understood his purpose, but the absurd fellow pretended that he had nothing but hunting in mind. He was pretending to be chasing the bushbuck or shooting birds. Now and then he beckoned and asked her to come. She was so disgusted by his feeble deception that she refused to answer.

"Go find food," the grandmother said.

"No."

She had no word for please, but even if she had had such a word, it was not her way to coax. She was one who gave commands. But now, looking at this self-willed woman, she knew that commands would be futile. Threats, too, might do no good, but she would try one. Pointing to the great blue home of the Moon Woman, she said:

"She will be offended."

Barren looked at the sky but she saw nothing there of which to be afraid. Anyway, the Moon Woman had never given her a child, and there could be no unfriendliness worse than that.

"She will kill you," the old woman said, speaking as a seeress able to look into the future.

Hearing those words, pronounced as a solemn judgment, the woman faltered and looked away. She glanced at Raven, and at once he renewed his entreaties. Recognizing that she was about to yield, he hastened over and grasped her arm. Before she could shake his hand off, the grandmother, looking like a remorseless avenger, thrust a withered finger at her daughter and spoke again.

"Go away!" she said.

266

Raven tugged at the woman's arm. Caught helplessly between hunger and fear, she allowed him to lead her toward the hills.

The moment they were out of sight, the grandmother decided to hasten the birth and get it over with. She went to Rose and asked, "Are you ready?" That was not a strange question. Birth for these people was not a matter wholly determined by physiological processes. It occurred in moments chosen by the Moon Woman, with the grandmothers assisting as midwives. As for the Moon Woman, she was not in sight, but the grandmother knew she was hiding and watching. She could have told what part of the sky she was in; if urged a little, she could have pointed to the tree behind which she was hiding. She knew that the hour for the birth had come.

Entering the hut, she returned with several skins and laid them in full view where the Moon Woman could see. Then Rose lay on the skins, and her mother knelt by her. After feeling over the belly, the old woman lowered an ear to listen. Gently she began to massage, using both hands and rubbing downward.

Raven meanwhile was trembling with joy. Imaginative and somewhat introverted men of his time, and in all the centuries since, have found deep egoistic fulfillment in sexual conquests. They have been more ravished by conquests that were difficult, and so have preferred the sly contriving which, in recent times, and in certain parts of the world, has become known as romance. In his own way Raven was quite an artful and cunning wooer, and because, in this instance, the measure of his success was unpredictable, the prospect was all the more tantalizing.

The woman at his side was sullen and unresponsive, and

so obsessed by thoughts of the child that she was hardly aware of him; but she was allowing herself to be led, and that in itself was a marvelous triumph for him. He was a crafty rascal and he took extreme pains not to alarm or enrage her. His fingers grasping her arm were gentle, and his covetous gaze was so furtive that she would not have sensed it, even if she had been less preoccupied. He was leading her across the rolling hills that lay between their home and the river, and he allowed her to take the path, such as it was, to protect her feet from sticks and thorns, while he waded through the grass and shrubs that bordered it.

From time to time he glanced to the right or left, looking for an inviting thicket and hoping she could be prevailed on to enter it. She went so meekly that he was sure she would be receptive; and when after a few minutes he sensed in her no reluctance or protest, he became convinced that she knew the purpose in his mind. Then he became a little bolder. Taking her arm firmly, he led her off the path and toward a jungle of large trees and flowering plants, but he let her walk slowly and pick her way, because the soles of her feet were not so tough as his own. If he felt her flinch or hesitate, he would pause for a moment and then gently urge her forward.

And so they came to the grove and entered it. On looking round her and seeing an extravagant richness of summer bloom, she gave a cry of pleasure and ran to a great hanging wall of pink and lavender. When Raven perceived that she intended to strip off an armful of the blossoms, he acted with extraordinary insight. Instead of showing impatience and trying to hasten her surrender, he helped her pluck flowers and chose only the largest

268

and most attractive ones. When he took an armful of bloom to her he saw that she was pleased, and at once he hastened away to find other flowers of a different color and fragrance. His face was touched by artful cunning. He was behaving, indeed, much like the romantic lover of a later time.

Obedient to her whims, he helped her gather so many flowers that when at last she sat to hug them to her she was almost lost in their glory. She laid them across her hair; she filled her lap; with both arms she hugged them to her breast and buried her face in their delicious wonder; and Raven, a little impatient now, sat on his heels and watched her.

"You want more flowers?" he asked.

She said yes, and he dashed away to strip another armful, and when he let the flowers fall on her, he heard her gasp with delight. He did not know that for her flowers and fragrance were symbols of life, or that, like rain, they helped a woman to become fertile. He did not know that an abundance of such symbols made a woman more receptive to the man's approach. Watching her luxuriate in her huge sweet-smelling bed, he felt baffled because now she seemed to be lost to him. Not knowing what else to do, he went away and gathered more bloom and piled it on her until she cried with joy and seemed to be more flower than woman.

Looking round him a little desperately, he wondered what else he could do to please her. He could think of nothing else, and so, looking owlishly bewildered, he stared at her while she crushed the blossoms to her face and breast, trying to draw into herself all the fertility and sweet smells of life. In her fragrant bed she turned sensuously, as if bathing herself, as if rubbing the essence of the flowers into her skin. That in a way is what she was doing. For her the experience was a delighted preparing of herself so that she could have a child; but also, because she was a healthy woman, the fragrance was exciting. A sweet hunger flooded her senses.

When at last she looked up at Raven, her eyes soft with happiness, she smiled at him, and Raven, reading the meaning in her eyes and face, gave a low cry that was like a sudden spilling of his waiting hunger. Quickly he dropped to hands and knees and reached out to embrace her. She did not resist. Drenched with the bloom and with her senses swimming, she turned gently under the pressure of his hands.

22

THE grandmother, acting as midwife, asked Rose to lie on her stomach, and she then massaged her firmly across the small of her back. And after a few minutes she said, "Turn over," and then massaged her abdomen, placing her hands high and moving them downward. She labored earnestly, in turn massaging back and belly, now and then looking at her daughter's face for a sign that birth pains were beginning. Each time she renewed the massaging of the abdomen she pressed more firmly, compressing the swelling with strong thumbs and fingers or resting a part of her weight on the moving heels of her hands.

When at last Rose gave a low cry and distorted her face, the old woman rested in her labor and waited. She looked round her to be sure that neither the sick one nor the barren one was spying. Then she fetched a jug of water and stood by Rose and sprinkled her with rain; and after the first labor pains ceased, she knelt again to massage her.

After a long while of convulsive effort, Rose delivered a baby. It was born dead, but the grandmother did not know it was dead. She took the wet and lifeless thing in her hands and studied it for signs of life and, seeing none, she laid it across her lap, belly downward, and massaged its back and slapped it gently. Exhausted, and with her eyes closed, the mother lay still. Clutching the baby under its arms, the grandmother held it up and looked at its face. Convinced that it was not breathing, she gave a cry of alarm and shook it and bounced it up and down.

Hearing the cry, Rose sat up. "Is it dead?" she asked, horrified.

"No," said the old woman, still bouncing the child.

"Does it breathe?"

"No."

With a cry of anguish Rose seized her child and for one swift moment hugged it to her. In the next moment she put her mouth to its mouth and tried to force air into its lungs. She would draw a full breath and then, her hands clasping the infant's cheeks and her mouth sealed to its mouth, she would exhale slowly, trying to drive her own life into the child. After three or four efforts, she not only strove to breathe in but also to suck breath out; and the grandmother meanwhile clasped the baby's chest, and when Rose tried to suck breath out, her mother would press in against the tiny ribs or against the stomach. In this manner they worked frantically for several minutes. Despairing at last, Rose abandoned her effort and began to sob, but the grandmother still struggled to make the infant breathe. She took it from the mother's hands and jounced it and slapped its back and, after failing in this, she put her mouth to its mouth and breathed into it.

Rose did not know that there was another child in her, waiting for birth. When she felt a renewal of the pangs

272

she yielded to them, not to eject a second baby, but in a desperate resolve to bring the dead one to life. This she hoped to do by continuing with the pains of birth, because for her, and for all the other women of her time, these were symbolic as well as real. They were a symbol of renewal and preservation. They were a form of magic. In the anguish and despair of the moment, she felt that in some way she had not completed the birth, that if she could resume the pangs and the convulsive movements, the child would begin to breathe.

And so she lay back and shut her eyes and encouraged the pain in her body, striving not to ease it but to increase it. Her suffering was so severe that she began to moan. Laying the child aside, the grandmother moved over to assist, though she did not know that her daughter was trying with symbolic pain to bring the dead child to life. Less distraught, and with her eyes open and alert, she sensed that another baby was coming; and when it came, announcing its birth with a lusty squall, the grandmother quickly severed the cord and held the child up, her wrinkled face alive with joy. Rose heard the cry and thought that the dead baby had returned to life. Too spent to open her eyes or move, she lay on her back with a deep warm happiness possessing her. Like one sunk in the memory of pain but slowly emerging from it to a realization of inexpressible joy, she listened to the babe's crying and thought of the wonderful thing she had been able to do.

When at last she opened eyes that were still dark with pain and memory, the old woman held up the child for its mother to see; and the mother smiled. She saw that her baby was puckering its face. It was breathing. It was alive.

273

She reached out to it with hungry hands and clasped it to her breast. While she held it and lay as quietly as a dead woman, the grandmother took the placenta of each child and carried them into the hut. These she would dry and preserve. They were precious because they were made of the same blood as the babies. She did not think of them as good luck amulets; they were simply a mysterious and wonderful thing, like menstrual blood, and were not to be wasted or thrown away. After hiding them between two skins, she returned to her daughter's bed.

Rose now felt strong enough to sit up. When she did so and saw the dead infant lying a few feet away, she uttered a terrible scream. With eyes wide and horrified, she stared at it and then screamed again.

"Look!" she cried, and pointed.

"It is dead," said the old woman. She did not speak calmly. She had been wondering why, in spite of all her knowledge and magic, one of the babies had been born dead.

"Is it mine?" asked Rose incredulously.

"Yes."

"Two babies?"

"Yes."

"Is it dead?"

"Yes."

"Ahhh!" cried Rose out of bitter grief.

"See," said the grandmother, and touched the miracle of the living child.

The mother looked at the living one, but after a moment she turned to gaze at the dead one; and while she looked her eyes filled with tears. Handing the live child to her mother, she moved over to clasp the dead one.

"Mine!" she cried, and murmured over it and again breathed into its mouth.

The old woman was gazing at the sky and wondering why a dead baby had been sent to her home. Her wrinkled and sallow face was strange to look at. There was no arrogance in it now, no hint of an imperious will; but neither was it a humble face. It was querulous and resentful and baffled. It was the face of an old seeress who seemed to feel that she had been tricked but who was not rash enough to suspect the Moon Woman of deceit. It was a face turned to the sky and asking questions. Neither expecting nor finding answers there, she laid the living child on her lap and searched it to learn if it was all right. She examined its hands and feet and limbs closely; she explored its whole body for signs of disease. Finding it healthy and vigorous, she was all the more baffled—because it was indeed strange that there should come from the same mother a child that was perfect and another that was dead. Perplexed and wholly at a loss for an answer to such a riddle, she again looked at the sky, her eyes winking thoughtfully. She knew that the others would ask her why such a dreadful thing had happened and she was searching her mind for an answer.

When it came, the answer was not hers, but she pretended that she had known it all the while. It seemed to her that she had. After all, as the maker of magic, as the only one in her family who had knowledge of many mysterious things, she could not possibly have placed any faith in the divining powers of her son.

After Raven came home, flushed by his triumph, and learned that a baby had been born dead, he intuitively sensed the reason. Thereupon, behaving like one who knew the answers to all things, he took the grandmother aside and told her he knew why the child was dead. His presumption outraged her, but she was forced to listen because his hands clutched and held her. He pointed an accusing finger at the thicket. He said it was the sick woman. There was a malicious ghost in her, he said, and in some dark night the ghost had left her and entered the pregnant woman. He said he had heard the ghost many times and had known it was up to mischief. Twice he had seen it in the form of a snake, crawling from bed to bed.

After hearing his story, it seemed to the old woman that she had known this for a long time. It was presumptuous of him to try to enlighten her in matters that were her own special province. Did the foolish man imagine that he could tell her anything about the ways of ghosts, or why babies were born dead, or in what ways a sick woman could harm a pregnant one! Annoyed by his whispering and his pretensions, she shook his clutch off her arm and pushed him away.

"You know nothing!" she cried.

"Look—" he began eagerly.

"Old woman know!"

"I know," he said.

Her face was so contemptuous that he felt angry. He wanted to explain to her that he had thought about these matters, that some persons were singled out for special punishment, but he had no words to express a notion of sin. He made emphatic gestures, beseeching her to understand that the sick one had offended the Moon Woman with her foolish and blundering behavior, and, again grasp-

276

ing the grandmother's arm, he strove to lead her into the thicket, there to face the sick woman and accuse her. But his hand was struck off. Because he was only an intolerable pretender, he was dismissed. It was his task to hunt. About hunting and the ways of wild beasts he knew a few things; but he was a fool to pretend to knowledge of birth and sickness and all other matters that were the special province of old and wise women.

"Go away!" she cried, infuriated by his arrogance.

"No," he said.

"Go find food! Go now!"

At once she forgot that he had told her anything. What he had told her had been a part of her own wisdom all the while; of course, she had known that the presence of the sick woman, and of the barren woman, too, had been bad for Rose. She ought to have driven them away. Some grandmothers did drive away such persons during a time of pregnancy, but this old woman, for all her tyrannies, was gentler than many who ruled families. Besides, she was half blind and by no means so alert as she had once been.

Appalled by the fact that another dead child had been born in her family, she resolved to discover and remove the malicious cause. This she must do at once because the girl was now pregnant, and her child might also be born dead if the destroying presence were not found and driven away.

After dismissing Raven she entered the thicket and knelt by her sick daughter. With rough hands she shook her and asked if she was awake. The woman stirred and opened her eyes.

"Dead baby out there!" said the old woman accusingly,

277

and leaned forward to peer at the sick face. She was studying it for a sign of guilt. The sick woman's eyes flickered
and then, as if very tired, they closed; and the grandmother, baffled and uncertain, arose to her feet. She looked
at the woman's swollen groin and realized that the ghost
was in her. She remembered that during dark nights it
had come out and crawled from bed to bed in the form
of a snake.

In times past she had tried all the magic she knew on
this woman but had not been able to frighten this ghost
away. She had massaged her; she had fed her a magical
broth of herbs and blood and the uterus of a rabbit; and
she had danced round and round her and made menacing
sounds. Now, staring at her, and feeling almost at the end
of her wits and her magic, she thought of one thing she
had never done. Some wise women among her people
operated in such extreme cases. If a ghost could not be
driven out by any other means, they cut the body open
so that they could get at the spirit, quite as a man, out
hunting, would dig into a burrow to force a creature to
the surface. This old woman had never employed surgery.
Just the same, she could if she must, and she had surgery
in mind while she looked at her sick daughter and considered the problem.

But other matters had to be taken care of first. There
was a baby to bury, and placentas to dry over the fire and
then wrap securely in a piece of skin. There was food to
be found for a hungry mother who was nursing a child.

Of these tasks the burial was the most urgent. The dead
baby must not be left above ground during the night or a
malicious ghost would spy it out and creep into it; and
so she left the thicket and called to the girl, and the two

278

women took the baby and the digging tools and went away over the hills.

All this while, the barren woman had been hiding and peering out. Only Raven knew where she was. Only Raven cared. When Barren saw the grandmother go away, she came out of hiding and went softly and quickly to the hut. Looking inside, she saw the mother there, holding her child. Rose had nursed the babe and was now rocking it, swaying gently back and forth while hugging it to her breast. The sight of this baby aroused in the childless sister such longing that she began to tremble; and though she knew very well that she would not be allowed to touch it or even to sit near it, she went inside, moving as noiselessly as a shadow. The moment she entered the doorway she darkened the room and Rose looked up. The woman she saw was her own sister but she did not think of her as a sister. She thought of her as something malicious and dangerous.

"Go away!" she cried.

Barren did not go away. She quietly advanced, determined to look at the baby, and when Rose recoiled as if from something repulsive and made a move to cover the infant with a skin, Barren continued to advance. If Rose had looked at her sister's eyes, she would have seen in them such yearning as she had never seen in eyes before. There was the same hunger in the woman's empty arms, in her taut throat, in the open hush of her mouth.

"Go away!" said Rose, speaking in a frenzied whisper.

Barren stretched her arms to the child. "Let me hold baby!" she said.

"No!"

Barren swallowed as if choked. She did not look at the

279

mother. Her eyes were fixed on the child, as if she had no power to take her gaze away. And in a hoarse and desperate voice she said again:

"Let me hold baby!"

Thoroughly alarmed, Rose struggled to her feet and backed away, clutching her child with such fierce possessiveness that it began to cry. She withdrew to a wall, and then, like one who expected to be attacked, she moved toward the open door. The barren one did not follow her. She watched the mother reach the doorway and vanish outside, and only then did her empty and outstretched arms relax.

During those few minutes she had been a starved woman, obsessed by a wish to touch a baby, but now, when she looked round her, she was deliberate and cunning. She was cunning, but she was still a woman driven by a will stronger than her own. She thought of the placentas and she suspected that they were hidden somewhere in the hut; and now, moving quickly, but noiselessly as a practiced thief, she dropped to hands and knees and began to search. She came to one bed after another and lifted the skins and shook them. In her mind was the thought that if she ate the placentas she would become fertile and have a child of her own; and so, never pausing, save now and then to glance at the doorway, she searched swiftly until she found them.

But now cunning failed her; instead of slipping outside with them and into hiding where she would have been safe, she began to eat like a ravenous she-beast, biting off pieces of the membrane and swallowing without pausing to chew. Knowing that the grandmother would return soon, she was pressed for time. She engorged like a glutton but she was not eating food; she was devouring the precious fertility of which some women had so much and some had none.

She was still gulping and choking when the old woman's stooped form darkened the doorway. Rose had told her of Barren's unreasonable behavior, and she was now peering in to see what the woman was doing. The moment Barren saw her she gasped and felt stricken. Her mouth was full, and her hands clutched the small portion that remained. She tried to swallow, but fear constricted her throat, and so she sat, like a guilty thief, and looked at the old woman, and the old woman looked at her.

Perceiving that this daughter was up to mischief, the grandmother entered the hut and slowly crossed the floor like an avenger; but when she saw what the woman was doing, she did not scream with rage as Barren had expected her to. For one thing, she was too astonished to utter a sound; but even stronger than amazement was the feeling that this woman knew what she was doing, and was doing it for a good purpose. Though the grandmother had never known a woman who ate the afterbirth, and had never thought of doing so herself, she was not horrified or angered.

It was as if she was again face to face with an eternal truth which somehow she had overlooked during her busy lifetime. After all, in an effort to become fertile, women did eat many things. To eat the very substance of a mother in which a young life had been clothed seemed to her a very sensible thing to do; and if for a moment she did not speak, that was because she was amazed to find this woman gifted with such insight.

When there was no outcry, nor even any rebuke,

Barren relaxed and swallowed the mouthful; and then she looked in turn at the portion in her hands and up at the old woman, wondering whether to swallow it or lay it aside.

In a gentle voice the grandmother asked, "You swallow it?"

"Yes!" said Barren, and gasped with relief.

The grandmother bent over to peer at the uneaten portion. Pointing, she said, "Swallow it."

"Yes," said Barren eagerly. With strong teeth she tore off a morsel and swallowed it. Then she hesitated and looked up, wondering if the old woman really approved or was plotting some mischief.

"Swallow it."

Barren gulped one piece after another until it was all gone. She licked her hands and waited anxiously, still afraid that the old woman would strike her. But the grandmother said:

"Come outside."

She left the hut and the bewildered daughter followed her. Though she behaved with extraordinary calm, the old woman felt very sly and secretive. She was unwilling to have any member of her family think that she was not wiser than all of them put together, but she was at a loss to know how to claim credit for so remarkable a piece of wisdom. And so, being at a loss, she acted mysteriously, having learned with cunning ripened by long practice, that she could enhance her prestige with baffling behavior.

She slowly walked across the yard and looked up at the sky. Dusk had come, and soon the Moon Woman would be visible. She needed her presence. Though she gave no sign of it, she felt deeply anxious, not knowing

282

if the Moon Woman would approve; but after reflecting on the matter she had little doubt of it. The Moon Woman wanted babies above all things, and she would be pleased to know that the placentas had been hidden where the childless one had found them. Having seen her way through that part of it, she felt more at ease; and while the members of her family watched her, baffled and waiting, she walked back and forth in the dusk, her head bowed, her gestures mysteriously deliberate. With calculated purpose she was acting like one who was consulting invisible meanings. That, indeed, is what she was doing in her own way. In her unconscious mind the experience was being shaped and revised and made reasonable; it was becoming a part of the lore and wisdom that all old women possessed. But though she moved like one sunk in thought, she was alert and sly and, the moment the Moon Woman came in sight, she knew it. One quick glance told her that the childless one was approved.

Turning, she faced the members of her family and slowly approached them. Her gaze was fixed on the barren one. She went up to her and for a long moment looked in her eyes; whereupon, in the voice of one who divined all things, she said:

"You will have child."

Barren gave a gasp of amazement and delight. Wondering if she could have misunderstood, or if the remark had been addressed to another, she looked in turn at all the faces and then, in a voice trembling on the brink of a cry, she asked:

"I will have child?"

In the grandmother's face there was a flicker of annoyance.

"You will have child," she said.

"Ahhh!"

Now the grandmother reached out and touched the childless woman's belly, and in the voice of one who knew all things, she said:

"Child is there."

"Now?" gasped Barren.

"Yes."

With a face as radiant as the Moon Woman's above, Barren turned to her sister and looked at the baby.

"Can I touch it?" she asked.

"Yes," the grandmother said.

Gently Barren touched the child. The touch burst the dam that held back the flood of her hunger, and with her face like a thing of light she cried:

"Can I hold it?"

The grandmother's face softened and she smiled. "Yes," she said.

Rose proffered the baby, and her sister took it and hugged it to her breast. Then, as if the glory of the moment were insupportable, she sank to the earth and bowed over the infant as if to absorb it into the substance of her being. The others could hear her talking to it in a voice that was full of tears.

23

For all the women, save the one who was too ill to care, the task now was to preserve and protect the baby. Though it was a healthy child, none of them could forget that its twin had been born dead, and therefore they felt that the living one needed special care.

For a newborn child there were always many things to be done. The first of these was to hold it up to the Moon Woman so that she could shed her smile of approval on it and communicate to it a sense of her own marvelous health and youth. This was the grandmother's privilege, because there existed a more intimate understanding between her and the Moon Woman.

Taking the babe, with one hand under its shoulders and the other under its knees, she held it up to expose it; and then, instead of standing in the yard, where all growing things had been trampled into dust, she went to the garden in which the barley and corn stood tall and strong, with filling heads. Her two daughters and the girl followed her. Raven went over and sat by his tree to watch them. Old Man turned wearily to seek his bed.

Standing in the garden, the grandmother held the babe up to the radiance of the Moon Woman. She uttered no sound, but her lips were moving. She was asking the giver of children, the mother of all people, to smile on this infant and fill it with health and strength and fertility. If it had been a boy, she would not have asked for fertility, but only for strength and health. She asked her to protect it from ghosts and all other malicious things; to make it grow into a vigorous woman, with menstrual blood for the making of babies and full breasts for nursing; and to prompt it to choose the kind of food that would be best for it. From time to time she turned it over so that every part of it would be exposed to the light.

Then she went up and down the garden rows, brushing the child gently against the barley and corn. These growing things would impart to the child a little of their vigor. When this part of the ritual was finished, she laid the babe in the arms of the girl, and now the girl walked back and forth by the rows of grain, holding it to the light and whispering to the sky. Then Barren took the infant, because she, too, was pregnant, and it was good for the child to have pregnant women touch it. The Moon Woman had moved up the sky and now looked down with a face that was gentle and approving. The grandmother knew that she was pleased. Nowhere around her in her enormous home of the night was there any sign of anger.

"She is pleased," the grandmother said, squinting up at the Moon Woman.

"She is pleased," said Rose.

"Your child will be strong!"

"My child will be strong!"

"She will be healthy."

286

"My child will be healthy!"

"She will be fertile."

"My child will be fertile!"

Over by the tree, Raven heard the chant and stared curiously at the women. If he had ever seen this rite of fertility and thanksgiving before, he did not remember it, and though he sensed its purpose there was no warm response in his being. He felt resentful and shut out. The miracle of birth was a special glory of women in which a man had no part. Raven knew very well that if he were to go away and never return, nobody here would care. The women owned the child, the fire, the home, the bedding, the garden; a man owned nothing but his hunting tools. He wanted to go over and hold the babe and brush it lightly against growing things and feel that it was also a part of his meaning, but he knew that if he went over, the old woman would scream at him. And so, listening to their rapturous chanting, he sulked and hated them.

He hated them the next morning when the four women took the child and went to a stream. Keeping out of sight, he followed them and spied on what they did. The grandmother sat in shallow water and held the babe, and the other three sprinkled it with rain. Cupping their palms together, they would fill them with water and toss the water high above the old woman's head; and the water would scatter like drops of light and fall. They took turns holding the child and bathing it with the fertilizing water. Then the two pregnant women sat in falling rain that was made by the others; and at last the old woman sat on the bank and held the child, while the other three sat in water to their waists and splashed like certain birds Raven had seen. Then he saw the grandmother dipping the babe's legs into the water, and its arms, and then all of it but its head. Next, she held it up, and the other women, using their hands as shovels, made a great shower of rain above it. Raven could see the multitude of drops fall like bright leaves spinning in sunlight. For what seemed to him a long time, the women made rain or splashed in the water, crying with delight all the while, and when they turned homeward, he saw that they were smiling.

In the afternoon of this day they began to dress the child with amulets, and he understood very clearly what they were doing. He was happy and proud. The old woman might know more than he about the magic of rain and herbs and many other things; but amulets to keep ghosts away were a part of his own special knowledge. It was he, and not the women, who had contrived such cunning protection against malicious spirits, and in his opinion he knew more about such matters than all the women in the world. It was this belief, and the vain joy in his knowledge, that impelled him to unwonted boldness. He approached the women to enlighten their ignorance and to give advice.

They had fetched a lot of bright pebbles from the stream, and they were choosing the oddly shaped ones around which they could tie vines or thongs. They were unaware of Raven, who stood back a little and stared at them with philosophic eyes. He perceived at once that they were ignorant, quite as he had expected them to be; they did not understand that some stones were potent and some were not. Paying no attention to color or brightness, or to qualities even more subtle and elusive which only Raven understood, the grandmother was choosing any kind of pebble, no matter how unattractive, around which she

288

could tie a thong. Raven was amused. He felt scorn for her but he did not intend to enlighten her at once. He would let her fumble for a while and discover in her own time, with clucking and dismay, that in some matters she was very stupid and needed a man's help.

But presently his gloating was turned to chagrin. The grandmother did not remember that he had once come home, with stones in his mouth, in his nostrils, and hanging by his ears. As the one in whom, at least within this family group, all knowledge was to be found, she thought she had been the first to use amulets. Not for a moment could she have believed anything else. The most cherished thing in her life was her own prestige and the awe in which she was held; that was an old woman's chief meaning, in this family or in any other, and she jealously maintained that prestige with all the guile she had. When guile was not enough, her unconscious mind played tricks on her memory and so came to her rescue. She would have been incredulous if Raven had told her that he had been the first to use amulets as a protection against malicious spirits. She would have seen in him an impostor who was trying to usurp her functions.

Raven suspected nothing of all that. With sly joy he watched the old woman and looked forward to the moment when he would explain to her that some stones were no good. He savored that anticipation and waited. But at last, overcome by a wish to humiliate her, and to convince her that he also had knowledge of mysterious things, he thrust a finger at a pebble with a thong affixed and said:

"That is no good." When the grandmother ignored him, he took the rawhide string and held the stone up. "Look!" he cried. "Stone is no good."

The grandmother turned to him and their eyes met. In his eyes she saw what she took to be sly mischief; in her eyes he saw only impatience and scorn.

"Why?" she asked.

Raven saw that the other women were now listening. He was pleased. Still holding the dull and irregular pebble, he stared at it, and for a while was at a loss to explain why it would not serve as well as any other. Perceiving, then, that it was dull and unattractive, he picked up a stone that gleamed with imbedded crystals. He turned it like a jewel to show how its facets reflected the light.

"Ghosts can see this," he said.

"Ahhh!" said Rose.

"Look!" Raven cried. He went about fifty feet away and then, holding the pebble close to his ear, he turned it in the sunlight to let them see how it would sparkle and shine. Hastening back, he seized the dull pebble, ran away and held it to his ear and turned it over and over. His argument was so persuasive that anyone less set in her ways than the old woman, and less jealous of her powers, might have been convinced. Indeed, the other women were convinced; they perceived that a bright stone would be better magic than a dull one. But the grandmother clucked with disdain. It was presumption for this man, whose knowledge was confined to matters of the hunt, to advise her in that sphere where she alone was supreme. She marched over to Raven and snatched the stone from his hand.

"You do not know!" she cried.

"I know—"

"You are foolish! Go away!"

Hating her with the pain of a genius whom nobody admired, Raven went away, a sullen and vengeful man, but he was not wholly vanquished. After a few minutes he thought of something to do to make the old woman envious; he took his weapons and hastened across the hills.

The younger women were troubled because they had seen the logic in Raven's choice, but the grandmother, grunting and clucking as if her labors were oppressed by memory of a very foolish and impudent man, continued to choose pebbles to which thongs could be securely tied. After a while she understood that she could tie one long string around several stones in a series, and she did this, thereby making a necklace, which she fastened around Rose's neck. Then she made a small necklace for the child. Raven's doubt of her wisdom had driven her to do some thinking, and presently she went away to a forest and returned with an armful of the shining black strands of a fungus. Raven's emphasis on that quality in stones which made them gleam had lurked in her unconscious mind and had moved her to gather the fungus, not only because it shone with a black and polished luster, but also because she had learned in earlier experiments that it had magical properties. Of the black strands she made another necklace for the mother, as well as one for the babe, and when these were finished she made a kind of apron to hang down the mother's belly. And all the while she wondered what else she could do to protect them both from harm.

Late in the afternoon Raven returned, and even the grandmother had to admit, with a twinge of pained astonishment, that his appearance was extraordinary. Using green vines as strings, and gathering all the shining and colorful stones he could find, he had made for himself

291

several necklaces and girdles and bracelets, as well as a handsome tiara. For the tiara he had chosen the most attractive stones, all ingeniously held in a circlet by a vine; he wore this crown on his black hair, with a shining stone hanging as a pendant by either ear. Around his neck were two necklaces; there was a girdle of larger pebbles around his waist; and there was a bracelet on either arm. He was so loaded down with jewels that he walked with slow and impressive dignity; and when the younger women began to oh! and ah! at him, he pretended not to see or hear them. Like one back from the realms of magic, fully equipped against all evil and arrogantly sure of his knowledge and his power, he walked back and forth in the yard, admiring himself.

His sisters and his niece admired him, too. They came up to him, crying with delight, and gently touched the more brilliant jewels. Their gaze was candid and covetous. The grandmother pretended to be unaware of him but nevertheless she watched him, her mind troubled less by his resourcefulness than by his wanton invasion of a sphere that was very specially her own.

"No ghosts bother me," Raven said, speaking with insolent pride to the women. He gestured, with a tinkling of stones, at the earth and the sky. "Look!" he said, and touched a pendant by an ear. "Look!" he said, and called attention to pebbles hanging in a protective covey by his genitals. Like one before mirrors, he turned round and round to show off his splendor.

The women were dazzled by the brilliance of his jewels. Rose touched the more handsome necklace and said:

"I want this."

"No!" he shouted.

292

"I want this," said the girl, and pointed to a stone with a tiny basin in it full of yellow radiance.

"No!" he yelled.

Realizing that entreaties did no good, the women looked at him, their eyes bright with envy. Raven stared at the unattractive necklace that Rose was wearing. He pointed a scornful finger and said:

"That is no good. Look! See mine."

Rose was chastened and downcast. Perceiving that she was ashamed of her own dull pebbles, he mocked her triumphantly. He made it known to her that he would never wear such stones. He told her that such colorless things would never frighten a malicious ghost. He was so abusive and contemptuous that tears came to Rose's eyes, and with a gesture of disgust and self-abasement she tore the necklace from her throat. For a while she looked at the dull stones and then tossed them away.

Raven was bored. He had humbled these women. He now went over to the grandmother, who all this while had pretended to be busy with the infant. He walked round and round her, asking her to look at his splendid ornaments; and when she could no longer ignore the insolent fellow, she turned on him in blind fury. Before he could divine her intent or make any move to flee, she tore his jewels from him and flung them out to the yard.

"Go away!" she shouted, goaded beyond endurance.

Raven dashed out to recover his stones, but the women were there first; and after swiftly gathering the broken vines, each tied to its own series of jewels, they ran into the hut, mocking him with shrill cries of delight. The girl peered out and held a necklace up for him to look at.

"See!" she cried. "It is mine!"

Raven shrugged. Again there came over him the oppressive feeling that the old woman was in league with malicious spirits. He went over and sat by a tree. An hour later he watched the Moon Woman come out of hiding and flood the earth with her omniscience, but for a long while he sat there, trying to think of a better way to protect himself.

24

ONE morning when the grandmother entered the thicket, carrying water and a little food, and saw that the sick woman was dead, she felt overwhelming distaste for this spot where she lived; and even after the body had been buried, she could not rid herself of the oppressive feeling that she had lived here too long. There had been too much sickness here and too many unhappy experiences. Three members of her family had died since she had built this hut, and out on the hills there were four graves. She felt as if she were living in a burial ground.

Returning from the fourth grave, she looked round her with unhappy eyes and liked nothing that she saw. Water was too far away; most of the dead wood in this area had been used; and there was some kind of blight on the kernels of her grain. Her house smelled of sickness. Looking at the yard and remembering that a baby had been born dead there, or at the jungle where two had died, or out at the hills where she had dug four graves, she felt that this area was the home of many ghosts. It was too familiar with pain and loss.

She decided to move again, but this time she would do more than to go aimlessly to a new spot. She would first explore the country roundabout and find a site that was fresh and fragrant and better suited to a family's needs. She gazed toward the sun and thought of the river, and of its bayou, full of fish. Along the river, as she had learned in former wanderings, there were gardens of fruit in this season, and edible roots in the earth. There were mushrooms in the dank woods. To be sure, other families lived in that area beyond the river and perhaps claimed most of the food there, but she believed she could find a better place to live if she took her time.

"We will move," she said, turning to Rose, and indicated with a gesture that she was weary of these things around her.

"Now?" Rose asked.

"No. I will walk."

"Far away?"

"Yes."

"We need food," said Rose, whose breasts were starving her child.

"Food!" cried the old woman impatiently, and looked round her to see what Raven was doing.

But Raven was nowhere to be seen. He had gone away to find more potent amulets; but after a while he had yielded to hunger and at this moment was sitting by his canoe and eating a fish. He had been playing with the notion of deserting his family—and he might have done so without hesitation or remorse if he had not been a slave of habit. He was captured and held in the pattern of a home fire, a bed, a roof above him, and the familiar paths that always led back to the hut. Besides, he was afraid to venture far, and he knew that no other family would accept him. At least none would if there was a strong man in it. And so he ate the raw fish and licked his fingers, winking thoughtfully at the still water and telling himself that he would take his weapons and the canoe and go far away. He thought of building a home for himself here by the bayou, but he knew that he would never dare to sleep alone in a house.

His mother was not so timid. She told the women that she would go away and find a new site; and when they argued, saying that she should not go far, alone and unprotected, she gestured impatiently. She was not afraid. Sometimes there is little fear in old persons who sense that they are close to death. As with certain beasts, there may be in them an unconscious wish to go off alone and wait for the end. Perhaps there was such a wish in this old and weary woman. Perhaps she was deceived by the notion that she wished to find a new home and was moved instead by a desire to withdraw deep into her own loneliness. This morning she was racked by pain. There was a kind of patient and engulfing sickness in her tired body, as if she were being remorselessly hushed and absorbed. In the hut were some of Raven's weapons, but she refused to take even a knife with her. When Rose proffered it, she impatiently brushed it aside and looked round her for a couple of sticks, and with a staff in either hand she helped to support her bent frame.

Her resolve to go far away alone was so unusual that Old Man left the hut and stood with the younger women. All of them were distressed and frightened.

297

"Will you come soon?" Rose asked anxiously.

"Yes," said the grandmother, and moved feebly toward the sun.

"Ahhh!" said Rose, and looked at her sister.

Baffled and apprehensive, the four of them stood in the yard and watched the old woman go away. She went slowly, like one whose naked feet were tender. She walked on two skinny legs and on the two sticks clutched in her hands, and now and then she paused and lifted her face as if to sniff or to choose her path. For a little while she stood on a hilltop and then went downward and out of sight.

Rose turned and met her sister's eyes. Nothing like this had ever happened in her life before. She said that someone ought to go with the old woman, and eagerly the girl spoke.

"I will follow her," she said. She took the stone knife and quickly went up the path.

When the girl disappeared, Barren turned to Rose and took the fretting babe from her arms. Knowing that it hungered, she offered it a nipple, though her own breasts were empty. It was a custom for all the healthy women in a family to take turns nursing a child. Barren sat with the babe and gave it the other breast, and Rose sat by her. Again their eyes met.

"Will she come home?" Barren asked.

"Yes," Rose said, but her voice was only a whisper.

Raven had eaten his fish and was coming up the path toward home when he saw the grandmother. He ducked into hiding but almost at once he peered out. He thought she was coming to find him and to demand food for the others and for a moment he considered dashing to the bayou to spear fish. But then he noticed that she was walking queerly. When she set out to find him she was always angry and she walked rapidly, swinging her arms and pointing her face like a beast on the scent. He sensed now that she was not angry. She was not looking round her as if to spy him out. She was moving slowly on two sticks, with her head bowed and her shaggy gray mane almost hiding her face.

Securely hidden, he watched her and waited. After a few moments he was startled by the girl who suddenly appeared on the crest of a hill. She paused there, and Raven realized, with another start, that she was spying on the grandmother. She was following her. The grandmother came along the path and now he could hear the gentle sound of her feet. Without looking to right or left she passed him and went down the path and out of sight; and then the girl came down the hill and in a few moments she also passed Raven and disappeared.

Completely mystified, he came out of hiding and looked down the path. They had gone toward the river. Perplexed, he considered the strange matter and decided that the old woman intended to steal his canoe. It was an unreasonable thought, but Raven was an unreasonable man. He set off down the path, going quickly but softly; and when he came within sight of the girl and perceived that she had not overtaken the old woman but was still spying on her, he was more baffled than ever.

Meanwhile the grandmother had come to the bayou. She looked at the canoe and the expanse of still water, and then up and down the beach, wondering which direction to take. Because the country here was densely wooded it was unsuitable for a home. She wanted a site not far from wood and water, but out in the open and at a safe distance from the jungles in which dangerous beasts might lurk. As far as she could see to the right or left there was only deep forest, with no sign anywhere of a large clearing open to the sky. Undecided, and curious about the beached canoe, she went over to look at it; and her son, slyly peering out from hiding, was convinced that she had come to steal it or to shove it out and let it float away.

While gazing at the log the old woman heard a sound. To the south of her, flamingos had been wading in shallow water, and the sound she heard was of their great wings. A hundred of them had taken to flight and were now crossing the sky above her, with the sun flashing on the pink and rose and scarlet of their plumage. She could see the black bands on their wings. Peering up with dim eyes, the grandmother watched the birds as they moved across the forest, their dangling legs almost touching the tree-tops.

Turning upstream because the forest looked less impenetrable in this direction, she followed the shore of the bayou and presently came to orchards of wild fruit. The vines were laden with raspberries, gooseberries, and currants. There were other berries, too, with which she was not familiar and, knowing that some fruits were poisonous, she explored cautiously for a little while before she began to eat. She would gather a handful of fruit and peer at it, smell it, and then experimentally taste it. Because she could not see it clearly, or be sure by the fragrance what was poisonous and what was not, she was

300

guided chiefly by the flavor. She would chew a few berries and then, with the juice saturating her mouth, she would wink her eyes thoughtfully and consider; if she was not sure, she would move the crushed fruit with her tongue, striving to recapture the first gushing taste of it. The raspberries and currants she recognized and ate, but some of the other fruit she spat out after chewing. While eating, she looked round her at the taller plants and wondered if there were cherries along this river. There ought to be mushrooms, she decided, and knelt to move exploring hands over the moist earth.

Then she grasped her two sticks and went forward through the brambles, paying little heed to thorns that gouged her tough hide. For perhaps a hundred yards she moved through a berry patch, noting, as she went, that the bushes were laden. She was still in deep growth, but she could hear running water, and in a few moments she came to the river. Though it was a small stream, the jungle along its banks was so dense that she could not tell how deep the river was or how far it was to the opposite bank. Never in all the years of her life had she crossed this river. She was determined to cross it now. She had a notion that on the far side of it there would be no graves, no ghosts, no unfriendly beasts. She liked to think of it as an unknown land, fresh and untroubled, with streams of pure water and an abundance of food and firewood. Over there she would find a broad clearing, claimed by no one, with gardens of fruit around it, and with mushrooms and edible roots and small animals, like rabbits and grouse, in the wooded parts. She was old and weary with so much striving, and for her last years before death she wanted the

301

security of food and fire and the peace of an untroubled home.

Following the bank upstream and fighting her way through a jungle of bramble bush and vine, she searched for an open place where she could descend to the river. She found none, but at last she did come to a big tree that had fallen across the river, and she walked across on the tree and entered a wilderness on the far side. The growth on both banks was so lush and tall that it arched above the stream, making a ceiling that hid the cool waters. Ahead of her was deep forest, but she plunged into it without hesitating.

Behind her the girl was struggling through the brambles and licking blood off her arms; and beyond the girl was Raven, dismayed and frightened, and wondering if both women had been driven crazy by the drinking of some strange juice. Never before had he been in such a mess of brambles and thorns. Unlike the women, he did not have free hands to protect himself; he carried his bow in one hand and his lance in the other. Again and again the bow became entangled, as if malicious hands were reaching out to seize it, and when he observed that his sexual amulet was gone, he knew that an invisible hand had snatched it away. He thought of retreating from this terrifying jungle and going home, but when he looked behind him, the way out seemed no less difficult than the way ahead. And so, despairing and sweating with fright, he persisted, trying all the while to keep within sight or at least within sound of the girl.

The grandmother was also faltering. After going so deep into the forest that she could no longer hear the sound of the stream, she paused and looked up, hoping to catch a glimpse of the sun. She realized that if she were caught here when darkness came, she would not know her way home. Nevertheless, she decided to go a little farther and after another hundred yards or so she suddenly emerged from the woods and was startled by the scene before her.

Her gaze went down and across a narrow valley and up a gentle hill, almost barren of vegetation, and on the crest of the hill she saw several persons. The sight of people where she had expected to find none was in itself enough to amaze her; but she saw more than people. Her gaze rested on a man who seemed to be leading a beast. She thought at first that it was a wolf-dog but, after staring at the creature and observing how it moved, she knew it was not a dog. So far as she could tell, it was nothing that she had ever seen before. While she leaned on her sticks and watched, the man seemed to kneel by the beast and to be doing something with it; and then the other persons came over and stood by him and gestured as if talking. Lifting her gaze, the grandmother looked beyond the people and their home and saw a range of mountains that stood high against the sun.

Raven had been startled, too. While struggling in the bramble thicket, still undecided whether to follow the women or to go home, he heard a scream of terror. Turning rigid and holding his breath while he listened, he then heard the sobbing cries of someone who seemed to be in extreme pain. It did not occur to him at first that it was the girl whom he heard, though he did recognize the voice as a woman's. Guided by the sound, he pushed forward more quickly and presently he could see the girl, cowering by a bush and looking toward him. Her eyes in that moment were wide with terror. She was ready to flee because she thought the sounds Raven made were those of a jungle beast. When she saw that it was Raven coming toward her, she uttered a cry of joy and ran toward him, her arms outstretched and her cheeks wet with tears.

"Ahhh!" she cried, and touched him with trembling hands.

"Where is she?" asked Raven, meaning the grandmother.

The girl pointed to the forest beyond. "Out there!"

"Is she lost?"

"Yes!"

Raven doubted that. The old woman was a wise one who had often prowled alone through forests to seek her precious herbs and wild honey. He was not worried about her. Indeed, when he perceived that the girl was unharmed and realized that she was alone with him, securely hidden from all eyes, he began to tremble with eagerness. His own fear left him; he was now a sly and a calculating man. But before moving to possess the girl he listened, afraid lest the grandmother might slip back to spy on him. Still, if she were to return, he thought he would hear her long before she came in sight. He felt safe enough. Impatiently, he moved toward the girl, but she drew away.

Pointing to the forest she said, "Go find her!"

"No," he said.

"She is lost."

"No!" said Raven angrily. It was foolish to think that the old woman was lost.

He looked at the girl, and the girl looked away at the

forest and listened. Raven had not learned that a woman was sometimes receptive to a man's embrace when deeply moved by grief or terror, but he was cunning enough to realize that the longer he hesitated now, the more unwilling the girl would be. He thrust his lance into the earth. He hung his bowstring over a limb and unfastened his quiver of arrows and laid it aside. Then, looking at her, he still hesitated, and the girl, meeting his stare, read the purpose in his eyes.

"No," she said, backing away, but she did not speak sharply. She was a terrified person who still felt the need of his presence.

Raven sensed in her voice, in the way she was looking at him, and in the way her body was poised, that she would yield if he laid hands on her; and so, after listening again for a sound of the old woman, he moved swiftly and grasped the girl and forced her to the earth. Her resistance was feeble. She cried out in protest and made an effort to escape, but his hands were rough and determined, and when he forced her to her knees, she gave a low cry of surrender.

After he had embraced her, she laid her forearms on the earth and bowed her head to them, and Raven, who had got to his feet to peer and listen, now gazed for a long moment at the girl, who seemed to be abjectly waiting, and embraced her again. Whereupon, having spent his hunger, and feeling triumphant and fearless, he fastened the arrows to his waist, grasped his bow and lance, and looked round him for something to eat. When the girl did not rise, he stared at her curiously, wondering for a horrified instant if she was dead. He knelt by her and tried to see her face. Unable to, he placed both hands against her and shoved her off her knees.

"Go away!" she cried.

Feeling resentment and anger, he arose and looked down at her. "I will go away," he said; and when, after he had waited a while, she did not move or speak, he added maliciously, "You are lost."

That statement fetched her to her senses. She sprang up and looked wildly round her, having forgotten where she was.

"Go find her!" she said, and pointed to the dark forest.

"You wait here," said Raven.

"No!"

"You go home."

"Which way?"

"That way."

"Will you find her?"

"Yes."

"This way?" asked the girl, pointing back to the bayou.

"Yes."

"She went that way," said the girl.

"I know!" said Raven impatiently.

He thought of embracing her, knowing well that he might never again find her in a place like this, but he felt spent. What he wanted now was food. The girl moved away through the bramble patch, going as quickly as she could because she wanted to emerge from the jungle while Raven lingered here. Raven watched her with crafty and triumphant eyes. When she was out of sight, and a little later when he could no longer hear the sound of her, he turned in the opposite direction and looked for signs. The girl was not a hunter and had lost the old woman when

306

she could no longer see or hear her. Raven saw everywhere the signs she had left. He saw twigs that she had broken. He could bend to the earth and see footprints where she had turned the old leaf depth. And when he came to the tree across the river, he had only to sniff its bark to tell that she had gone that way.

25

EAGER to learn what the people were doing, the grandmother crossed the valley and climbed the hill; and all the while, as if unaware of the curious stares turned her way, she kept her gaze on the strange beast. Never before had she seen one like it. What she saw was a goat, a very shaggy creature with curved horns, a mantle of long hair, drooping ears, and a great handful of beard hanging from its chin. And it was tethered to a bush by a long rawhide string.

Wondering where these people had found such an animal and what use they made of it, the grandmother turned to a woman, intending to ask her a question, but the woman's appearance was so startling that the question died on her tongue. She was huge and she was very fat. Her buttocks were enormous. The grandmother was used to rather slender women whose shape was not very unlike that of a man; this woman seemed to be all curves and bulges. Her broad face was well fleshed and lightly bearded. Her dugs, broad and brown, and hanging almost to her waist, looked like big moss pads.

"Where is your home?" the woman asked, and like her body her voice was large and deep.

Turning, the grandmother looked back toward the river. Pointing, she said, "Over there."

"Far away?"

"Yes."

There was silence. Beyond the big woman were several other persons, watching and waiting. The grandmother sensed that they were curious but not unfriendly. Nevertheless, she felt ill at ease and, after peering again at the woman's face, she turned to the goat.

"What is it?" she asked, her voice sounding thin and old in comparison with the other's deep tones.

The woman said it was an animal, using their word for any living thing except human beings. The grandmother gestured impatiently. She had known all the while that it was an animal. She wanted to know what sort of beast it was and why they did not kill and eat it. She had perceived that the long-haired skin would be excellent for a bed.

The big woman had been enjoying her visitor's bewilderment. She was very proud of this goat; it was her property and, save human children, it was the most precious thing she knew of in life. Going over to the beast, she laid a hand on its shaggy coat. She looked at the old woman, standing grotesquely on two thin legs and two sticks, and waited for her wrinkled face to show curiosity and impatience. Then she lay down by the goat and rested on an elbow and put a teat in her mouth. For a few moments she sucked. Glancing up at the old woman to see what she made of that, she said

"Food is good." She ran her tongue over her full lips. "Look!" she said. Then she knelt and milked into a palm and drank the milk. "It is good," she said.

The grandmother knew that the food from breasts was good food but she had never known that any people ate such food from beasts. This was indeed amazing. Her eyes were so wide and her face so breathless with astonishment that the woman smiled. She arose and went into the hut and came out with a small boy, and now she milked a little into her palm and the child drank. The other adults came up, resolved to claim their share. Again and again the woman milked as much as her cupped palm would hold, and in turn the others drank. In turn, too, they looked at the old woman after drinking as if to ask, "What do you think of that?"

What the grandmother thought was written plain in her face. She went over and said, "Give me some," and the woman milked a little for her. After swallowing the milk, the grandmother kept moving her tongue and pursing her lips, the more fully to savor the taste. She knew the taste of human milk. This beast's milk was not unlike it.

"Is it good?" the woman asked.

"Yes."

"Very good?" she asked, teasing her.

"Yes."

"Look!" said the woman, and milked another palmful. This generosity fetched a cry of protest from a man. He wanted a second helping, too. Morning and night they all shared this goat's milk and looked forward to it as the most savory part of their meals. After he had drunk a little more, the others, including the small lad, clamored for another serving, and the woman gave a little to each of them.

"Bring baby," she said, and after a few moments the man came with a small kid. The woman let it suck a full teat which she had not milked.

Perceiving that these people had two of these beasts, the grandmother felt covetous.

"Is it yours?" she asked, pointing to the kid.

"Yes," said the woman proudly.

"Ahhh!"

"Mine!" cried the woman, gloating over her possessions. "You like them?"

"Yes!" said the grandmother eagerly; and after a moment of hesitation she added boldly, "I want one."

The woman's face turned hard and cold. "Mine!" she said.

The man hastened away and returned presently with a full-grown ram. When, back in the mountains, he had trapped the mother goat in a pit, she had had a kid with her, and after it grew up, the two beasts had mated. The ungainly little creature standing by its mother was their offspring.

When she saw that they had three animals, two of which were grown, the grandmother hoped they would give her one of them, and with greedy eyes she looked in turn at the two large ones, wondering which she would prefer to have. She observed next that they were not alike. Becoming suspicious of the ram, she knelt to peer under its belly and in a voice of disgust said:

"This is man-beast!"

"Yes," said the woman calmly.

But the man hastened over and grasped the kid and

fetched it to the old woman. He turned it upside down and pointed. "Woman-beast," he said.

With her hands itching covetously, the grandmother examined the kid to learn if it had teats and, when she learned that it was indeed a female, she stood up and looked at the mother goat, still struggling to decide which of the two she would take. For so many years she had had her way that it did not seem to her that she was unreasonable and greedy. She had always taken what she wanted if she could get it. That was the way with all her people. Persons were born then, as they still are, with theft and covetousness in their hearts.

After tortured indecision, the grandmother was unable to make up her mind and so, craftily, she asked a question. She wanted to know if the mother beast was very old. But the other woman was also full of guile.

"Why?" she asked.

Nonplussed by the answer, the grandmother resolved to settle the matter quickly. Pointing to the one giving milk, she said:

"I will take her."

If she had said she would tear down their home or take a human child, she would not have aroused more anger and resentment. The man exploded with rage. The big woman narrowed her eyes and looked at the grandmother as if she were plotting her death. In another moment the old woman would have been beaten and driven away if the man had not looked across the valley and seen Raven coming. He was running toward them, his lance flashing in the sunlight.

"Look!" the man shouted, and pointed to the stranger.

"Man is coming!" cried another.

The grandmother also turned to look. The man of this family dashed into the hut; and when Raven came up, out of breath and looking bold and impudent, the man rushed over to face him with his lance poised. Then the two men looked at one another, and Raven lost his air of bravado. He let his lance fall, he laid his bow aside as a gesture of peace, and he looked very humble and abashed.

When the others realized that he belonged to this old woman's family, they were suspicious. The woman and her man went off a little way and spoke together; they were convinced that these two persons had planned to come here and steal one of the beasts. Too possessed by covetousness to sense the unfriendliness, the grandmother grasped Raven's arm and led the astonished fellow over to the mother goat, intending to milk a little so that he could taste this wonderful new food, but with a shout of rage the big woman rushed toward her. She ran against her, thrusting with both hands, and knocked the feeble old creature head over heels.

Thoroughly frightened, Raven glanced toward his home and then at his weapons. He was on the point of fleeing, but the big woman called to him, and when, moving like one who expected to be knocked down, he went over to her, she milked into a palm and asked him to drink. He bent over her hand and made a noisy sound of sucking.

"Is food good?" she asked eagerly.

"Yes," he said, and smacked his lips.

"You want more?"

He nodded. She milked a little more and he drank it; and when he straightened, his eyes met her steady gaze. Raven felt ill at ease because he was standing so close to her, realizing, with senses painfully acute, that she was

313

a woman. His gaze fell to her large breasts and down across her abdomen; when his eyes returned to her face and she read what was in his mind, she stepped back and spoke sharply.

"Go away!" she said.

Feeling ridiculous, Raven turned away. A quick glance told him that the man was still poising his weapon, as if ready to attack. Looking round him and feeling the menace everywhere he looked, he saw that the old woman had risen to her feet and recovered her sticks. Observing the ram next, Raven went over to the beast and almost at once perceived that this animal was a male. Kneeling, he stared under the belly at the huge testicles and, like a man fascinated by a sudden and strange discovery, he pointed to them and cried, "Look!"

When nobody spoke, he arose and looked down at his own genitals. All the members of this family were now watching him closely, as if they suspected that he was trying to deceive them. Speaking to him and the grandmother, the big woman said:

"You go home."

But Raven was not ready to go home. Like his mother, he was feeling very covetous. Glancing slyly round him, and observing that this family seemed to have no wolf-dog, he wondered, with naïve guile, if he could steal the mother beast. He saw that the man had laid his lance aside. Raven asked him:

"Where did you find her?" He pointed to the goat.

The man gestured at the distant mountains. "There," he said.

"More there?" asked Raven.

"Yes."

314

Raven looked at the mountains. They seemed to be far away—much farther than he would ever dare venture from his home. He admired the boldness of this man who had gone so far into strange country.

The big woman left the mother goat and went over to stand with her family. She had been happy in showing off her property and making these visitors envious; now she looked at them as if becoming aware that they were strangers. The more she thought about them, the more convinced she became that they were malicious thieves who had come here to steal; and in turn she looked at one and the other, keeping a sharp eye on both.

Raven sensed that they wanted him to go away, but he was so possessed by greed, and so confused by his desperate effort to figure out a way to steal the mother goat, that he stood like a man lost in bewilderment. His head turned on his shoulders, looking now at his mother, now at the members of the strange family, and now at the beasts. He behaved like a witless fellow, but those watching him closely saw that his eyes were bright and searching. Covetousness had so robbed the old woman of her senses that she had blandly asked for one of the goats. Raven was too cunning for that. Though he glanced around him like a confused and foolish man, he was a sly rascal nevertheless; he was assuring himself that there was no dog in this family and he was wondering where they hid these beasts after darkness came.

The grandmother had heard the man say that there were other milk-givers in the mountains. She now came over to Raven. Though she had been knocked over, and ought to have been subdued and chastened, there was more greed in her than prudence. She wanted a food-giver, and

315

she wanted it soon. Pointing to the mountains, she said to her son:

"Go find beast!"

Raven was dismayed. A glance told him that the sun was halfway down the sky and the mountains were a long day's journey from his home. He went over and picked up his weapons. When he turned homeward, the old woman was so angry and so obsessed by a wish to own a food-giving beast that she ran to the mother-goat and jerked at the tether. This indiscretion brought the big woman rushing toward her, but the grandmother saw her coming and shuffled away. After she and her son had gone a little distance, with Raven hastily leading, the others began to yell at them, telling them to go home. It was as if they realized at last that they had been kind to two thieves.

After crossing the valley and coming to the forest's edge, the old woman called to Raven; when he came back and stood by her, she turned and with squinting and baffled eyes looked at the people she had left. She asked Raven to bring the mother beast while she waited here.

"You go," he said.

Frenzied with impatience, she struck him, but when he ran into the forest, she limped after him, calling to him to stop. Going through the woods and crossing the stream, they picked their way through the bramble thicket; not until they reached the bayou where the canoe lay did they pause. Exhausted, the old woman sat down to rest, and Raven, feeling starved, pushed his boat out, intending to spear a fish. When he saw the woman struggle to her feet and turn homeward, he quickly beached the canoe and followed, because he wanted to be present when she told of the wonderful things they had seen. He had known of the bushbuck and the waterbuck, because the dead uncle had hunted these creatures, but he had never dreamed that there were animals which give food for human beings to eat.

The moment she entered the hut, the others asked the grandmother if she had found a spot for a new home. She was not thinking of that. Moving in a slow and mysterious way, she stirred the fire and then looked round her, as if spying on intruders. She went out to the yard, calling to them to come, and when they were gathered round her, she pointed to the south, where the invisible mountains stood, and told them of the marvelous things she had seen. Her voice quavered with emotion. Because she had so few words with which to talk and so few symbols to express this strange new meaning, she turned to Rose and, grasping a nipple with thumb and forefinger, squeezed a drop of milk into her palm. Solemnly she pointed to the drop and talked again, striving to explain that a family far away had found a beast that gave food like this which they all ate. She said it was very good food; and from time to time Raven interrupted, adding with thought and gesture to the story. For almost an hour they told of their amazing adventure and of the wonderful advantages enjoyed by these people, and before the tale was done, the other women were gasping with astonishment. As for the grandmother, so for them the meaning of the story was of a time to come, and perhaps soon, when their way of life would be more secure, with an abundance of nourishing food such as babies had, and long-haired skins of which to make their beds.

"Will we have one?" Rose asked eagerly.

"Yes," said the old woman.

"Where is it?"

She pointed toward the hidden mountains and said that Raven would go and find one.

"Soon?"

"Yes."

In a crude basket woven of vines and leaves, the girl had fetched some berries home, and now the women ate the fruit for their supper, as well as a few mushrooms and roots, but they were all thinking of the time, soon to come, when they would have beasts tethered close to their home that would give food for the asking. Never doubting that this would be so, they looked happily at one another and smiled.

26

THE next day, from early morning until dusk, Raven was urged by the women to go to the distant mountains and find a food-giver. Deeply resenting their indifference to the perils of such a long journey, he tried to figure out a safe way to steal the mother-goat he had seen—because if he were successful in that, he could then pretend that he had been to the mountains. Under persistent urging, he did make a gesture of inspecting his weapons and of setting forth like a bold man fully resolved on a long and hazardous march. But he never went farther than the bayou. There, sitting on his pirogue and gazing at the forest beyond the river, he fancied himself in reverie as a man of extraordinary courage who, in broad daylight, strode up to the people and drove them cowering into their hut and took all their beasts. After a while of such blissful fancies, he would spear fish and gather berries and take the food home to appease the women.

They were overjoyed by the food but never for a moment did they falter in their resolve to have a milk-giver. Deciding that Raven needed more boldness, the grandmother gathered herbs and fruits and honey and fermented another pot of courage; and when it was ready he drank deeply, feeling like a man goaded by tyrants to seek his death. He became so drunk that he staggered and made menacing gestures, but he was still unwilling to go forth alone; whereupon, in disgust, the women went with him as far as the bayou.

"Go find beast!" the old woman cried; and while the girl held the baby, the three women dragged the drunken fellow over to the berry patch. This, said the grandmother, pointing, was the way he should take; he would go through the thicket and cross the river; he would cross the valley and go past the home of the people and into the mountains beyond. There he would find many of these food-givers and would trap one and bring her home.

Raven solemnly wagged his head as if he understood very well what he was to do, and he allowed the women to push him into the thicket. Then, with the women shouting entreaties and commands, he picked his way slowly among the vines and persisted in his journey until he was out of sight. Feeling secure, he sat on his heels and blinked drunkenly at nothing at all. Suspecting that the sly rascal would balk as soon as he was beyond sight of her, the grandmother had followed him. Presently, with a start of dismay, he was aware of her angry voice, shouting abusively; and so he arose like a man lost in a stupor and moved away. When he thought he was hidden again he sank to his heels, but almost at once, it seemed to him, the dreadful old creature rushed up and pushed him over. Then she tried to drag him to his feet.

"Go away!" he cried, but she pursued him to the tree

320

and drove him across the river. Determined to outwit her, he now went more quickly and soon vanished deep into the forest. Crawling under a hanging wall of ferns, he pulled his weapons in after him and listened; in a few moments he could hear her, scurrying around in the woods. He lay quietly, hoping she would think he had left the forest and gone to the mountains. After a while she decided that he had, and she returned to the bayou to wait there with the others.

Feeling blissfully wise because he had tricked her, Raven peered out when he could no longer hear any sound and, convinced at last that she had gone home, he began to think about himself. He was very drunk but he knew where he was. He knew he was lying in a forest on the sun-side of the river; that the home of the strange family was toward the sun and not far away; and that he was expected to bring home with him a food-giving beast. He was expected to go to the mountains and find one, but even when he was drinking the liquor he had not intended to risk his life in such a perilous journey. In fact, he had had no clear notion of what he would do and now, realizing that he was not far from the mother-beast, he wondered if he could steal her.

This thought excited him. It challenged his opinion of himself as a resourceful and cunning man. Sitting here, safely hidden and aware that no one could divine his plans, he was encouraged to unwonted boldness in trying to devise an attack; but after considering a daylight foray and realizing that he might be beaten and killed, he shuddered a little, as if he had been exposed to sudden danger. Like one sleeping alone in a cold night and trying under chilled bedding to withdraw snugly into himself, so Raven, shivering at the thought of a daylight advance, hugged his arms against his ribs and drew his legs up, all in an effort to recover a sense of security.

He was a crafty rather than an intrepid man. He liked to think of himself as a dauntless hunter, but even when as drunk as he was now, he knew better than that. He knew that if he were to steal the beast, he would have to do so not by intimidating the owners but by outwitting them. The sly and stealthy attack suited him best. And so, dropping the notion of a bold foray, he tried to think of some plan by which he could slip up, undetected, and lead the beast away. This kind of plotting delighted him, and especially now when his fancies were stimulated by alcohol. He had a vision of himself moving as noiselessly as a serpent.

Such a sense of extreme stealth possessed him that he made a move to act out the drama. He turned over quietly to his hands and knees and crawled forward a little to peer out of his hiding place. Though still so drunk that his senses swam, he knew very well what he was doing; as a kind of symbolic preparation, he was acting a part that would become real enough when the world darkened. It was as if he were feeling out and testing his sensory capacities. Crawling out of hiding, he observed with joy that he was making no sounds. He lifted his face and peered and sniffed like a jungle beast preparing to leave the woods; but when he arose to his feet he staggered and, to save himself from falling, he turned blindly and clasped a tree. His senses had been engulfed by a slightly nauseous darkness. Feeling alarm, he sank gropingly to hands and knees and crawled back into hiding.

Because an idea quickly became a fact for him, after a

while there was no doubt in his mind that he would steal the beast. It did not seem to him that he had ever doubted that. In the experimental stage of feeling out his intentions, his own cunning acting had betrayed him; he had moved to the fixed purpose. He would have said that when he left his home he had known what he would do and that, without being urged or driven by the women, he had come here to do it. His task now was not to question his intentions but to establish the pattern of his after-dark adventure by constantly imagining it.

And this until darkness came he did. He was not quite so drunk then, and it almost seemed to him that he had stolen many beasts and was about to take his way along a familiar path. Before the forest darkened, he took his weapons and went softly to its edge; and there he peered at the home beyond the valley and tried to foresee all the risks. He was sure that this family had no dogs. He could think of nothing that might announce his coming if he went as noiselessly as he intended to. Having forgotten whether the Moon Woman was old or young tonight, he looked at the sky, but there was no sign of her. He wondered next where the beasts were tethered after darkness came. Then he considered the matter of his weapons and decided to leave them here. If he were surprised he would run, and weapons would only encumber his flight.

As the night darkened and the time approached when he would leave the protection of the woods, it cannot be said that he felt less bold. It was not boldness that sustained him. It was the fixed idea that he had done this sort of thing before, and had always been successful, and would have no trouble in doing it again. During most of the afternoon he had been living the adventure in his fancies.

The landscape at which he looked now seemed as familiar as his own dooryard. He knew he would cross the valley, skirt the hill, approach from the rear, and quietly lead the beast away. But he waited until the night was very dark and there was only a faint reflection of light in the open doorway of the hut. He believed that the people would be asleep now. After hiding his weapons and marking the spot with broken twigs, he went forward on naked feet that explored like hands before accepting his weight.

And this man, accustomed from early boyhood to stealthy movements and practiced in all the wiles of the hunter, crossed the valley and climbed the hill without making a sound audible to human ears. He went around the hill and approached from the far side. The goats were tethered in a thicket behind the house and fenced around with an interwoven hedge of branches and vines. When Raven slipped close enough to look over the hedge, he was startled for a moment to realize that the beasts had heard him coming and were now looking at him. In the darkness he could see their large anxious eyes. Waiting a little while to let them become accustomed to his presence, he crawled under the hedge, pausing there to make an opening through which he could lead the goat; and then, moving as softly as a shadow, he reached out to find the rope that held her. He untied the end fastened to a bush and gently pulled on the rope to draw the beast to him.

She was stubborn and held back. The man-beast shook his great curved horns and gave a low snort, and for a long moment Raven stood still and listened. If he had heard a person coming he would have dashed through the aperture and fled, but the beating of his own heart was the only sound he could hear. Straining his ears to catch the faintest whisper and deciding that the family was still asleep, he again pulled on the rope, dragging the obstinate animal to him step by step. When she was within reach he grasped her horns and, backing away slowly, pulled her through the hedge. Close behind her came the kid. Outside the enclosure, Raven looked back at the male goat and saw him straining at his leash. Afraid that he might snort again or, worse still, begin to cry with alarm, Raven considered entering the pen and choking the creature, but that, he decided after a moment, might cause enough sound to awaken the family.

Backing away, he dragged the goat after him. Her feet made an alarming noise in the leaves and twigs, but it was not so loud as his hypersensitive ears imagined it to be. He was moving away from the house and down the hill on the far side; after he had gone fifty yards or so, he tried to move more swiftly. The goat was stubborn, but now and then she eased the strain and led without being dragged. All the while the kid followed like her own shadow.

Perhaps an hour had passed since Raven first looked into the goat pen. He was down the hill and across the valley, and he was feeling safe and triumphant when he heard a sudden and terrifying sound. It was the man-beast crying for its mate. Knowing that the family would be aroused, Raven burst into the sweat of terror and, dragging the goat after him, plunged for the deep forest, never pausing in his desperate efforts until he reached it. Quickly tying the mother to a tree, he ran back to look out.

The Moon Woman had not risen yet, the sky was dark save for a few stars, but Raven's eyes, accustomed to the darkness, could see people running around on the hill. He

325

could hear the frantic bleating of the male goat. Afraid that the people might track him by the scent—for he had never known a beast with such a strong odor as these animals had—he untied the leash, plunged with frenzied haste deeper into the woods, and did not pause again until he came to the river. Wildly confused now and undecided how to take the animals across the fallen tree, he tied the mother to a limb, seized the kid, and started away with it; but a low bleat from the mother stopped him. With amazing nimbleness she had leapt to the tree and was pulling at the leash in an effort to follow. Sensing that she would follow her child, Raven dashed back and untied her; and when, carrying the babe, he hastened to the far side, the mother nimbly followed him.

Overjoyed by this unexpected solution of his problem, he clutched the kid in his arms and headed for the bayou, and close on his heels came the mother-beast. When, gouged and bleeding, he emerged from the brambles, he was delighted to learn that the women had waited here for him. They had been sitting by the canoe but had heard him coming, and the moment he appeared, they rushed toward him, uttering low cries.

"Be still!" Raven said in a frantic whisper. He gestured wildly in the direction of the dangers he had left. Whispering hoarsely, he made them understand that he was being pursued, and the grandmother realized then that he had not been to the mountains but had stolen the beast she had seen. That made no difference to her; like all the people of this time, she had no sense of property right, at least of none that was inviolable, except her own.

She grasped the leash but after a moment handed it to the girl; and with Raven leading, still clutching the kid,

326

and the girl going next, with the anxious mother-goat close on her heels, the women fell in behind, the grandmother hobbling frantically to keep up. Like persons who knew that they were thieves who might at any moment be overtaken and punished, they went swiftly until they reached their home. Then, realizing with dismay that he had left his weapons, and believing that the outraged owners would soon come in sight, Raven dashed around like a wild man, seeking a place to hide his loot. With anguished words and gestures, he explained to the others the predicament they were in. In carrying the kid, he had discovered that the strong odor came from the forefeet, and he now asked the women to sniff them.

"They will come!" he whispered, looking back into the darkness.

Wagging her wise old head, the grandmother considered the problem. She said they would hide the animals at a safe distance away and then, even before morning came, they would move their possessions and abandon their hut. But to take the beasts safely away, leaving no scent behind them, she realized that they would have to be carried; and so, after making her plan known, she gave the human baby to the girl, she took the goat-baby herself, and she told the other three to carry the mother-beast. Then she summoned Old Man from the hut and they all set out.

Through thickets and across open places they journeyed for about two miles, going into the north. Not once did Raven and his sisters let the mother-goat touch the earth. When they paused to rest, the three of them would sink to their heels and lay the beast across their knees. And after making her and the kid secure in a dark and almost im-

327

penetrable jungle, they left Old Man to watch them and hastened back for their things. A golden sun was standing above the treetops before, exhausted and famished, they had gathered the ripened heads of their barley and corn and moved all their belongings to the new site.

27

THEY made a breakfast of roots and mushrooms, and then the younger women began to build a new home. Alternating between feelings of anxiety and elation, Raven assisted them; and not until several days and nights had passed did he dare to go back for his weapons. On the way he perceived that persons had come to the old hut and walked round and round it and back and forth across the garden, and at the bayou he discovered that someone had been riding in his canoe. But darkness followed light and light followed darkness until the Moon Woman was again old and weary, and nobody came to their new home.

During these first days all of them but Old Man gave almost as much attention and care to the food-giving beast as to Rose's child. They vied with one another in learning what she preferred to eat and in finding it for her; in bringing water for her to drink; and in providing a bed for her of old grasses and dry moss. They spent many hours simply looking at her and trying to realize more fully the miraculous fact that they had a beast that gave them food.

But after a while the grandmother took over the care of the goat, allowing no one else to feed and water her or to milk her. Milking her became almost a ritual for the old woman. She looked forward eagerly to the chore, and when she knelt to squeeze milk from the udder she was as solemnly mysterious as when she planted corn or made magic to bring rain. She left one teat for the kid, but the food from the other three she gave to her family, carefully measuring each portion and giving to the baby its share. They were fond of the milk, not only because it was rich and nourishing but also because it was new and strange. Milk was the food babies ate; there could be nothing better for anyone. They smacked their lips after drinking and looked at one another with glad eyes.

And after becoming accustomed to the miracle, they foresaw the time when they would have many beasts. The kid would grow up and become a mother, and the mother-goat would have another child. They did not know that they would need a man-beast to mate with these. With faith resting on ignorance, and on the old woman's power of magic, they looked forward to the time when they would have at least as much as they hungered for of one kind of food; when it would be with them in all seasons, close by their home; and when, they dared to hope, each member of the family would have his own food-giver to nourish him. Their lives then would be happy and care-free. Their meaning would be enriched by property that would nourish them, that would be a constant anchor among the hazards of life, and—though only Raven sensed this—an advantage over their less prosperous fellows.

For this family those dreams would never come true, but their hope did anticipate the future. Though defeated

330

by ignorance and superstition, they perceived, even if only dimly, that the milk-givers would alter the patterns of human life. Their vision of a happier time for themselves was a window that looked upon a less menacing world and a brighter morning.